MONA
PASSAGE

Veterans
Writing Award

Sponsored by the Institute for Veterans
and Military Families and Syracuse University Press

In keeping with Syracuse University's longstanding commitment to serving the interests of veterans and their families, Syracuse University Press, in cooperation with the Institute for Veterans and Military Families (IVMF), established the Veterans Writing Award in 2019. The mission of the Veterans Writing Award is to recognize the contributions of veterans to the literary arts, shine a light on the multivalent veteran experience, and provide a platform for unrecognized military writers.

This biennial contest is open to US veterans and active duty personnel in any branch of the US military and their immediate family members. This includes spouses, domestic partners, siblings, parents, and children. We encourage women veteran writers, veterans of color, Native American veterans, LGBTQ veterans, and those who identify as having a disability to submit. Although work submitted for the contest need not be about direct military experience, we seek original voices and fresh perspectives that will expand and challenge readers' understanding of the lives of veterans and their families. Posthumous submissions are eligible.

Previous Winners

2019

Revolutions of All Colors:
A Novel by Dewaine Farria

Honorable Mention:

Mona Passage:
A Novel by Thomas Bardenwerper

Thomas Bardenwerper

MONA PASSAGE

A Novel

Syracuse University Press

∞ The paper used in this publication meets the minimum requirements
of the American National Standard for Information Sciences—Permanence of Paper
for Printed Library Materials, ANSI Z39.48-1992.

For a listing of books published and distributed by Syracuse University Press,
visit https://press.syr.edu.

ISBN: 978-0-8156-1139-4 (hardcover)
978-0-8156-5536-7 (e-book)

Library of Congress Cataloging-in-Publication Data

Names: Bardenwerper, Thomas "Buddy", author.
Title: Mona Passage : a novel / Thomas "Buddy" Bardenwerper.
Description: First edition. | Syracuse, New York : Syracuse University Press, 2021. |
"Sponsored by the Institute for Veterans and Military Families and Syracuse University
Press." | Summary: "Selected as the runner-up for the inaugural Veterans Writing
Award, Bardenwerper's novel explores the friendship between Pat, an officer in the
Coast Guard, and Galán, a Cuban emigrant"— Provided by publisher.
Identifiers: LCCN 2021018790 (print) | LCCN 2021018791 (ebook) |
ISBN 9780815611394 (hardcover) | ISBN 9780815655367 (e-book)
Subjects: LCSH: United States. Coast Guard—Officers—Fiction. | Cubans—
Puerto Rico—Fiction. | Friendship—Fiction.
Classification: LCC PS3602.A7752647 M66 2021 (print) |
LCC PS3602.A7752647 (ebook) | DDC 813/.6—dc23
LC record available at https://lccn.loc.gov/2021018790
LC ebook record available at https://lccn.loc.gov/2021018791

Manufactured in the United States of America

To Alie and Leni, for the love.
To my parents, for the belief.

Contents

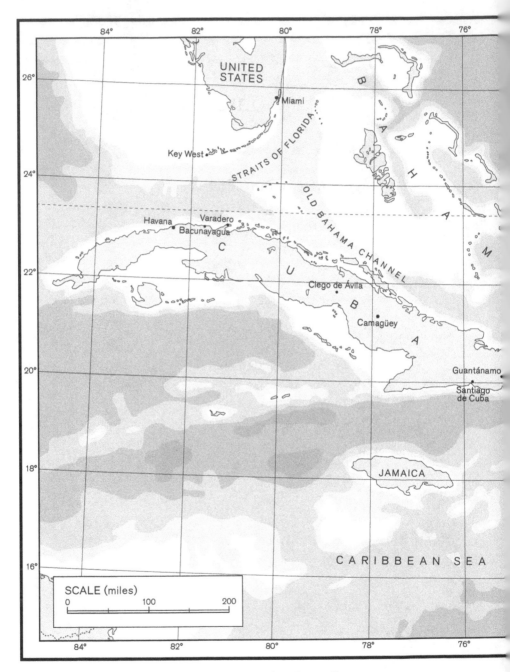

Map 1. Map of the Caribbean. Courtesy of Mike Hall.

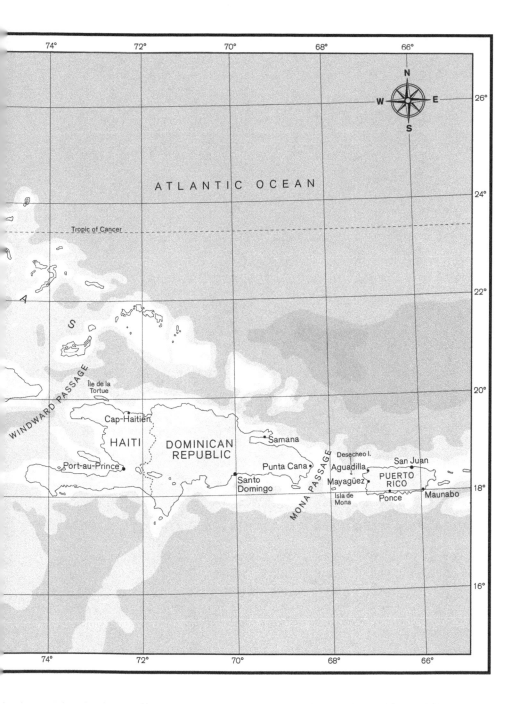

MONA
PASSAGE

Prologue

Bacunayagua, Cuba ~ 1991

The stake-bed truck rattled down the dirt road in the early morning darkness. The fifteen passengers braced themselves against the cab and rail, and the jungle sped away in the red glow of the taillights. Twelve-year-old Galán Betances sat over the rear axle, his younger sister's head in his lap. Gabriela clutched her Winnie the Pooh stuffed animal to her chest in her sleep.

The truck groaned to a stop, and dust settled over the passengers. Some began to whisper, while others rubbed their eyes or craned their necks to get a better view. They had departed from the underpass just outside of Ciego de Ávila six hours earlier.

"Gabi," said Galán, no longer sleepy. "Wake up. We're here."

Gabriela blinked and wiped the saliva from the corner of her mouth. She smiled at Galán, the birthmark on her upper lip barely visible in the darkness.

Galán stood and pulled Gabriela up with him. They waited, hand-in-hand, for their parents.

Gustavo, their father, peeled away from the rail and leaned down. His face, greasy from the diesel fumes, shone in the faint moonlight. "Are you ready, Galán? Remember, I need you."

"Yes, Papá," said Galán, crinkling his nose to avoid his father's stale breath. At least it didn't reek of cane liquor and vomit.

"Good." Gustavo squeezed Galán's shoulder with his calloused hand. He slung his olive green backpack from his Angola deployment over his shoulder and stepped off the tailgate.

1

Galán looked up at his mother, Josefina, who wore a red bandanna around her normally unkempt hair. She didn't return his smile. In fact, she hadn't said anything since they had passed the exit for Cienfuegos just after sunset.

Galán passed Gabriela to his mother and jumped off the tailgate. The dirt here was softer than the dirt in Ciego de Ávila. Or maybe it was sand? It was too dark to tell.

As the group proceeded single-file into the jungle, Galán thought about how he would never play catch again with his father in front of their sagging bungalow. Indeed, he would never be a center fielder for los Tigres de Ciego de Ávila. But then he thought about the evenings he'd spent behind the house holding Gabriela, waiting for the alcohol to put his father to sleep, waiting for his mother to stop crying. Maybe life could change in other ways, too?

A flashlight broke through the darkness from the head of the line. The group stopped, the only noise coming from the frogs and crickets. The beam strafed back and forth across the jungle floor before stopping on a large pile of branches and palm fronds.

"There," said Ramón, the overweight carpenter doubling as captain. "Just where he said it would be. Thanks be to God."

Josefina pulled Gabi closer.

Gustavo's fingers dug into Galán's shoulder.

Ramón, wearing a ball cap emblazoned with the American flag and the word BICENTENNIAL, scrambled through the brush toward the pile. Two younger men followed. As the threesome removed branches and palm fronds, a blue tarp came into view. The skinniest man grabbed a loose corner.

"No, wait, wait," said Ramón, stepping between the skinny man and the tarp. "I'll do it." He raised his jean shorts up under his ample belly and pulled on the tarp. It snagged. "Damn," he muttered, getting a better grip. He pulled again. There was a ripping noise, but the tarp came off.

Galán swallowed. The raft looked like something he and his friend Juani would have built to fly to Mars. Rebar and sheets of corrugated metal held together a collection of large Styrofoam blocks.

In the center, a tractor engine sat in a shallow depression, somehow connected to a homemade propeller. The whole thing was no bigger than the back of the stake-bed truck.

"She may not be pretty," said Ramón, wiping his face with the bottom of his shirt. "But we don't need pretty."

With the raft sitting not more than ten feet from him, Galán could no longer ignore that the trip was really happening. He remembered his nightmare, the black water closing in over his head, the last air he would ever breathe trapped in his lungs. He reached for his mother's hand and could feel her fingers trembling.

"What is that thing?" asked Gabi, her voice still sleepy.

"A boat," said Josefina.

"Oh."

Galán took a deep breath and reminded himself that Ramón knew what he was doing. Ramón was the finest carpenter in all of Ciego de Ávila. He had almost single-handedly rebuilt the neighborhood after the hurricane. Putting together a raft was nothing for him.

"Let's go," said Ramón, waving the rest of the men toward him. "It's not like it has wheels."

The call to action broke the stillness. The men half-pulled and half-lifted the raft down the trail. Galán, Josefina, and Gabriela followed.

"You're telling me this heavy bitch is going to float?" said a straining voice Galán didn't recognize.

"It's called physics," said Ramón. "And to think our country leads the world in education."

"Physics. Gravity. Same shit."

The group plodded along for several more minutes until the trail spilled onto a small, secluded beach. The ocean was blacker than the sky, but a streak of moonlight shimmered on the surface. Galán strained his eyes toward the horizon to see if he could make out Florida, but there was only darkness.

Ramón inspected the engine while a few of the men, Gustavo included, watched over his shoulder. They spoke in hushed tones until there was a loud backfire followed by a steady hum. The engine accelerated for a moment and then went silent.

"Good," said Ramón, satisfied with the test. "Let's go."

The men pushed the raft into the gentle surf. Gustavo turned, the water up to his waist, and waved for his family to join him.

Galán hoisted his and Gabriela's backpacks over his head and waded into the warm water. His sandaled feet dug into the squishy, shapeless mud. Gustavo helped him aboard the raft, which shifted beneath the weight of the embarking Cubans.

As Galán crouched into a tight space between his parents, goose-bumps formed on his wet legs. He tried to rub himself dry. Rivulets of seawater ran through the dead leaves and dirt that coated the Styrofoam.

Galán looked up to force a smile at Gabriela, but she was asleep in Josefina's arms. He couldn't understand how she could sleep at a moment like this, but then again Gabriela was different.

Ramón handed out four oars. "We're not firing up the engine until this damned island is just a memory. You know how sound travels on water. If the Border Guard hear us, we're screwed."

"You're worrying too much, Ramón," said a voice from the other end of the raft. "The third time's the charm."

Gustavo laughed, but Josefina didn't. She just wiped a wet streak from her cheek.

As the four oars dipped rhythmically into the gentle swells, Galán tried to distract himself by thinking about his cousins in Miami. He had only ever seen them in photographs, but they were waiting for him, for Gabriela, for his parents. Yankiel, the oldest, played on a baseball team with blindingly white pinstriped pants and royal-blue stirrups. And then there was the field at Yankiel's school. Straight white foul lines, perfect rows of cut grass . . .

Galán felt rapid breaths close to his ear. His mother was looking over his head at Gustavo.

"What?" said Gustavo.

"I can't," she said. "I can't. Tell him to turn it back."

"What? Are you crazy?" said Gustavo. "Take a deep breath and calm yourself down."

"I can't, Gustavo. I won't. Tell him to turn it back."

"No," said Gustavo through gritted teeth. "You have to calm down."

"Ramón," said Josefina loudly. "Turn it back."

"Be quiet!" said Gustavo. "Have you lost your mind?"

Galán's heart pounded.

"Turn the raft back, Ramón," said Josefina, even louder. The other migrants murmured. "Ramón, I said turn it back!"

"For the love of Christ, Gustavo," said Ramón. "Control her! We can't have this noise."

Josefina shifted her weight, bumping her hip into Galán. There was a splash as she dropped her foot into the water. Gabriela, who was still in Josefina's lap, started to cry.

"Come on, Galán," said Josefina, grabbing his arm. "Let's go."

Gustavo grabbed Galán's other arm.

"What are you doing, Josefina?" said Gustavo. "Get back on this boat!"

"Let's go, Galán," said Josefina. "We're going home. Let's go. Now!" She tugged Galán toward her but he didn't budge.

Gustavo held Galán's arm so tightly that the boy's eyes watered.

"Let go of my son," yelled Josefina to Gustavo. "That's my son. Get your hands off my son!"

"Get back in the goddamned boat!" said Gustavo. He reached for Josefina and Gabriela with his free hand.

Galán didn't know what to do.

Ramón appeared in the darkness above and put his wet sneaker against Josefina's back. He kicked her and Gabriela into the black water.

"Mami!" screamed Galán, sticking out his arm. It was no use— his father now had him in a bear hug.

As the raft slipped away, Josefina and Gabriela popped above the surface, coughing and choking.

"What the hell, Ramón?" yelled Gustavo, not taking his eyes off his wife and daughter.

"You have a problem?" said Ramón. "Then go with them! I don't care. But we're not having this!"

"Turn this thing around and pick them up," said Gustavo. "Josefina! Get back here!"

Ramón clambered to his spot next to the engine. "North," he said to the rowers.

Galán tried to struggle out of his father's arms. "Let me go, Papá!" he yelled, no longer afraid of the deep black water. "Let me go!"

Gustavo only tightened his grip. "Josefina! Josefina! Get back here! Get back here now!"

The only response was Josefina and Gabriela's frantic splashing toward shore, a splashing that grew quieter until all Galán could hear was the dipping of oars. He tried once more to lunge away from his father, but Gustavo was too strong. Galán fell back against his father's broad chest and began to sob.

☆

As the sun crept overhead, Cuba receded toward the horizon until only its green mountains protruded from the sea. The tractor engine hummed, and the men took shifts using a milk carton to scoop seawater into the coolant system—all the men except Gustavo, who sat silent, his face twitching.

Galán remained next to his father, his stillness masking his frantic thoughts. Were his mother and Gabi alive, hitching a ride back to Ciego de Ávila to move in with Aunt Teresa? Or were they floating face down just beyond the break? And if they had somehow survived, would he ever see them again?

Even though the seas were kind, Galán had to focus on what was happening around him to keep from vomiting.

Those migrants not on coolant duty slept. Despite the heat, they covered themselves with loose clothing to avoid the pounding sun. Ramón, however, periodically glanced upward and adjusted the aluminum pipe that served as a tiller. "I'll be damned if we end up in the Bahamas," he said to himself.

Galán swallowed the bile lurking in the back of his throat. Bahamas? United States? What difference did it make? Gabi and his mother wouldn't be there.

Around noon, Gustavo's face finally broke. He blinked and furrowed his brow. Pointing toward the horizon, he nudged Ramón with his foot. It took several seconds before Galán noticed the dark speck.

"It's okay," said Ramón, squinting. "Probably just an American fishing boat." He removed his ball cap and wiped the sweat from his brow with the bottom of his shirt. The fabric had become stretched.

Those who had been sleeping stirred. They watched Ramón. Their captain glanced back and forth between his watch and the sun and appeared to be performing some kind of calculation. He grabbed the tiller and altered course away from the other boat, but the raft was moving too slowly to open the distance.

As the minutes inched by, the other boat grew larger until Galán could make out a high green bow, a white pilothouse, and a trailing ribbon of black smoke.

"Yup, fishermen," said Ramón, nodding. "Still, we have to be smart. I don't want these bastards radioing the Coast Guard."

White waves rolled off the fishing vessel's bow. A name was written in white paint across the starboard side, but Galán couldn't read it. Still, the fishermen had to be able to see the raft by now. God willing they would call the Coast Guard, and Galán would be reunited with his mother and Gabriela. After a few days, the whole ordeal would be nothing more than a bizarre, fading nightmare.

"That's close enough," said Ramón, killing the engine. "Get the tarp."

Two men pulled the large sheet from the space in front of the engine and began unfolding. Others took the loose ends and spread the tarp over themselves and the raft.

"Jesus Christ," said Ramón. "Not the white side up! Put the blue side up! Shit! You think these Americans are expecting to see a goddamned iceberg out here?"

The migrants flipped the tarp. Once they had it secured to the edges of the raft, they waited underneath. They were silent but for the occasional whisper. Ramón, who had kept a corner of the tarp folded back, was the only one who could see out.

The temperature rose. Not only did the sun cook from the outside, but the tractor engine radiated heat from within. Sweat dripped from Galán's face onto the gouged Styrofoam. He thought about shouting to the fishermen until he noticed the hilt of a knife protruding from Ramón's waistband. Galán had never seen Ramón truly angry.

The minutes dragged on, and the steady rumbling of the fishing boat's engines became audible. Gustavo murmured something that sounded vaguely familiar to Galán. Was his father, the same man who laughed at Josefina when she went to Sunday Mass, praying the Our Father?

"What does it look like, Ramón?" a frightened voice asked.

"Shut up," said Ramón.

"Ramón—"

"I said shut up!"

The approaching engines grew louder. Galán waited for an American fisherman to reach down and snatch the tarp away, or worse, for the snub-nosed green vessel to plow over the flimsy raft. He dug his fingernails into the Styrofoam.

Ramón laughed.

"What, Ramón?" asked the same scared voice.

"There's nobody on the bridge," he said. "Autopilot. Those Americans have that thing going on autopilot. They're probably taking a damned nap. I should have known. Lazy bastards."

The other migrants laughed, but Galán closed his eyes and buried his forehead into the Styrofoam. He bit his lip to keep from crying out.

★

Galán awoke disoriented beneath a dark sky. He lay still until he recognized his father snoring beside him. The wind had picked up, and the raft rose and fell with the waves. On the port side, a silhouette defecated into the water. Ramón, hunched but still awake, poured water into the engine.

Galán, afraid of standing and being pitched into the sea, slid on his backside across the Styrofoam toward the captain. "How much farther is it, Don Ramón?" His voice cracked from dryness.

"I don't know, kid," said Ramón, reaching the milk jug into the salt water. "Depends on the currents, the winds. But I'd say we're more than halfway."

"Halfway" would've been more helpful if Galán hadn't lost track of the hours that had passed. He scratched his head before giving up on the uncertain math.

"You want me to pour for a little bit?" Galán asked. He wanted to do something, anything, even if it meant helping the man who had kicked his mother and sister into the sea.

Ramón looked him up and down. "Sure," he finally said, handing Galán the jug.

By focusing on the scooping and pouring, Galán managed to briefly forget that his mother and sister were gone. But the trick only lasted so long. When the memory of their wild splashing inevitably exploded into his consciousness, his breath caught, and his pulse quickened.

Galán was about to start crying again when he noticed the oldest man in the group staring at him from beneath the wide brim of a straw hat. Galán looked away. He didn't like how the man stared so intently, how he didn't blink. But with each passing minute of pretending to be engrossed in coolant duty, the more Galán felt like an animal in a zoo. He finally stole another glance.

The old man seemed to have been waiting. He smiled and pointed a long finger toward the black sky. "Olokun will bring her back." With that, he pulled his hat down over his face and laid back onto the Styrofoam.

Galán didn't know much about Olokun—his mother always said that the *orishas* were "sacrilegious"—but something about the man and his strange, knowing statement made Galán's heart race even faster. And why did the old man say *her* and not *them*?

Trembling, Galán spilled the water onto the hot engine block. The water hissed into steam, scalding him back into the moment.

☆

When Galán woke again, the sky was still dark, but the winds had calmed. The other migrants appeared to be sleeping—all except Ramón. The hefty carpenter, his shirt wrapped around his head, fussed over the sputtering engine. A disconnected hose hung uselessly.

Galán turned away and tried not to think about what would happen if the engine failed. His stomach grumbled and his mouth felt like sandpaper. He retrieved a water bottle and a package of crackers from his backpack. He drank slowly, letting the water soak into his parched tongue before swallowing. Then he ate one of the crackers in small bites. It did little to satisfy his hunger, and its saltiness made him thirstier.

As Galán stowed his bag, he noticed Gabriela's pink backpack jammed between two blocks of Styrofoam. He pulled it out, its familiar texture and heft bringing back memories of carrying it for her on the way home from school. Wherever Gabriela went, so did the backpack, along with Winnie the Pooh and the plastic horse that was missing a hoof and the tip of its tail. Galán had hated being the one boy with a pink backpack, but now he would do anything to walk his sister home again from la Escuela Primaria Vargas Hernández.

The raft lurched. Galán looked to his left and right but saw nothing unusual—only the shapes of several other migrants sitting up. The bump had felt like a wave hitting the raft broadside, but the seas were calm.

After a minute of nothing but the normal rocking, Galán returned to inventorying Gabriela's backpack. He had just uncovered the plastic horse beneath a package of cookies when he heard a loud splash behind him. He turned but again didn't see anything.

"Did you hear that?" somebody asked.

"Yeah," said Ramón, "probably some kind of fish."

"It must be a big-ass fish."

The raft lurched again, this time in the opposite direction. By now, all of the migrants were awake, murmuring to each other and staring at the dark ocean. The skinny man who had helped Ramón pull the branches from the raft made the sign of the cross.

The raft jumped a third time, violently enough that Galán dropped Gabriela's bag onto the deck. The only woman aboard sobbed, and the skinny man clasped his hands in prayer.

Galán remembered again his nightmare about the black ocean. His breaths became rapid and shallow. He felt like he was going to suffocate.

"Control yourself," said Gustavo, turning away from the sea toward Galán. "Be a goddamned man."

Galán managed a nod.

A blinding light burst through the darkness. A man on the other side of the raft was wildly scanning the waves with a flashlight.

"Put that shit away," yelled Ramón. "They'll be able to see that from Miami!"

Whoever had the flashlight didn't listen.

"My God!" the solitary woman screamed. There in the beam of light, not ten feet from the raft, a fin cut slowly through the water. The skinny man dropped to his knees in the engine depression, his hands outstretched toward the heavens. More than a few of the other men cursed.

Ramón clambered across the raft and snatched the flashlight. He flung it into the sea, where it sank beneath the waves, the glowing orb dropping into the shadowy depths. The night seemed even darker than before.

Now that he could barely see, Galán couldn't stop himself from imagining sharks circling the raft. They didn't even have to bite anybody to make his nightmare come true. They only needed to thrash the raft into pieces. His hyperventilating worsened, and he felt like he was already drowning.

"For the love of Christ," said Gustavo, grabbing Galán by the shoulders. "Pull yourself together!"

Galán nodded again. He tried to hold his breath, but the effort just made him choke.

Gustavo slapped Galán across the side of the head. Galán's ears rang, but the shock knocked his breathing back to normal. He blinked away the tears and was surprised not to see anger in his father's eyes.

"It's going to be okay," said Gustavo, his forehead touching Galán's. "You have to trust me. It's going to be okay."

Galán collapsed into his father's arms. He gave up fighting the sharks and the darkness and the sea. He surrendered.

Once he finally fell asleep, Galán dreamt that he was eating breakfast with Gabriela before school. He could smell the eggs his mother fried on the camp stove and could hear the roosters crowing behind the house. His father's stained fluorescent-yellow work vest hung from the hook on the front door. For some reason, though, the bench he shared with Gabriela kept shifting beneath his weight. The floor was moving.

But Galán didn't mind. They were together.

Part One

1

Every time the Coast Guard interceptor slammed into a wave, Lieutenant Pat McAllister felt the midnight coffee slosh in his belly. In the darkness, he couldn't anticipate the jolts that rocked the thirty-foot boat and reverberated up his spine. Smugglers loved moonless nights.

The radio buzzed. Gripping the navigation console, Pat strained to hear the transmission coming from the Customs and Border Protection airplane, but the rushing wind and inboard engine were too loud. It didn't matter. He knew they were within a mile of the suspicious speedboat heading north toward Puerto Rico.

Pat took a deep breath and exhaled slowly. He had been making these interdictions for two years. While his knees no longer shook, he still had that unsettled feeling in his stomach.

Pat reached into his pocket and felt the Velcro patch that he brought on every boarding. It was a McAllister nametag in army camouflage, not Coast Guard blue. It had gone to Iraq and back with Pat's older brother, Danny. Upon receiving his discharge and coming home, Danny had jammed his duffel bag full of uniforms under his childhood bed. Pat had taken the nametag one afternoon when Danny was drinking at the American Legion.

"Got 'em!" yelled Petty Officer Wallace, a wiry Texan and one of the other three members of the interceptor crew. "Just off the starboard bow."

Pat turned up the volume on his headset and wiped the salt spray from his goggles. Below the faint horizon, a ghostly rooster tail of water trailed a barely visible speedboat. Chief Landis, the coxswain and most seasoned crewmember aboard, must have seen it too. He pushed the throttle forward, causing Pat to slide back in his seat.

"Cutter Strickland," radioed Pat. "We have eyes on the target." He didn't bother waiting for a response, as he knew the watch standers in the ship's pilothouse would only complicate things.

Chief Landis maneuvered the interceptor just outside of the speedboat's wake. "Going overt," he said, flipping a switch on his console. A white floodlight and a blue strobe pierced through the darkness. A siren wailed.

The smugglers' speedboat, which had been nothing but an eerie gray shape, stood out in vibrant detail. It had a high, sharp prow, two outboard Yamaha engines, and the name *el Angelito* written in red cursive along a blue hull. Two men in black rain jackets and ski masks stared momentarily before turning to each other and yelling. The man who was not driving made his way toward the stern.

Petty Officer Martínez, the muscle-bound Puerto Rican engineer seated behind Pat, called out to the smugglers in Spanish over a bullhorn. Pat didn't understand the words perfectly, but he knew Martínez was telling the smugglers to stop or else they would shoot.

The smugglers turned abruptly, cutting across the bow of the interceptor. Chief Landis reduced speed, careful not to overshoot the smugglers and become a ramming target. A senior chief had been killed that way off the coast of California.

"All right, Martínez," said Chief Landis. "Let's go with those warning shots."

"Roger." Martínez pressed the pyrotechnic rounds into the shotgun's tube with his thumb. He slid the pump forward, chambering the first shell.

Chief Landis positioned the interceptor alongside the speedboat. Only twenty feet separated the two bouncing, roaring vessels.

Martínez shouldered the shotgun. "On target."

"Batteries release," said Chief Landis.

The warning shots exploded into small fireworks in front of the speedboat. It didn't stop. Pat wasn't surprised. The smugglers had too much to lose.

"Disabling fire, Martínez," said Chief Landis. "And don't fuck it up like Wallace."

The rest of the interceptor crew laughed over the internal communications system except Pat. He didn't know what Wallace had done.

"We got a problem," said Martínez, as he secured the shotgun and loaded a magazine into the M16 rifle. The smuggler who had been crawling aft was now draped across the closest Yamaha outboard, his face turned away from the spraying wake.

"You know what to do," said Chief Landis.

"Roger," said Martínez, raising the rifle. "On target."

"Batteries release."

These two bangs were louder and sharper. The red tracer rounds streaked ten feet behind the engines. The smuggler shielding the Yamaha yelled at his partner with more fervor than before. Pat couldn't hear him, but he could see the man's mouth moving through the hole in the ski mask.

"Two more," said Chief Landis.

This time, the rounds darted only five feet aft of the engines. The smuggler acting as a human shield stopped yelling, but he didn't move, either. He stared at the interceptor, his eyes wide and his exposed belly hanging over the transom.

"Two more," said Chief Landis.

"You sure, Chief?" asked Martínez. "That's going to be close."

"Your call, XO," said Chief Landis to Pat.

The last thing Pat needed was to accidentally kill a smuggler on his first patrol as executive officer of Coast Guard Cutter *Strickland*. He'd learned enough during his tour on his first cutter to know that one unforeseen wave could send a round dangerously off target. But he also couldn't afford a reputation of doubting his new crew. Pat licked the salt water that ran down his face. If Chief Landis trusted Martínez, so did he.

"I'm good with it," said Pat.

"Aye, sir," said Martínez. He sighted in and squeezed off two more rounds. They barely danced past the stern of the speedboat. The smuggler released his grip on the Yamaha and scrambled forward, despite the screaming from his partner at the helm. Pat exhaled.

"Finish it, Martínez," said Chief Landis, his voice still calm.

Martínez fired four rounds in quick succession into the Yamahas. A small orange flame licked its way out of one of the bullet holes, and the speedboat slowed to a stop. Chief Landis turned the interceptor away from the smugglers in an easy loop.

Pat unbuckled his seatbelt, removed his helmet and goggles, and pulled off his headset. He could finally hear the frantic voices of the smugglers. Touching the McAllister nametag one more time, he reminded himself not to become complacent. He didn't know what the cartel had threatened to do to the smugglers' families as punishment for a failed delivery. He licked his lips and drew his pistol from his thigh holster.

"All right," said Chief Landis, completing the circle and pointing the bow at the speedboat. "Just like we talked about. You ready, XO?"

"Ready, Chief," said Pat, wiping salt water and sweat from his face.

"Martínez?"

"Ready."

Chief Landis slowly brought the interceptor alongside the speedboat, and Pat moved forward to the bow.

"*Manos arriba!*" yelled Martínez. "*No se muevan!*" The smugglers congregated in the middle of their boat with their hands over their heads.

Just as the two boats made contact, Pat jumped. He landed tailbone first on a plastic fuel drum and crawled across several more to the nearest man. Martínez followed and approached the other smuggler. Wallace stood in the bow of the interceptor and provided cover with his pistol.

Pat handcuffed his man, who was muttering under his breath. Pat slid an orange life preserver over the man's neck, buckled the straps together, and frisked him. He didn't find anything except pockets soaked with salt water and gasoline. The man smelled about as ripe as Pat would have expected him to smell after a three-day journey from Riohacha, Colombia.

Pat removed the man's soaking ski mask and froze. The smuggler wasn't a man so much as a boy. He looked younger than Pat. Younger by a lot. And he had tears in his eyes.

The boy said something in Spanish that Pat didn't understand. The kid touched his ear to his shoulder as if he were speaking on the telephone.

"*Mi mamá,*" he said. "*Mi mamá.*"

Pat looked away from the boy's pleading eyes. "I'm sorry, brother," he finally mumbled. He tried to think of something calming to say, but he didn't have enough confidence in his Spanish. He patted the handcuffed boy's knee and moved away.

While Martínez searched the bow, Pat climbed aft. Behind the fiberglass center console, Pat found the usual provisions and garbage. Tins of Vienna sausage and pink bottles of Postobón Manzana soda floated on a shallow mixture of salt water, gasoline, and vomit. Two backpacks were strapped to the driver's bench, each stuffed with soaked clothing and a toothbrush.

"Hell yeah," said Martínez from the bow.

Pat pulled his head out of the battery compartment and looked forward. Martínez was bent over a flapping blue tarp, the veins in his arms bulging. When he stood, he held a tightly wrapped bale of pressed cocaine the size of a carry-on suitcase. "I see about twelve, maybe fifteen," said Martínez, grinning. He set the bale down with a thud that rocked the boat. "That's how we do, sir. That's how we fucking do."

"I knew you could shoot," said Pat, sitting down on the driver's bench. He did the math—probably just under a thousand kilos.

"Yup," said Martínez. "Wallace would have jacked it all up, though."

Pat laughed. He leaned over the gunwale to clean his hands in the salt water when he noticed the fat, older detainee signaling to him. The man said something in Spanish.

Pat turned to Martínez.

"He says his teeth," said Martínez, counting the bales. "He says give him his teeth. They're in that jacket stuffed into the console."

Pat pulled out the jacket and opened a pocket. Nothing but a piece of paper covered in latitude and longitude coordinates. Good intelligence. He kept digging until he found a set of dentures. He picked them out carefully and put them into the handcuffed man's mouth. The man nodded as he seated them with his tongue.

Next to where the jacket had been sat a waterproof bag. Pat picked it up, hoping to find a GPS or a satellite phone. Instead, he found a wooden figure of la Virgen de Altagracia, her eyes down-turned and her pale hands clasped in prayer.

Pat took the religious icon out of the bag and turned it between his fingers. He pictured the old man—it was probably the old man and not the kid—taking the statue down from a shelf in his home before setting sail from his fishing village. Or maybe the old man's wife had given it to him. Maybe they had even said a prayer together.

Pat slid the statue into his pocket next to Danny's nametag for safe keeping. He noticed the old man watching him. Pat wanted to tell the man that la Virgen would be safer with him than she would be inside a wet evidence bag cooking under the Caribbean sun, but when Pat looked up the man quickly turned toward the coming dawn.

And maybe if Pat looked out for la Virgen, she would look out for Danny.

2

San Juan, Puerto Rico

Galán, squinting against the late afternoon sunlight that streamed in from la Calle San Francisco, flipped the window placard from ABIERTO to CERRADO. He popped open the cash register and counted the money. Not bad, he thought, especially for a Monday. With an inclination of his head, he told Sefora, the new waitress, that she could go home.

Armed with his savings from Key West, Galán had opened la Fonda del Ciego shortly after his arrival in Puerto Rico ten years earlier. He had poured himself into all facets of his new diner, and la Fonda had earned a reputation amongst Old San Juan's locals as a reliable breakfast and lunch spot. The only mystery was the name— *Ciego* was a place, not a person.

Sefora shouldered her purse and waved good-bye. Galán smiled. There was no point saying anything because she was wearing headphones just like all of the other kids. He shook his head as the glass door closed behind her. Maybe he was just getting old.

Back in his windowless office, Galán tidied the card table that served as a desk and unplugged the fan that had long ago lost its protective screen. He refused to throw it away, as it reminded him to never forget where he came from.

After turning off the lights, Galán stepped out of the diner and into a wall of humidity. *Reggaetón* thumped out of a Mazda hatchback parked nearby. Something about *perreo*. Galán pulled down the mesh gate and snapped the padlock closed.

After visiting the grocery store on la Plaza de Armas, Galán climbed the stairs of a pink Spanish colonial building on la Calle Luna to his third-floor apartment. He entered his musty quarters and threw open the hurricane shutters. The Atlantic breeze rushed in from across his terrace. Galán looked around outside for the black cat but didn't see him.

With leftover rice and beans on the stove, Galán cracked open a gold can of Medalla. He knew he should cut down on his drinking, but a few beers here and there numbed the loneliness and regret. And even so, it wasn't like he was turning into his father—Gustavo's cirrhosis had put him in a Florida cemetery only a few years after he'd completed the naturalization process.

Galán stood at the edge of his terrace and looked down at la Plaza de la Barandilla. Young women in scrubs walked out from between the Roman columns of la Universidad de Albizu. Don Eduardo, the one homeless man to whom Galán regularly gave a few dollars, fed pigeons from a concrete bench. Galán appreciated how Don Eduardo still shined his shoes and wore a threadbare fedora. But now even Don Eduardo wore headphones. Galán chuckled and returned to the kitchen.

Galán spooned the rice and beans onto his plate and opened a second beer. He ate in silence on the terrace, enjoying the warm breeze. The sky turned orange over el Castillo San Felipe—also known as El Morro—one of the two massive Spanish fortresses buttressing Old San Juan. Just as Galán returned to the fridge for a third beer, he remembered.

"Shit."

It was the second time that week that he had started drinking too early. He retreated into his dark bedroom and lit the Virgen de la Caridad votive candle. As he crossed himself, the faces of Josefina and Gabriela looked back at him from wallet-sized photographs in the flickering light. Galán closed his eyes.

"Hail Mary, full of grace . . ."

The words flowed automatically, and Galán's mind traveled back to Ciego de Ávila. He was pacing across the living room of the bungalow, his bare feet leaving footprints on the dusty floorboards. Galán had been watching Gabriela while his mother prepared the chicken and plantains, but he had stepped away to kick a soccer ball with Juani in the rutted street. Now the stroller on the porch was empty.

When his father came through the door in the afternoon twilight, his yellow work vest from the state-owned gas station covered in oil and sweat, Galán stopped pacing. He looked at his cracked and dirty toenails and fought the urge to cry. He knew that crying would only make his father angrier.

"What did you do this time?" asked Gustavo, hanging his vest on the nail next to the door.

"It's Gabi," said Galán. He didn't have to look up to know that his father's eyes were already slightly bloodshot.

"What about her?"

"She's missing."

Gustavo dropped his leather work gloves. "What?"

"She's missing."

Gustavo stared at him unblinking before heading back out the door. Galán collapsed against the rusty refrigerator and sobbed into his hands. The sun set, and he eventually fell asleep.

Galán awoke to shouting in the street. He stood and peered outside. A small group of neighbors surrounded Gustavo and Josefina, and in Josefina's arms was a baby. Galán dashed outside, broke through the crowd, and hugged his mother's legs. He didn't care that other children were watching.

"I'm so sorry," Galán started to say, but he was interrupted by a nearby commotion.

"My girl!" wailed an older lady who lived down the street. "My girl!" Her toothless gums flapped, and her eyes darted about. A young man held her close and attempted to usher her away from the others.

Gustavo stared at the old lady with his lip curled.

"It's okay, Gustavo," said Josefina, holding the back of her husband's shirt with her free hand. "It was a mistake. She's not right in the head."

"Then she shouldn't be allowed out and about," said Gustavo. "She's a threat to public safety!"

The old lady continued to wail as she struggled against the young man. "They can't take my baby! They can't take my Esmeralda!"

"Esmeralda is okay," said the young man. "She'll be home from work any minute." He steered his teetering grandmother down the street, and the group of neighbors slowly dispersed.

The Betances family went back inside. Galán had hardly crossed the threshold before his father grabbed him and spun him around. Gustavo squatted down in front of Galán, his eyes remarkably focused.

"You have no idea how lucky you are," said Gustavo, his fingers digging deep into Galán's shoulder. "You will never, ever leave your sister like that again. Do you understand me?"

Galán nodded.

"Do you understand me?" Gustavo's voice shook. "I want to hear it. I need you to promise me that you will never leave her again."

"Yes, Papá," said Galán, blinking away the tears. "I understand. I promise."

3

San Juan, Puerto Rico

Pat awoke in a dark room. Little lines of sunlight snuck through the shutters, and an air conditioner whirred overhead. As the fog of sleep receded, Pat realized that the patrol was over. He was home.

Even though it was almost ten, Pat still felt groggy. The *Strickland* had moored at the Coast Guard base on la Puntilla at midnight, but Pat hadn't granted liberty until the crew had sprayed down the weather decks, stowed the .50 caliber machine guns, and tidied the berthing areas.

As Pat brushed his teeth, he heard a knock. He swished water around his mouth and walked down the narrow hallway. He fumbled with the unfamiliar lock and opened the door.

"*Buenos días*, Patricio! How do you find yourself?" An older man with a gray ponytail hustled inside and set a brown paper bag on a nearby table. He wore a dozen bracelets and necklaces, some gold, others silver, and a few made out of wooden beads.

"Hello!" said Pat, shaking the man's hand. Pat had no idea who he was, but he already liked him.

"I'm Edwin, Edwin Peña, your landlord," said the man in English. "*Landlord* is a funny word to me, but you Americans seem to like it. Maybe because your country was birthed by the Brits!" He let out a cackle. "Either way, I consider myself a benevolent landlord."

"Well, that's better than the alternative," said Pat. He had first arrived in Puerto Rico just days before the recent patrol and had yet to meet the man to whom he paid rent.

25

"Yes, yes!" said Edwin before lowering his voice in a conspiratorial tone. "But I had to be a bit malevolent to the last young man that lived here. He was a real rat's ass. You? I already have a better feeling about you!"

"Oh yeah? Why's that?"

"Because on this day in 1812, Johann Galle was born."

"Johann Galle?"

"Johann Galle. He discovered Neptune. And you, my friend, are a sailor, no? So I believe this bodes well for both of us."

Pat laughed. "I believe it does."

"And, on this day in 1964," Edwin continued, "I lost my virginity in this very building!" He let out another gleeful cackle, this time shuffling his feet in a little dance. "So, how do you like your new home?"

"How do I like it? The view alone is worth the $1,500." From the roof, Pat had a panoramic vista of the colonial skyline, the San Juan Bay, and the distant mountains.

"Be careful what you say, or else I will start charging you double. But yes, Puerto Rico is the most beautiful sight in the world. Other than women, of course!" Edwin broke into another shuffle, his bracelets and necklaces jangling together.

Pat smiled as Edwin wheezed to a stop.

"Anyway," said Edwin, pulling out a cigarette, "I'm glad to finally meet you, and I'm sure you are eager to make yourself at home. I, too, have a busy day planned. So busy, that I am already two cigarettes behind!"

Edwin walked toward the door but stopped short. His mischievous grin disappeared. "And Patricio, you should know that these are complicated times for my island. The economy is in the shitter, as you might say, and life is hard for some of my countrymen. So if you run into any problems, knock on my door downstairs." He paused, a lecherous look spreading across his face. "Unless I am entertaining."

"I appreciate that," said Pat, laughing. "And don't worry, I won't interrupt your entertaining. I think that's part of a code or something."

"Yes, a code amongst neighbors—or better yet, a code amongst friends. Ah! I almost forgot the whole reason I came up here! I brought you a housewarming gift." Edwin pulled a bottle of Ron de Barrilito from the paper bag. "This is the best Puerto Rican rum. See, three stars. I figured a sailor like you could use some."

"That's for sure," said Pat, turning the clear bottle over in his hand. The white label depicted a cherub holding a barrel. "Thank you."

"You're welcome, my friend." Edwin opened the door and stepped into the humid stairwell. "Remember, Patricio, I have a good feeling about you." He closed the door and cackled his way down the stairs.

Pat shook his head, still smiling. He would have to tell Danny about this guy. A few laughs would do his brother some good.

★

Pat's first Saturday night in Puerto Rico found him on his couch watching the Houston Astros play the St. Louis Cardinals on WAPA Deportes. He had taken Spanish in high school, but Señora Jiménez's hands-off approach of playing grainy VHS recordings of dry, Latin American history documentaries hadn't paid dividends.

Pat checked his phone just as Yadier Molina, the stocky, tattooed Cardinals catcher from nearby Bayamón, stepped to the plate. No new messages. Pat wasn't surprised.

As the *Strickland*'s executive officer, Pat existed in a social no-man's-land between the enlisted crew and junior officers on the one hand, and the captain on the other. Traditional maritime hierarchy, not to mention the Uniform Code of Military Justice, made intermingling of the ranks awkward even under the best of circumstances.

Pat thought about going downstairs and knocking on Edwin's door. But what if his landlord was presently engaged in some amorous acrobatics? And even if Edwin wasn't, what would the two of them do together—separated as they were by half a century in age?

To hell with it, thought Pat. He had to get out of the apartment. He screwed the cap back on the bottle of Ron de Barrilito and checked himself in the bathroom mirror. Coast Guard regulations didn't leave him with a whole lot of hair to work with, but he wet his fingers and pushed his black bangs to the side nonetheless. No matter how tan he became, his blue eyes would always give him away as a *yanqui*.

Pat was sweating before he even emerged from the dark stairwell onto cobblestoned la Calle Luna. The streetlamps cast an orange glow, and stray cats darted out from behind parked cars and dumpsters. They appeared unfazed by the ubiquitous salsa and *reggaetón* coming out of open windows and passing cars.

Thinking of Michaela and her love of cats, Pat sent her a picture of a tabby reclined on the canvas roof of a Ford Mustang. Michaela had cried when she had heard about Pat's orders to Puerto Rico. If he wasn't enough of a draw for her to leave her nursing job in Philadelphia and move to the island, maybe the cats would be.

Closer toward the harbor, loud tourists armed with absurdly tall alcoholic drinks stumbled out of bars and into the middle of the narrow streets, blocking traffic. Hucksters worked the corners. A menacing, scrawny man in a green top hat carried a lethargic iguana over his shoulder. Perhaps the man's Taser explained the reptile's pale, sickly complexion. Even in their inebriated state, the tourists gave the duo a wide berth.

Underwhelmed, Pat changed course and weaved his way back up the hill toward la Calle San Sebastián. The tourists thinned out, only to be replaced by young locals. Like high school young. Then Pat remembered the drinking age was eighteen.

Pat hesitated outside Humberto's Spot. Inside, young Puerto Ricans drank Medalla and Redd's and shot pool. Pat liked the beat of the *reggaetón*, but he didn't like how the patrons stared at him in the doorway.

He continued down la Calle Norzagaray, the high road that paralleled the Atlantic. In the distance, a glowing cruise ship sailed east to Saint Thomas. Down below were the weather-beaten tin roofs of la Perla. Medalla and Sangriiia banners hung from the walls of the closely packed buildings. Pat had been told that white boys like himself weren't welcome at the bottom of those dark, winding stone steps.

Pat turned right onto a well-lit pedestrian street. Older people danced salsa to the rhythms emanating from large outdoor speakers. The revelers could have been the parents or even the grandparents of the kids he had seen a few blocks before. Pat squeezed past them into an adjacent bar and realized why everybody was outside. The lone ceiling fan didn't stand a chance against the tropical heat.

Pat waited to order a drink, beads of sweat running down his nose. Photos of local heroes covered the red walls, including a life-sized poster of the boxer Félix "Tito" Trinidad. As a kid, Pat had watched Tito wage pugilistic war in his blue-and-red Puerto Rico trunks. Little did Pat know that he would one day live on the welterweight's island.

A spot opened at the bar, and Pat ordered a Medalla from a sober-faced woman with a nose ring. As he walked away with the cold can wrapped in a napkin, he heard her greet the next customer with a joke in Spanish.

Out in the alley, Pat found a spot against the wall and sipped his beer. As he watched the old couples dance, he wondered what Michaela was doing a thousand miles to the northwest. He wondered how long it would take to swim to her if he were endowed with some kind of amphibious superpower. Maybe a couple of weeks? That was assuming he didn't get stabbed in la Perla on his way into the surf.

The enormous speakers went silent, and the crowd began to whoop. Pat craned his neck. A live band had assembled under a small tent. An older man in a tweed flat cap and linen shirt stood at the microphone, while a younger tattooed man with dreadlocks sat on a milk crate behind a drum.

With a shout, the younger man smacked the drum with his palms, creating a machine gun–like beat. The singer chanted at a frenzied pace. One courageous woman gyrated in front of the band, but the rest of the crowd only yelled words of encouragement.

Pat leaned back against the wall and sipped his beer. Puerto Rico, he thought, smiling. He couldn't really believe he lived here. And to think it all began on the banks of the muddy Chattahoochee River.

Marinating in the music and ocean breeze, Pat remembered that weekend in Columbus, Georgia. He remembered his father hunched over the steering wheel of the rented Buick and his mother staring out at the passing blur of scrub pines. Nobody spoke.

For eight weeks, thirteen-year-old Pat had been counting down the days until Danny's graduation from US Army basic training. He would reread Danny's letters, picturing his brother in green fatigues rappelling from towers or sending 5.56 rounds downrange.

Pat's father, fumbling with a map spread across his lap, exited US 185. The McAllisters entered a world of pawn shops, strip clubs, and payday loan businesses. The neon signs competed with each other for young soldiers' paychecks.

"Are you sure this is right?" asked Pat's mother, her brow furrowed. "This doesn't look right to me. Where did you see a sign for Fort Benning?"

"I didn't," said Pat's father. "But look—Victory Drive. I'll be damned if Victory Drive won't take you to Fort Benning."

"We're not going to be late, are we?" asked Pat. "Doesn't it start at one? We can't be late."

Mr. McAllister looked at the dashboard clock. "No, we'll be fine. Everybody just relax." He gunned the engine to beat a red light. "See. There it is. 'Welcome to Fort Benning. Home of the Infantry.'"

Pat's pulse quickened.

At the gate, the McAllisters encountered a tired-looking military policeman with a rifle slung over his shoulder. Pat's father handed over his New Hampshire driver's license, but Pat's mother realized she had left hers at Logan Airport. The military policeman accepted a Costco membership card instead.

"Imagine that," said Pat's father, winding the Buick around the serpentine barricades. "Saved by a goddamned Costco card. We should write them a letter."

Pat was too distracted to laugh. Up ahead were the large, T-shaped towers for the Airborne School. Danny had mentioned that he might be going there soon.

Mr. McAllister followed the signs to the Morale, Welfare, and Recreation Center. He parked the Buick, and the McAllisters hustled into the musty gymnasium. They found seats at the top of the bleachers, and Pat scanned the rows of shaved heads below for Danny. Even though Pat had never seen Danny with a buzz cut, he narrowed the search to five suspects before a tinny recording of martial music burst from the sound system.

The color guard marched in with the American flag. Everyone stood. Pat had heard the "Star Spangled Banner" at sporting events, but this time it was different. This time the flag and the anthem seemed fragile.

Pat sang along until he realized he didn't know all of the words.

After the anthem, the audience sat, and a succession of commissioned and noncommissioned officers delivered scripted remarks. Pat finally understood what his teacher meant when she said clichés kill good English. Still, he liked it. He liked all of the references to sacrifice and brotherhood and camaraderie and victory.

Pat looked around the cavernous gym. The graduates, seated at the position of attention, seemed to be listening, but the same couldn't be said for the rest of the audience. Most of the attendees fiddled with cell phones or disposable cameras or attended to wailing toddlers.

Pat turned back to the soldiers to keep looking for Danny. By the time the ceremony ended with an unnecessarily loud recording of "The Army Goes Rolling Along," his search was down to two.

Pat kept his eye on the potential Dannys as he and his parents clambered down the bleachers and out onto the parade field. Sure enough, his hunch was right. One of the soldiers turned and smiled a crooked smile.

"I see him!" said Pat, breaking into a run and leaving his parents behind.

Danny's dark-green dress uniform looked good on his wiry yet muscular body, but the massive brown-framed glasses didn't. Before

Pat knew what was happening, he had his arms around Danny like when they were kids. A cold, gold button from Danny's jacket pressed against his temple. So much for the manly handshake he had planned.

"I missed you," said Pat. "I can't believe you did it."

"I missed you too, Patty," said Danny, laughing. "But you really had that little faith in me? Come on, man!"

Pat let go and allowed his father to deliver the manly handshake. Mr. McAllister's eyes were watery, something Pat had only seen once before, at his grandmother's funeral. "You look great, Specialist," said Mr. McAllister. "Man, you look great."

"I should hope so," said Danny, laughing. "I only spent an hour last night making sure this monkey suit was put together within regs."

Mrs. McAllister hugged her son so tightly that she knocked her glasses askew. When she finally stepped back, she was crying, too.

A drill sergeant in a Smokey the Bear hat approached, and Danny popped to attention. "Good afternoon, Sergeant Waters!" he said in a deep voice that Pat didn't recognize.

"At ease, Specialist McAllister," said Sergeant Waters, a heavily muscled man with a bulging neck. He shook Danny's hand and congratulated him. "Enjoy the weekend, because on Monday it's back to work. And you thought I was bad!" He laughed from somewhere deep in his chest. "You're going to love the infantry!"

"Yes, Sergeant," said the new Danny, as Sergeant Waters and his booming laugh disappeared into the crowd.

"Do you think you could introduce us to your friend from Chicago that you were always telling us about in your letters?" asked Mrs. McAllister. "You know, the guy that made the chessboard out of the napkin?"

"Yeah, I don't know," said Danny, his voice back to normal. "I don't really want to spend any more time here than I have to. I've only been waiting to get off this infernal base for eight weeks." He picked up a green "McAllister" duffle bag from in between "Matos" and "McDowell."

As they approached the rental car, Pat peppered Danny with questions about his ribbons, his marksmanship, the morning work-outs. He talked so fast that Danny didn't have a chance to answer.

"I'll tell you about it later," said Danny, smiling. "I promise. But first, we have to find that Chick-Fil-A. It should be out the main gate to the left. You don't even know how long I've been dreaming about a spicy deluxe."

They found the Chick-Fil-A, and Danny demolished two sand-wiches. Pat was too excited to even finish one. Afterward, they returned to the Sheraton in downtown Columbus.

"Damn," said Danny, looking at the redbrick textile mills that had been converted into bars, coffeeshops, and loft apartments. "I had no idea any of this was here. This isn't a bad town at all. Not a lot of girls, though."

"That's true, but you could do a lot worse," said Mr. McAllis-ter, parking the Buick. He tried to extricate himself from behind the steering wheel. "It's like a nicer version of Manchester. Hey, Patty. Why don't you give Danny a hand with his bag?"

Pat already had it over his shoulder. Danny chuckled as Pat stag-gered across the parking lot. "Come on, private," said Danny, open-ing the glass door to the lobby. "Put a little ass into it. We don't got all day."

Danny and Pat arrived at their room. The previous occupant had left the thermostat at sixty-five degrees. Pat dropped the bag onto the carpet, and Danny collapsed onto the bed, his arms stretched wide. "This is one hell of a nice bed," he said, smiling, his eyes closed. Instead of falling asleep, though, he got up and poured the contents of the duffel bag onto the floor.

"Hey, Patty," said Danny, as he dug through the pile of green, tan, and camouflage. "I have something for you. Yeah, here. This is it." He held up a gray crew-neck sweatshirt with ARMY written on the front in block letters. "We wear this during PT. Don't worry, I need to buy a bunch more. And if you're lucky, it might still smell like my sweat." He laughed and tossed the sweatshirt to Pat.

Pat pulled it over his head and looked in the mirror. The sweat-shirt was big, but not so big that he couldn't wear it.

"Thanks," said Pat. "It's awesome."

"Don't thank me, thank my recruiter."

Pat laughed. He was glad it would still be cold when he got back to New Hampshire.

4

San Juan, Puerto Rico

Pat climbed the circular staircase from his terrace to his roof and sank into his solitary lawn chair. The afternoon sun felt good after spending the day below decks preparing for the *Strickland*'s next patrol, a three-week stint in the Mona Passage between Puerto Rico and the Dominican Republic. The forty-mile stretch of ocean was home to la Isla de Mona, an uninhabited plateau that belonged to Puerto Rico and thus the United States. Because Cuban migrants became legal residents upon touching American soil, Dominican traffickers delivered them to Mona's beaches regularly. Haitians and Dominicans, on the other hand, as well as bales of cocaine, had to be smuggled directly to the Puerto Rican mainland.

The *Strickland*'s job was simple: Prevent these landings.

Pat slid further down into his chair—better to forget about the patrol and enjoy terra firma while he could. The red exhaust stack of a cruise ship slid behind the Banco Popular tower toward el Morro and the open ocean. Pigeons cooed and the wind rustled a potted palm tree. Pat closed his eyes and drifted off.

"*Oye! Vecino!*"

Pat blinked and looked around.

"Over here!"

A man waved from the adjacent terrace below. His salt-and-pepper hair was cut short, and he had the broad shoulders and narrow waist of an athlete. Pat stood and approached the edge of his roof.

"You just move in?" the man asked.

35

"Yeah. About a month ago. You probably hadn't seen me before because I'm always coming and going."

"That must be it," said the man. "Well, come over and I'll give you a welcome-home beer. Better late than never."

Pat descended his staircase and swung himself over the chest-high plaster wall that separated the two terraces. A vaguely familiar Spanish pop song emanated from a portable speaker. Pat landed with a thud and extended his hand. "Thanks for the invite. I'm Pat."

"Galán," said the man, smiling. "*Mucho gusto*. Here, take a seat. And a beer." He tossed Pat a sweating Medalla and removed a black cat from the table by the scruff of its neck. "Don't worry about him. He's only angry because I increased his rent."

Pat laughed and opened his beer.

"Speaking of rent," said Galán, "how do you like Edwin?"

"You know Edwin? Edwin's the man. He cracks me up."

"Who doesn't know Edwin?" said Galán. "He's like, how do you say it? The mayor? He's crazy, but he's a good man." Galán sipped his beer. "So, what is a North American like you doing in Puerto Rico?"

"I'm in the Coast Guard," said Pat. He pointed toward the harbor. "I work on one of the ships down there. I'll be here two years."

The black cat eyed him from the corner beneath the water tank.

"Oh, the Coast Guard," said Galán. "You know, if it were up to you, I would still be in Cuba."

"Really? So you're not from here?"

"No, no. I may look Puerto Rican to you, but I'm *cien por ciento cubano*. It's a big difference." He laughed and took another sip of his beer, and then became serious. "Yeah, I came over as a kid. Well, not to here. To Florida. I stayed there for a few years, and then I came here. It's okay. Sometimes this island reminds me of home."

Pat nodded. "And the cat? He lives with you too?"

"Oh, him? He's just trying to get a free meal before he chases the ladies all night. He's a lover." Galán called the cat to him, but the creature remained under the tank, his eyes unblinking. "So, Pat. Are you hungry?"

"Oh, no, I'm all good. Thanks though."

"If that cat eats for free, I think my neighbor should too," said Galán, standing up. "Let's take a look."

They walked inside the sparsely furnished apartment, tidy and organized. Pat walked past the votive candle and photographs, his gaze lingering on the two small faces. They must be dead.

"Oh, you've found my roommates," said Galán as he removed two steaks from the refrigerator.

"I'm sorry." Pat flushed. "I was just trying to see what the candle said. I didn't mean to be getting up in your business."

"That's for the patroness of Cuba, la Virgen de la Caridad. Basically, the Virgin Mary appeared on the sea to some poor fishermen and saved them during a storm." He pulled the adobo seasoning out of a cupboard. "You know, I feel like she may have helped me make it to Florida without your friends noticing."

"Oh yeah?" Pat had heard the stories. With the Florida Straits, the Windward Passage next to Haiti, and the Mona Passage, the Coast Guard had no problem keeping its cutters busy.

Galán carried the steaks out to the grill, and Pat followed with extra beers. Blue clouds obscured an orange sky. Down on the plaza, toddlers chased each other around the trees and concrete benches while their mothers conversed from behind empty strollers.

"So, Pat, is it just you here? Any wife? Girlfriend?"

"No, no wife. I'm too young for that. But I do have a girlfriend back in the States." He didn't say that his countdown to Michaela's first visit to the island stood at twenty-six days. Well, twenty-five and a half to be exact.

"A girlfriend, huh? And she let you come here? This town can be dangerous."

"She didn't have much of a choice," said Pat, laughing. "Neither did I. So I'm of the opinion that you can look but can't touch. What about you?" It was a dumb question since he could see the man's entire living space from where he was sitting—there wasn't much of a feminine presence.

"No, no," said Galán, shaking his head. "One day there was, but that was years ago." He gestured toward the cat. "Now, it is just me and him."

Pat, unsure of what to say, let Galán fill the silence instead. Six beers later, he shook his neighbor's hand and returned to his unlit apartment, a smile still on his face.

✶

The night before Pat returned to sea, he finally had plans. He set the case of beer on top of the wall and swung himself onto Galán's terrace.

"There he is," said Galán without looking up. He was dangling a shoelace inches above the seated cat, who eyed the dancing string with malice.

"Yes, sir." Pat noticed the grill was cold. "No grilling tonight? What's up? You on a diet?"

Galán laughed. "No, no diet, *hermano*. I think instead it's time you meet your city."

Pat put the beer into the fridge and followed Galán down to the street. They walked through la Plaza de la Barandilla and into a small bar called Mamajuana's. The doors were open to the street, and some kind of music far smoother than *reggaetón* played. Coors Light, Presidente, and Medalla banners covered the wall, as did a painting of a red *flamboyán* tree signed by an artist named Cajiga.

"Galancito, *mi amor*!" said the bartender, making her way around the counter. "*Cómo estás?*" She gave Galán an air kiss on the cheek. She was about fifty with hair dyed bronze. Unlike most bartenders, she had a genuine smile. She must have been a heartbreaker in her youth—maybe even still.

"Pat," said Galán, beaming, "I present to you Yadira, the most beautiful woman in all of San Juan." Yadira made a face of mock embarrassment and shook her head. "I can introduce you to nobody else in this city, and I will have done my job."

Yadira leaned in for an air kiss, Pat's first on the island. "*Mucho gusto*," he said, self-conscious of his accent. Yadira responded with a dizzying flurry of Spanish. Pat didn't understand, but he couldn't help but smile.

Yadira brought over two frosted bottles of Presidente. "A taste of *la República*." She had a strong accent, but an even stronger voice.

Galán and Pat toasted Yadira.

"*Mira*," Yadira said to Pat, "In my country, you would say *dos cervezas vestidas de novia*." She said the words slowly, enunciating each syllable. "Two beers dressed like brides. See the white ice?"

Pat nodded and mouthed the words. "And this music?" Pat asked. "This isn't *reggaetón*."

"No," said Yadira, her eyes wide with horror. "*Reggaetón*? Very bad music. Very bad. This is bachata. This is music." She grabbed Galán's hand and began dancing with him in the narrow space between the bar and the street. "See, you can dance bachata. You can't dance *reggaetón*."

"The young kids do," said Galán.

"That is not dancing. That is sex with clothes on."

As Pat laughed, he noticed two older men at the end of the bar who stared hungrily at Yadira from beneath greasy ball caps and sipped from the straws poking out of their rum and Cokes. One of them pursed his lips toward Galán, and the other chuckled.

When the song ended, Galán kissed Yadira's hand and returned to his wicker stool. "When I first moved here," he said to Pat, "I didn't know anybody. I didn't understand Puerto Rico, and I didn't understand *puertorriqueños*. Yes, I looked like them, but that was it. To them, I talked funny. They knew I wasn't from here. But Yadira took care of me. Yadira is like family."

"I can see that for sure," said Pat. Yadira attended to her two suitors, but she smiled less frequently and less fully than before. When she turned in Pat's direction, he looked away and caught a glimpse of himself in the bar mirror. "And I think I kind of know how you felt."

"I bet," said Galán, chuckling. "You stick out worse than me."

Pat laughed. "But your actual family? Where are they? Florida?"

"My father was in Florida," said Galán, "but he passed away. I have some cousins there, too. But everybody else is in Cuba."

Pat nodded. "Do you ever see them?" Another dumb question.

"It's difficult with the laws and everything," said Galán, taking a sip of his beer. It was no longer dressed like a bride. "Sometimes, if the stars are lined up, we talk on the long-distance phone. You have to get these special calling cards, and it's expensive as hell." He bit the inside of his cheek, staring at the lineup of liquor bottles. "But to try to see them? I don't know. They have their own lives. I think maybe it's better not to shake everything up."

"I'm sorry," said Pat, briefly putting his hand on Galán's shoulder. He didn't know how displays of male affection went over at Mamajuana's. "Hopefully things will change. The laws, I mean."

"I've been hoping for that for like twenty, twenty-five years. My mom isn't getting any younger, and my sister . . ." Galán's voice trailed off.

Pat remembered the second photograph in Galán's bedroom shrine. Based on the sepia tint, Pat never would have guessed that it depicted Galán's sister. But maybe that was the norm in Cuba, where cars from the 1950s still prowled the streets.

Galán sipped his beer before continuing. "My sister is different. I was a little kid when she was born, but I can remember my parents talking. Something about how my mother had dengue."

"Dengue?"

"Yeah, you get it from mosquitoes. Your bones hurt. When you shit, your shit comes out white. I had it once. But anyway, my mom had it when she was pregnant with my sister."

Pat nodded.

"The doctors said dengue doesn't cause problems, but Gabriela? Gabriela is different. She's like a child still."

Pat nodded again.

"I don't know why I'm telling you all this," continued Galán, looking over at Pat. "Maybe because you listen better than the cat."

Pat chuckled. "Don't worry about it. I'm happy to hear about your family anytime. Family is what matters most."

Galán raised his beer to that, and they both drank.

"And you, my friend?" asked Galán. "What about your family?"

"My parents and my older brother live in New Hampshire. It's a tiny state. You've probably never heard of it. It's near Boston. Do you know Boston?"

"Yeah," said Galán, mimicking a baseball swing. "Big Papi."

"Yeah, right," said Pat, smiling. "Big Papi. He's the man."

"So, do you miss them?" asked Galán. "They are all the way up there freezing their asses off, and you are here drinking beers with me, a *cubano* who lives with a cat."

"I used to be stationed up there, on a ship out of Boston actually, so I saw them all the time. I do miss my brother, though. He's kind of having a rough go of it."

"What do you mean?" asked Galán, glancing at Pat.

"He was in the war. In Iraq. I'm not sure exactly what happened, but all I know is that he wasn't himself when he got back."

Galán nodded. "War can do that. It's a bad, bad thing."

"It really is."

As they finished their beers. Pat's mind drifted back to the day Danny came home from Fort Lewis and moved into his childhood bedroom. Danny once again slept beneath his posters of Mo Vaughn and Drew Bledsoe, but now his calloused feet hung off the end of the bed. The setup was only supposed to be temporary.

Galán pulled out his wallet. "How about we leave Yadira to her two friends, and I show you somewhere else. There's a lot for you in this neighborhood if you know where to look."

"Please," said Pat, pushing back his barstool. He was thankful for the distraction.

☆

Pat and Galán ate their *pastelillos* as they threaded through the crowds on la Calle San Sebastián. Pat was surprised by how many of the locals favored the hipster look. The men sported manicured beards and floral shirts, and the women wore dark lipstick and oversized glasses. If Pat ignored the colonial buildings and tropical breeze, he could have been with Michaela in Center City.

A group of girls passed by on the opposite sidewalk in tight jeans and midriff-baring shirts. Two of them glanced at Pat and giggled.

He smiled, unused to the attention.

"Remember," said Galán, noticing Pat's wandering eye, "There's a reason *esposa* means both wife and handcuffs." A flake of *pastelillo* crust fell from the corner of his mouth as he laughed.

They arrived at el Colmado de Manolo. The sound of *reggaetón* and the smell of hookah poured out of the front door. A large man with a neck tattoo frisked Pat and then Galán as they entered.

Inside, a cluster of girls gyrated on the tiny dance floor while several boys waited against the wall and sipped from plastic cups of clear alcohol. There were no hipsters, and certainly no white boys either. Stares came Pat's way as he followed Galán to the bar, but he didn't look down. He wasn't alone anymore.

Galán said something to the bartender in Spanish and pointed at Pat. The bartender looked skeptical but produced two cans of Medalla from a cooler covered in red-and-blue Dominican flag decals.

Pat moved his head to the thumping *reggaetón*.

"That's Williams," said Galán, jutting his chin toward the sullen bartender. "He's friendlier than he looks. He was just surprised to see you here."

"Williams?" Pat wiped the sweat from his forehead.

"Yeah, Williams," said Galán, laughing. "What? Is that a strange name?"

Pat smiled and drank his beer. The music switched to bachata, and some of the more intrepid boys sidled onto the dance floor. The surplus males continued to look on, their faces fixed in tough guy scowls, as high heels and Jordan sneakers glided across the linoleum floor.

"You really like these Dominican bars, huh?" asked Pat. "Shit, I didn't even know there were Dominicans in Puerto Rico. So what is it? You like the girls better? The bachata? It can't be the beer, because it's the same beer everywhere. Medalla for breakfast, lunch, and dinner."

Galán laughed. "I don't know. That's a good question." He paused, furrowing his brow and drumming a cigarette on the bar. "Maybe it's because when you're an outsider, it's nice to be with other outsiders." Galán lit the cigarette. "Yeah, that has to be it."

Pat nodded.

"You'll see what I mean."

5

San Juan, Puerto Rico

Under the glow of the terrace floodlights, Galán celebrated his birthday with the black cat. He sipped his beer and looked south over the shoulder of his less than festive companion. Beyond the colonial skyline and the harbor, lights twinkled in the mountains. Esperanza would have liked this view. Gabriela too.

Galán stood and opened the grill. He cut off a piece of pork that smoked above a bed of cherrywood chips. Almost. He cut off another piece for the cat, who carried it to his hiding spot. Ever since returning from a nocturnal adventure with a laceration above his eye and a piece of his ear missing, the cat had been spending more time than usual under the water tank.

Galán looked over at Pat's dark terrace and empty roof—two weeks until his neighbor returned from sea. Galán liked his peace. He always had, especially after Esperanza had left. But with Pat around, he'd recently caught himself watching the clock above the diner's espresso machine. There was a new richness to his life that distracted him from his usual grind, a grind that revolved around sending remittances back to his mother and Gabi.

As Galán finished his beer, the cat emerged from beneath the water tank and rubbed against his leg. Galán scratched him, careful not to touch the wounds. The cat jumped onto Galán's lap, purring. As Galán waited for the pork, his mind wandered to another birthday.

Even though he was turning twelve, he was still only in the fifth grade at la Escuela Primaria Vargas Hernández. Galán knew that

Señora Vargas had played some kind of role in the Revolution, a role that Gustavo said involved sleeping with leaders of the July 26th movement. Josefina, however, said that those rumors were nonsense, and that to insinuate such a thing was disrespectful to poor Señora Vargas. Galán didn't understand why the lady wasn't allowed to sleep, but he did know that she lived across the street from the school and would appear from time to time in hair curlers and a revealing nightgown.

Just as he did every afternoon, Galán waited for Gabriela outside of the school's main gate. The mural behind him read, "Our children are our dominant natural resource!" Cartoonish boys and girls, wearing the same white blouses and maroon bandannas as the actual students, danced beneath the wavy script.

Gabriela, pigtails bobbing, finally emerged. Her oversized skirt almost reached her socks.

"What's up with you?" asked Galán, taking her hand. "Why are you smiling so much?" He looked down the street to see if the Fortuño twins were laying an ambush.

"I'm happy," said Gabriela, her eyes blinking in the warm wind. "I'm happy that it's your birthday. It's my favorite day of the whole year. Well, besides my birthday."

"Yeah, I'm happy too," said Galán, unsmiling. There was no sign of Eddy or Rody.

"Galán, do you think Mami will make you a cake?"

"Of course. She always does. You know that."

"I know," she said, hustling to keep up, "but I didn't see any flour or eggs when we left this morning."

"Yeah, but she will. You know Mami."

As they turned down their street, Galán saw their father sitting in his folding chair on the front porch. It was early. Gustavo's shift at the gas station wasn't supposed to be over for another two hours.

"The birthday boy arrives," said Gustavo, smiling. "Señor Echeverría, when he heard it was your birthday, said to go home early. Why? Because he said you could use some batting practice." He stood and revealed a scratched aluminum baseball bat, the rubber grip long gone.

"Whose is that, Papá?" asked Galán, bounding up the steps. "Where did you get it?"

"Don't worry about that. It's a birthday present. If you're going to beat the shit out of los Industriales one day, you need a real bat. No more of Mami's mops."

Galán examined the bat. He took a few practice swings. It was perfect.

"Can I see it?" asked Gabriela, who watched from a safe distance.

Galán took another swing before handing her the bat.

She awkwardly imitated his swing before giving it back. "It's really beautiful."

"Gabi," said Gustavo, "why don't you go inside and help Mami? She's getting everything ready for the party."

Gabi, still moving her arms in a swinging motion, smiled her closed-mouth smile and went inside.

Galán and Gustavo walked the four blocks to the state-owned tire shop. The chain link fence that encircled the property was their batting cage. On the other side of the sagging mesh were stacks of used tires, some bald, others slashed by the potholes of Ciego de Ávila and the national highway. A few men milled about smoking cigarettes, carrying on a dispirited conversation as one of their colleagues applied a gelatinous substance to gouged rubber.

Gustavo knelt across from Galán and tossed the homemade baseball. It consisted of a round stone wrapped tightly with twine and covered with the palm of a leather work glove. Galán, using every bit of torque his small frame could muster, unleashed a violent swing, the bat launching the ball into the fence.

The tire workers turned. "Damn, that boy can hit."

Galán tried to keep from smiling too wide. Professionals didn't smile.

Gustavo picked up the ball as it rolled back to him. "Remember, explode your hips. And keep your weight back. The power comes from your lower body, not your arms."

With each cut, Galán's calloused hands blistered anew. He didn't notice the stinging, only the clean sensation of the bat's sweet spot tearing through the ball.

One hundred swings later, Galán and his father returned home. A dozen relatives and neighbors filled the living room, holding cups of guava wine. On the table sat a large cake, too big and perfectly frosted to have been homemade. According to Tía Teresa, Josefina had traded a pair of blue jeans for the cake with a pharmacist who moonlighted as a baker. Gabi's suspicions had been correct.

Galán blew out the candles as soon as his mother would allow, and each guest received a full piece. The thick vanilla icing was unlike anything he had ever tasted. He regretted how quickly he ate his slice, but he also wanted to get back outside. He smiled as the old ladies commented on how much he resembled a young Gustavo, all the while keeping his eye on his new old bat.

The sun was setting when Galán, Juani, and Juani's older brother were able to break away from the party and return to the tire shop. Even the older brother, who was usually too cool to hang out with the youngsters, smiled when it was his turn to hit.

Lost in the game, Galán didn't notice night fall. He just kept swinging or tossing in the moonlight, the singing insects the only cheering crowd. The stitching holding together the ball's leather cover began to break apart.

"Galán! Galán!"

From the other end of the block, Gabriela ran barefoot toward the three boys. She was still wearing her yellow party dress, but her smile was gone.

Galán grabbed the bat from Juani and started to run. He knew what was wrong.

Turning onto his street, Galán could make out the twinkle of a broken bottle in the front yard. Muffled screams came from inside the house.

Galán jumped onto the front porch and opened the screen door. Gustavo had Josefina bent forward over the plywood counter. Gripping her by the hair, he slammed her face into the dishwater.

"You bitch!" Gustavo screamed. "A fancy cake like that? Who the hell do you think you are?" He pulled her head back out, soap suds and food particles covering her face.

Galán stood frozen, his eyes wide. This was beyond anything he'd seen before.

Gustavo jammed Josefina's face back into the sink, splashing water onto the counter and camp stove. "You think this is Miami? Is that what you think?" He pulled her face out, grabbed a leftover piece of cake, and stuffed it into her mouth. "You wanted this damned cake? Well, it isn't going to waste! I promise you that!"

Josefina's arms flailed against the counter, knocking a plate to the floor.

"Now you're breaking dishes!" said Gustavo, laughing. "But that's okay. We live in Miami! We'll just go buy more!"

Galán, body trembling, squeezed the bat. He took a step forward and swung, striking his father behind the knee.

Gustavo sagged to the floor, losing his grip on Josefina. He turned, facing Galán, his eyes bloodshot slits. "What do you know? The birthday boy thinks he's a man!" He scrambled toward Galán, who took another swing, this time unloading on his father's shoulder. Gustavo crumpled.

Galán dropped the bat with a metallic clang and ran out the front door and around to the backyard. Gabriela would be there. That's where she always went. He found her sitting against the house covering her ears. Galán sat down and put his arms around her.

Josefina's sobs and Gustavo's cursing emanated from the kitchen window. After some time, both voices went silent. All that could be heard were the insects in the nearby cane fields.

A lizard darted tentatively from under the house past Galán and Gabriela toward the weeds. It, too, seemed afraid that the shouting would begin anew.

Galán, finally confident that his father was passed out, stood. He led Gabriela by the hand back around the house.

She held onto him tighter than usual.

"It's okay," said Galán. "It's over now. It's okay."

Galán and Gabriela climbed the steps and stopped at the open front door. Gustavo was still lying where Galán had dropped him, his belly rising and falling slowly beneath his untucked shirt. His crotch was wet. This wasn't the first time he had urinated on himself.

The green tablecloth that served as their parents' bedroom door fluttered, and Josefina emerged. She crouched down and hugged her children.

"I'm sorry," she said, kissing their foreheads. "I'm sorry." She smelled like dish soap, and there was a sticky spot on the crown of her head. Was it cake or blood?

Neither Galán nor Gabriela said anything as they got ready for bed. Galán left the baseball bat where it lay on the floor next to his father—he didn't want to touch it.

When Galán awoke for school the next morning, the bat was still there, but his father wasn't. Somehow Gustavo had managed to wake up in time for work. Rising from the mattress he shared with his sister, Galán noticed a cellophane package of cookies and a note sitting on the kitchen counter.

"Galán," the note read, "This is to reward you for your batting practice yesterday. Papá."

Galán threw the note in the trash and put the cookies in Gabriela's pink backpack. Sometimes he thought it would be better to have no father than two fathers.

6

Mona Passage

Pat reached around his rack curtain and silenced his alarm. Three in the morning, but he had to get moving. Guys who showed up late to watch earned a reputation, even if they were officers and could get away with it. He pulled on his blue cargo pants in the dark, the deck shifting beneath his feet. Even though the *Strickland* was under way in a perpetual summer, Pat also threw on his sweatshirt emblazoned with the cutter's crest of an ibis standing on a globe. Chief Landis kept the pilothouse thermostat at sixty-six degrees, and Pat knew better than to pull rank and adjust it.

Pat squeezed into the dark, narrow passageway that separated his stateroom from the captain's cabin. He ducked around the privacy curtain and onto the messdeck, which glowed a ghostly red—after sunset, only red lighting could be used so as preserve the crew's night vision. Somebody had left a plate of half-eaten chicken wings on one of the three aluminum tables. Cursing under his breath, Pat threw the bones into the trash and put the plate in the dishwasher.

Stepping back out of the closet-like galley, Pat poured himself some coffee. As soon as the thick, tepid liquid touched his lips, he realized an engineer had been the last barista. Engineer coffee always tasted like tar.

Careful not to spill as the cutter lurched to starboard, Pat exited the rear of the messdeck and climbed the aluminum ladder to the pilothouse, or bridge. As he emerged through the middle of the

50

pilothouse deck, he heard the laughter of the three off-going watch standers. Moonlight poked through the windows, and the multiple navigation and radar monitors were either dimmed or covered with red plastic screens.

Pat approached the chart table on the starboard side of the bridge and dug through his pocket for his red-lensed flashlight.

"Is that the XO?" asked Ensign Tim Anderson. He was the off-going conning officer and Pat's gangly roommate. Although Pat outranked the recent Coast Guard Academy graduate, Tim had spent more time aboard the *Strickland*.

"You're damn right it's the XO," said Pat. "What's the word? You standing a taut watch? I could hear you cackling from the messdeck."

"Cackling?" asked Tim. "No, sir. We were just talking about Wi-Fi."

"Oh yeah?" said Pat. "What did Fireman Jackson do now?" Fireman Jackson had earned his nickname by asking for the cutter's Wi-Fi password his first day under way. There was no such thing, and ever since the rest of the crew had delighted in asking him if he needed a turndown service for his rack, or if he had misplaced the room service menu somewhere in his locker.

"What did Wi-Fi do?" asked Tim. "I don't know if I can tell you, sir, you know, being XO and all."

"Do you want to get relieved or not?" Pat had found his flashlight and was studying the paper chart of the Mona Passage. Little triangles made in pencil marked the *Strickland*'s hourly positions over the last day. "I'm more than happy to go back to sleep. You know I'm not doing this for my health." He plotted a new position using the latitude and longitude coordinates from the GPS.

"All right, sir. If you insist," said Tim. "So Fireman Wi-Fi's been dating a girl back in San Juan for a few months now. Her family loves *Game of Thrones*, but apparently they refuse to pay for HBO. So Fireman Wi-Fi, being the gentleman that he is, offered to lend her and her family his underway hard drive because he has all of the episodes pirated on there."

"And?"

"Well, apparently that particular hard drive has tons of porn on it, too."

Pat laughed. "I guess it's the thought that counts. Who knows? Maybe the whole family will be into it." He double-checked his work. The *Strickland* was ten nautical miles southwest of Mona Island.

"See?" said the off-going engineer from the back of the pilot-house. "I knew XO would think it was funny."

Pat smiled. "What did Jackson's girlfriend say about it?"

"He doesn't know yet," said Tim, digging into a cellophane bag, which Pat knew contained Cheetos. Tim loved Cheetos and would leave orange fingerprints all over the monitors on the bridge. "He gave her the hard drive right before we got under way."

Shaking his head, Pat glanced out the pilothouse windows and saw the single white light from the Mona Park Ranger station blinking on an otherwise black horizon. It was right where it was supposed to be based on their location and heading. To their west, barely obscured by the curvature of the earth, was the Dominican Republic.

"So what do you have in the way of a pass down?" asked Pat as he walked toward Tim and the forward console. He held onto the aluminum overhead grab bars. "Anybody out here?"

"All quiet," said Tim, pouring the last of his Cheetos into his mouth. "The swells have been consistent. Running north-south has given us a pretty good ride."

"So I'll be sure to head east-west in about fifteen minutes," said Pat. "I'll find that nice trough and shake you out of your rack before you can close your eyes."

"That's messed up, sir. Why would you do me like that?"

Pat laughed and increased the brightness on the radar. Other than a splotch of green feedback at the center, the rest of the twelve-nautical-mile display was black. Pat zoomed out and then back in. Tim was right. No other vessels. Or, at least no other vessels large enough to show up on the finicky radar.

"So what else do we got?" asked Pat.

"We're running on the port-side generator and port-side engine. Eight knots has been smooth."

"Roger." Pat checked the radios to make sure that they were set to the correct channels and the volumes were turned up. "Anything else? Any planes up?"

"Oh yeah," said Tim. "Customs and Border Protection is up. We haven't heard much from them. I think they have another two or three hours before they return to base."

"Anything else?"

"No, sir. That's it. Nothing going on."

"All right," said Pat, turning to face Tim's silhouette. "I offer my relief."

"I stand relieved."

They exchanged informal salutes, and Pat assumed responsibility for the mission as well as for the safety of the *Strickland* and her crew.

"You all have a good watch," said Tim as he made his way down the ladder.

"Thanks, brother," said Pat, his eyes fixed on the black horizon ahead. "Get some sleep."

As Pat waited for the oncoming quartermaster and engineer to complete their reliefs, he fought the urge to look at his watch. Since he would be driving the *Strickland* back and forth in ten-mile-long straight lines for the next four hours, the last thing he wanted to do was slow time by checking it.

Driving was actually a misleading word thanks to autopilot. Pat would really just be staring out into the darkness with his arms folded.

"We're all set, sir," said Petty Officer Ricky Bartlett from the darkness behind Pat. Bartlett, a pudgy-faced engineer from inland Florida, was seated on a small retractable stool in front of a computer that reported engine room temperatures, pressures, and revolutions per minute. "I have the engineering watch, and Seaman Wilson is your quartermaster. It's like the '85 Bears up here."

"You're damn right it is," said Pat. He checked the electronic chart to see how the wind was affecting their progress north. They were crabbing slightly to the west. He adjusted the steering knob on the autopilot and sipped his coffee.

"Damn," said Pat, wincing. He had forgotten how bad it was. "Who made this coffee? Was it Martínez?"

"What, sir, you don't like engineer coffee?" asked Petty Officer Bartlett.

"Or maybe the XO doesn't like enlisted coffee," said Seaman Wilson from behind the bow cannon console.

"Yeah, yeah. Get your laughs. But for real, you can give me that watered-down instant stuff they have in motel rooms, and I'll be happy. This though?" He held up his mug, turning toward Bartlett and Wilson. "This is horrible. This is like drinking asphalt soup."

"I don't know, sir," said Bartlett. He had managed to squeeze himself between the bulkhead and his computer in such a way that he appeared to have become one with the ship. "Maybe it's you and not the coffee. Maybe you need some more sea time."

"Sea time?" Pat checked the radar. Still nothing. "How much sea time do you have?"

"One and a half years."

"One and a half years! And you're talking shit?"

"I think sea time can be a state of mind. So right now I feel like I have twelve years. By the end of this watch it will probably be more like thirteen or fourteen."

Wilson laughed.

"Don't you have some dipsticks to check?" asked Pat, turning toward the dark mass that was Bartlett. "Lay below to your engine room and when you come back, for the love of God, please bring some halfway decent coffee."

"Aye, sir," said Bartlett, peeling himself off the bulkhead and making his way toward the ladder. "Are you okay if it has caffeine?"

Wilson burst out laughing again.

"We've got a bunch of jokers up here," said Pat, smiling and shaking his head. "A bunch of goddamned jokers."

Pat was still smiling when he paced to his right and looked down at the electronic chart. In twenty minutes, the *Strickland* would reach the edge of the digital box that the captain had programmed into the navigation system, and Pat would have to turn the ship 180 degrees. Very exciting. Pat started to pull up his sleeve but caught himself. Not yet.

Instead, Pat tried to think about Michaela's upcoming visit and not the news that Danny had been fired from his job driving trucks for the Portsmouth Department of Public Works. You can't miss multiple shifts and then call your boss a dumbass. At least not to his face.

7

San Juan, Puerto Rico

Galán looked down at la Plaza de la Barandilla, which glowed orange under the streetlamps. A homeless man limped by using a PVC pipe as a cane, and a young couple listened to music from a cell phone. Two sunburned vacationers stopped to take a selfie. Galán's eyes darted back and forth, but he didn't see who he was looking for.

He finished his beer, dropped the can on the picnic table, and walked through his apartment to the stairwell. As he descended, he opened a package of catnip-flavored treats.

Galán crossed the cobblestone street to the plaza. Instead of making one of his usual commutes to la Fonda del Ciego or Mamajuana's, he ducked into the barrier-like bushes that lined the square.

"Come, kitty, kitty, kitty," he said in a high-pitched voice, crinkling the bag of treats. Nothing—only the wind whistling across the top of an old Heineken bottle.

Galán walked west on la Calle Fortaleza toward the governor's mansion, still shaking the bag. "Come, kitty, kitty, kitty." Two stray cats, one orange and one white, darted out through the front gate of an abandoned, crumbling house. A stooped, white-haired woman pushed her grocery cart to the opposite side of the street, all the while regarding Galán with a furrowed brow.

Other cats joined the procession, but not the one Galán was looking for. He passed through the red arch of the San Juan Gate and followed the pedestrian pathway toward el Morro. With the harbor lapping against the rocks to his left and the old city walls to his right, even more recruits joined the ranks. The stifling air reeked of cat urine.

Up ahead, a pair of headlights appeared. Some of the cats scattered, but a more determined, hungrier contingent remained. A National Park Service golf cart came into view.

"Sir," said the green-uniformed ranger, eyeing the cats. "The walkway is closed for the night. You have to go home."

"I understand," said Galán, pulling his cell phone out of his pocket, "but I'm looking for somebody. Perhaps you've seen him?" On the screen, the black cat was reclined on one of Galán's terrace chairs, his yellow eyes gleaming in the camera's flash.

"I'm sorry, sir," said the Park Ranger, glancing up from the phone, "but you have to turn around. The path is closed."

Galán didn't move.

"Now, sir."

Galán nodded. He turned and retraced his steps. A small band of loyal followers looked up at him expectantly.

"I'm sorry, my friends," said Galán, putting the package of treats in his pocket. "But this is for somebody else. If you see him, tell him to come home."

★

A few days after returning from patrol, Pat dropped down onto Galán's terrace. No music played, and there were more empty beer cans and cigarette butts than usual. Blue smoke wafted toward a crescent moon.

Galán didn't turn as Pat approached the picnic table.

"What's going on with you?" asked Pat. "I know Michaela's coming down to take me from you, but there's no need to get all emotional."

Galán nodded and continued looking out into the distance. His eyes were puffy.

"Don't tell me you're crying over that cat," continued Pat, laughing. "He was a mean bastard, and you know it. Plus, he's probably getting all kinds of tail right now. You should be happy for him."

Galán sniffed and smiled weakly. "No, no, not the cat." He held up one of the small photographs he normally kept in his bedroom shrine. It was wrinkled and delaminating. "It's my mother." He stuffed the cigarette into the ashtray and pulled another one out of the box of Ashfords. "She passed away."

Pat swallowed and sat down. He felt like a moron as he looked at the photo. "I'm sorry, brother. I'm really, really sorry." He put his hand on Galan's shoulder and left it there.

"I should have seen her," said Galán, wiping away a tear. "It's been almost twenty-five years. I could've seen her if I had tried. The last time I saw her was on that goddamned raft." Another tear followed the first. This one he let roll.

"How did you hear?" Pat didn't know what else to ask, but any conversation was better than none.

"From family in Miami." Galán exhaled another cloud of smoke. "She was young. She was too young."

"I'm sorry."

Galán shook his head. "What can you do?" He wiped his nose.

Pat thought about his own mother, and how she looked more and more like his late grandmother every time he saw her. He thought about how she teetered ever so slightly when she walked. He pictured the sneakers she had taken to wearing, even with dresses and skirts.

"The other thing now is my sister," said Galán, biting the inside of his cheek.

"What do you mean?"

"You remember how I told you that she's different? I don't know what's going to happen to her. My mother always took care of her and now she's gone."

Pat stared at the glass table. Again, he didn't know what to say.

"My aunt will look after Gabi for now. But my aunt's getting older, too. And another mouth to feed . . ." He shook his head.

They drank their beers in silence. Galán continued to bite the inside of his cheek in between puffs of his cigarette. The only noise was the crickets chirping from an abandoned building across the street.

Galán picked up the picture of his mother again. "You always know this day will come. But you never imagine how it's going to feel. Especially when you don't get the chance to say good-bye, to tell them how much you love them." He bit down on his shaking lower lip. "But that's bullshit. I had plenty of chances."

Pat squeezed Galán's shoulder and let go.

"The funeral's in four days," continued Galán. "My family in Miami says they know how to work it out for me to go."

"That's good. I'm sure that would mean a lot to your mom. And to your sister and everybody. You need to be with them right now."

Galán nodded.

Pat took another look at the picture. The woman was young and strikingly beautiful, with an angular face and a petite nose. She would be beautiful even by today's standards. And now that he really looked at her, he could tell without a doubt that her blood ran through Galán's veins. Pat could see the same sadness in her eyes.

"A beautiful woman, right?" said Galán, noticing Pat's gaze. "That's how I'll always remember her." He stuffed the cigarette into the ashtray and blew his nose into a dish towel. "Maybe I'm lucky in a way."

8

San Juan, Puerto Rico

The following Friday afternoon, Pat and Michaela lay next to each other on Pat's bed. The air conditioning hummed on the wall above them, and sunlight streamed in through the windows dirtied by the constant sea breeze. Pat's jeans and T-shirt lay on the floor, and Michaela's light cotton dress hung from the corner of the mattress.

"I still can't believe that you're here," said Pat, running his fingers through her silky brown hair. "You don't know how long I've been waiting for this."

"Are you kidding?" Michaela smiled up at him, her green eyes shining. "Of course I know. What did you think I was doing in Philly? Every other thought I had was about you. The only thing that made the time go faster was taking double shifts. My supervisor thought I had gone off the deep end."

Pat smiled. He loved her toughness and compassion. She never let the constant mayhem, sickness, and suffering at the Temple University emergency room bring her down. He didn't know how she did it.

"But now I'm here," she continued, her small yet pert breasts pressing against his broad chest with each unhurried breath. "We're together. And it's like the whole time apart never happened."

Pat kissed her on the forehead. "And now you'll finally be able to picture my world down here. It'll make things less lonely for me when you leave. Like Puerto Rico will be something we share, you know?"

"Don't talk about leaving. I just got here!"

"You're right," said Pat, holding up a lock of her hair and letting it drop slowly onto the silver necklace on the back of her neck. "I'm sorry."

"So what about your friend Galán? Will I get to meet him?"

"That was the plan, but he has to leave for Cuba early in the morning."

"A part of me is surprised you wanted to introduce me to him. Sometimes I wonder whether you're dating him or me." She laughed. "Hopefully he doesn't try to off me when nobody's looking." She made a face of mock terror, her eyes opened wide. "He's not going to off me, is he?"

"I don't know. If he is, he hasn't told me. You know, if he did off you, I would still have to be a character witness for him at his trial. That would be okay with you, right?"

"Terrible!"

Pat kissed her, and she smiled.

"So you said he's going back to Cuba?"

"Yeah," said Pat, his voice losing its playful lilt. "His mother passed away. He hadn't seen her since he was a kid."

"Poor guy."

"I think it will be good for him to go back. He'll see his sister, too. It'll be the first time since they were kids." Pat stared at the wood ceiling beams. "It's messed up. A brother and sister being separated like that."

"Yeah, I can't imagine."

"Like with Danny? I can go months without seeing him, no problem, but at least I always know I have the option. I can put in some leave and cough up some money for an airplane ticket. But to not have that option because of laws or whatever?" He shook his head. "That's not right."

"It's like that for a lot of people," said Michaela. "I'm not saying that makes it any less hard for Galán, but his situation isn't really that unique."

"Yeah, I know. That separation still sucks, though. Plus, Galán's sister has some kind of problem. I don't know exactly what. Like something mental. That's got to make it extra tough."

"It makes you realize how good we have it," said Michaela. "In terms of being born where we were born." She repositioned her head on his chest and closed her eyes.

"I know. It's amazing how arbitrary the world can be." He ran his hand down the curve of her warm back. "You know, when I think of people being born, I have this picture in my head of an assembly line up in Heaven, with all of these blank-slate people, or souls, or whatever, lined up. And every moment that there is an opening down on earth for a new person, the next soul in line drops down a chute and pops out as a baby, whether that opening is in Mexico or New York, or some rich London suburb or a slum in India. Everything depends on your number in that line."

"I don't know about that," said Michaela. "I feel like we were destined to be either who we are or nobody at all."

"Really? So if your parents never met, you just wouldn't exist?"

"Exactly."

"Huh," said Pat. "I guess we'll have to agree to disagree."

Michaela smiled. "Since when did you become a philosopher anyway?"

"You'd be surprised how much thinking you can do when you have the midwatch in the middle of an empty ocean. Lesser thinkers than me have turned to existential questions to pass the time."

"You're out of your mind!"

"Maybe," said Pat, laughing. "But anyway, about Galán, I was going to say that at least he has his cat. But then I remembered that the cat disappeared, too. The guy can't catch a break."

"Well, he does have you."

"Yeah, I'm sure having me around more than makes up for all of it."

"It better," said Michaela, her voice fading toward sleep. "Or else he doesn't know how lucky he is."

Pat pulled her closer to him until one of her legs rested between his and their cheeks touched. He knew that she was asleep by the soft puffing noises she made when she breathed. He wanted to sleep, too, but he was thinking about Galán and how it would feel to lose somebody he loved without being able to say good-bye.

It was the middle of a summer night after Pat's freshman year of college. Pat closed the front door of his family's clapboard house softly behind him, slightly buzzed from the three Narragansett tallboys he'd drank with his old high school friends at their spot on the banks of the Piscataqua. As he made his way to the kitchen to toast some frozen waffles, he was surprised to see his dad sitting on the La-Z-Boy in the dark living room.

Mr. McAllister smiled at Pat, his face awash in the muted television's blue glow. Pat sensed a sadness in his father's expression, even though Mr. McAllister normally found curfew violations irritating.

"I'm sorry I'm late," said Pat, opening the yellow box of Eggos. "Where's Mom? Asleep already?" She was usually the one who stayed up waiting for him.

"Yeah, she's upstairs. It's been a long night." Mr. McAllister stood. He was still in his work clothes—an untucked flannel shirt and Carhartt utility pants. He usually changed into his faded, unflattering blue jeans the moment his shift ended as a master electrician at the Portsmouth Naval Shipyard.

Mr. McAllister grabbed a Miller Lite from the fridge and sat down at the butcher board kitchen table. "We heard from Danny earlier."

"Oh yeah?" said Pat. "What did he say?" The toaster's metal coils glowed orange.

"He had a bad day yesterday," said Mr. McAllister, staring at the brown beer bottle. "His first bad day in Iraq. As far as we know, I guess."

"A bad day?" The blood rushed from Pat's face. The waffles popped out of the toaster, but he didn't grab them.

"He got hurt, Pat," said Mr. McAllister before taking a swig of the beer. He picked at the white label. "Not terribly hurt. But hurt."

"What happened to him?" Pat didn't feel buzzed anymore.

"We still don't really know. Something about being on patrol two days ago and the Humvee going over an IED. The driver got killed." Mr. McAllister wiped his eye. "Danny got a concussion and broke his back. I guess the fracture is really minor though, nothing horrible. He's able to move around pretty good. But his hearing seemed off. It sounded like he was shouting into the phone."

Pat shuffled over to the table and sank down on the bench across from his dad. He fingered that morning's *Boston Globe* and tried to steady his breathing. "Where is he now?"

"He's at this big air base called Al-Asad. They're going to get him back in shape and back to his unit." Mr. McAllister's knee bounced up and down like he was operating a sewing machine.

They sat in silence for a few moments.

"Danny's tough," said Pat finally. He was too superstitious to add that Danny would be all right.

Mr. McAllister nodded, his jaw clenched. He removed his bifocals and rubbed his eyes. His remaining gray hair was uncharacteristically disheveled. He looked like an old man.

"I just feel bad thinking it," said Mr. McAllister, staring at his glasses lying on the table.

"Thinking what?"

Mr. McAllister picked up the glasses and drummed them against the butcher board. The muscles in his forearm danced beneath skin pockmarked from his journeyman days. "For wishing that maybe it had been just a little worse. For wishing it was serious enough to get him out of there for good."

Pat nodded.

Later that night, as Pat lay beneath his plaid comforter, he was surprised to experience a feeling of profound relief. Some other family had received a soldier in a dress uniform at their front door earlier that day, but his family hadn't. Danny was still breathing.

Pat reached over to his bedside table and grabbed the plastic rosary. Just as he had every night since Danny's deployment began, Pat said ten Hail Marys. So far it was working—or at least had been working.

Pat prayed an extra decade. The more divine protection the better.

"God," said Pat, when he got to the last bead, "just bring him home. I'll do whatever. Just bring him home."

＊

Galán stood with his hands on his hips and studied the articles of clothing spread across his bed. He would wear the khaki suit for the funeral but was unsure about the rest. If he appeared too matching, too put together, there would be whispering in Ciego de Ávila. People would say he had forgotten where he had come from.

Galán picked up his navy-blue polo shirt. Somebody like his cousin Yunel would know that the shirt was too understated not to be a $65 real deal. It didn't look anything like the knockoffs that could be purchased with Cuban pesos. No, it wouldn't do.

Instead, Galán found a black T-shirt that he hadn't worn in years. ARMANI EXCHANGE was festooned across the front and back in shimmering fonts. He smiled, remembering how Esperanza had rolled her eyes when he had bought the shirt at the Marshall's in Big Pine Key. It would work just fine.

Galán finished packing the wardrobe suitcase and zipped it closed. He then eyed the larger, nearly empty duffle bag. Every cubic inch needed to be put to good use. So far he had over-the-counter medications, bandages, hand sanitizers, toothbrushes, sneakers, socks, men's and women's underwear, powdered laundry detergent, and towels. He still needed to get reading glasses for Yunel's father-in-law and diabetic supplies for Tía Teresa. And the sewing machine.

He checked his watch. Stores would be open for another hour. He grabbed his wallet and keys and descended the stairs to the street.

As Galán walked past the statute of Patricio Rijos solemnly playing his *guiro*, an unsettled feeling returned to the pit of his stomach. It had come and gone ever since he had purchased his airplane tickets. He had thought that he was just nervous to fly—it had been years since his trip from Key West, after all—but now he realized it was something else.

After twenty-five years of living in a different world, he was afraid he wouldn't be able to recognize any of the faces back in his old neighborhood in Ciego de Ávila, or even the neighborhood itself. To him, those people—family and friends, even some enemies—were no longer living, breathing individuals but rather faded memories.

But there was something more, he thought, crossing la Calle San Justo. Something even more unsettling. While he had nurtured his memories of Ciego de Ávila the best he could—the good ones at least—it was unlikely that anyone beyond his immediate family had done the same regarding their memories of him. In the one place on this earth that he considered home, he was, for all intents and purposes, dead and gone.

That thought marinated in his mind as he crossed la Plaza de las Armas. He took a deep breath.

To hell with it. He didn't need a home.

What he needed was to say good-bye to his mother. Who he needed was Gabriela.

9

Havana, Cuba

Galán stepped off the plane onto the portable stairway at Aeropuerto Internacional José Martí. The wall of tropical humidity possessed a certain tang that he had never experienced in Puerto Rico. After several breaths, he finally recognized the diesel.

The sole of Galán's shoe made contact with the warm tarmac, and for the first time in over two decades, he was home. He had a hard time reconciling the difficulty of his escape with the ease of his return—after all, he had been in his own bed that very morning, and the sun had yet to set.

"Sir," said a young officer from the Aduana General, her light-green skirt and blouse hugging her body. "I need you to keep moving. Let's go."

Galán nodded and followed the rest of the passengers into the red-walled terminal. Ten minutes, twenty minutes, thirty minutes passed before the baggage belt creaked into motion. Televisions, small refrigerators, and even a generator, all mummified in shrink-wrap plastic, emerged through the hanging flaps.

As Galán collected his suitcases and the sewing machine, a diminutive security guard approached from an unmarked door. I haven't been here ten minutes, Galán thought, and they're already going to give me shit. Once a worm, always a worm. He tried to avoid eye contact with the boy, but it was too late.

"Look," said the pimply-faced guard, his assertiveness disproportionate to his age, "you know there are taxes on items like that, right?" He tilted his head toward the sewing machine.

"Really?" asked Galán, feigning ignorance.

"Yes, really," said the guard. "But you look like you might be in a rush."

Galán glanced over at the long lines for customs inspections—a sense of urgency hadn't overcome the Cuban workforce during his years of absence. Rush or no rush, he may as well give his money to the kid as opposed to the state. Plus, he didn't know what kind of complications the kid could cause otherwise.

Galán reached into his neck wallet and pulled out a ten-euro note. He had changed his currency back in Puerto Rico because of the Cuban government's punitive exchange rate for American dollars.

The kid took the bill without hesitation, not even bothering to check if anyone was watching. "Follow me."

Galán, weighed down by his luggage, struggled to keep up with the young man. He expected one of the other officers from the Aduana General to say something as he skipped by the customs checkpoint, but none of them did. His heartrate slowed, only to accelerate again as he approached the airport's exit.

As Galán passed through the doors, he came face to face with a crowd of people waiting to reunite with long-lost family members. Galán lowered a shoulder and banged his way through to the taxi stand. Galán found a 1955 Dodge and threw his luggage onto the threadbare seats. "We're going to the national bus stop on Independencia."

The driver nodded and shifted the Dodge into gear.

As the land yacht groaned forward, Galán wiped the sweat from his face and peered through the window. Propaganda billboards passed by, some with generic images of Che Guevara and Camilo Cienfuegos accompanied by stale slogans like *Patria o Muerte* and *Venceremos*. Others, like an outdated one demanding the release of the five spies captured in Miami, were more specific.

The Dodge passed the zoo, low-slung housing, and warehouses as it covered the ten miles that separated the airport from downtown. The traffic, thick but moving, consisted of other cannibalized American mid-century classics, 1980s Ladas, and contemporary makes that Galán had never seen before. He had forgotten how the drivers here honked their horns more frequently but less aggressively than their brothers and sisters to the north.

Galán rested his head against the top of the seat and stretched out his legs. There was something surreal about being back. Sure, there were superficial differences, like the modern pay phones and the smoother highway, but the essence of Cuba was just as he remembered.

Except that his mother had died, and his sister was growing old.

✯

The air brakes hissed, and the bus slowed to a stop at the Ciego de Ávila station in the unforgiving hour before dawn. Galán, legs stiff from the seven-hour journey, staggered down the steps. Despite his interminable day of traveling, he was wide awake. Everywhere—the turnoff by el Parque Martínez Brito, the baseball field down la Calle Narcíso Lopez—was another memory.

Galán humped his luggage up the curb toward a cluster of people hanging out by a black and red Cerveza Bucanero vending machine. A short man leaned with his elbow cocked against the pirate's tricornered hat, his palm supporting his shaved head. Galán hadn't seen that pose in decades.

"Yunel?" asked Galán.

The man stepped forward, his sandals slapping against the concrete and his camouflage shorts hanging well below his knees. He studied Galán. "Wow. It really is you. Welcome home, cousin."

They embraced, Galán's back and neck stiffening—he had forgotten what it felt like to be hugged by family. He had forgotten what it felt like to be accepted for no other reason than sharing the same blood.

As they drove across the flat, dark city in Yunel's borrowed Lada, Galán's eyes devoured the scenery. The squat, concrete buildings set back from the street behind covered sidewalks, the gaping potholes, the Lycra pants favored by the women who were up and about before dawn—they were like the details from a long-forgotten dream.

"So," said Yunel, waving his hand from one side of the windshield to the other. "What do you think? How does your beloved Ciego de Ávila look?"

Galán didn't know where to start.

"Well, I'll tell you. It's the same. Completely the same." Yunel fumbled with a wrench to roll down his window. "But more importantly, how is Puerto Rico?"

Galán didn't bother answering the question. "Two decades have passed, Yunel. More, even. Can you believe that?"

"Can I believe that? Brother, it feels like it's been two centuries since I saw your skinny ass constantly throwing that baseball around." Yunel tapped the horn at a crossing chicken. "Anyway, time moves slower when every day brings with it some new bullshit. As a kid, you don't notice it as much."

Galán nodded, half-listening.

"But, hey. We get by." Yunel tapped his horn again, this time at a slow-moving 1956 Chevy, its most recent coat of red paint faded by the tropical sun. "Anyway, everybody is excited to see you, you know. You're a mystery man. Gabi's the most excited."

Galán's heart beat even faster.

Yunel downshifted and turned into the old neighborhood, which was darker than the rest of the city thanks to a rolling blackout. The Lada bounced down the rutted dirt road, its headlights casting a ghostly light on the few early morning risers. With the exception of a missing ceiba tree, several abandoned homes that had crumbled to the ground like wet cardboard boxes, and a new arcade and shooting gallery on the lot where Juani used to live, the neighborhood looked unchanged.

As Tía Teresa's house came into view, Yunel killed the engine and let the Lada coast down the block in silence. Josefina and Gabi had lived with Josefina's sister ever since they had emerged from the black water off of Bacunayagua.

In the dawn's first gray light, Teresa's bungalow still leaned slightly to the left. Somebody had replaced the front porch, and the yard looked smaller.

Yunel yanked up on the emergency brake and switched off the lights. Galán, his forearms frozen to his thighs and his eyelid twitching, didn't move.

"Well, here we are," said Yunel softly, stepping out. "Welcome home."

Galán swallowed and opened the door. As soon as he felt the familiar packed dirt beneath his shoes, he heard the screen door open. A small woman in a loose T-shirt stumbled down the steps, emitting a soft cry. She moved in a familiar way, with her head down and her feet taking short, choppy steps.

It can't be, thought Galán, as the woman approached. But then he felt her embrace. He felt the way her hands were balled up in that curious way against his back. It was really her. It was Gabriela. He held her tight.

The screen door opened again. Galán looked up and saw Tía Teresa shuffling toward him with a cane to compensate for her missing toes. From her silhouette alone, Galán could tell that his once lithe aunt had put on considerable weight.

"Galancito!" yelled Teresa, her face breaking into a wrinkled but still dimpled smile. She hurried across the dusty yard and threw her arms around him and Gabriela. Galán could feel the women's tears against his neck.

As if on cue, the town's lights buzzed back on, and a television turned on a few houses down. Teresa backed away from the siblings toward Yunel.

Galán couldn't believe Gabriela was standing in front of him smiling her closed-mouth smile. She still had the large, brown eyes that strangers rudely said looked vacant, and the birthmark on her upper lip. The gray strands in her curly black hair and the faint outline of breasts beneath her T-shirt reminded Galán yet again of just how much time had passed.

"I missed you, Gabi," he said, hugging her again. "I missed you so, so much."

"I missed you, too." Her voice was deeper than her childhood squeak, but not by much. "I was scared that I would never see you again. Every single day I'd ask Mami when you were going to come back, and she always said the same thing. She always said, 'Soon.'"

Galán felt a pang of guilt deep in his chest. "I'm sorry. I'm so, so sorry."

"It's okay. You're back now. You came back." She sniffed. "We're a family again."

"We've always been a family. We'll always be a family."

"Yeah," said Gabi into his chest. "We'll always be a family."

10

Off of Haiti

Pat turned on the computer, the brightness temporarily blinding him. Only the red overhead light was on since Tim was asleep. Pat's emails slowly loaded, and sure enough, there was Michaela's nightly dispatch. He read her words twice, but had a hard time imagining that at that very moment it was snowing in Philadelphia.

Pat had last seen snow a year earlier. He was on leave from his old cutter visiting Michaela, and the two of them were snuggled under her covers watching *Holiday Inn* as the streets turned white. Even though Pat hadn't shared her enthusiasm for Fred Astaire's tap-dancing shtick, he had never felt so content. He couldn't have cared less about what was going on in the world outside the four walls of her bedroom. Everything he needed was right there next to him.

With his fingers poised above the keyboard, Pat thought about his reply. He had stood two watches and hadn't even taken the ship off of autopilot. Such was cutter life—weeks of boredom interrupted by the occasional few hours of excitement. But whenever anything exciting did happen, like a drug bust, he couldn't talk about it.

He began typing, telling Michaela about his workout on the forward deck. The smell of burning wood that wafted over from Haiti's coastal villages reminded him of the bonfires that his dad and Danny made at Lake Winnipesaukee every August. He described Haiti's barren mountains, which jutted up from the sea like something out of *Lord of the Rings*. "It's beautiful in a haunting kind of way," he wrote.

Pat clicked SEND and leaned back in his chair, his hands behind his head. He began to drift off.

"Now, set the migrant bill! Now, set the migrant bill!"

Pat opened his eyes. The engines, which had only been clutched in, roared to life.

"What the fuck?" Tim grumbled from behind his rack curtain.

Pat didn't say anything. He just put on his boots and grabbed his gun belt. As he passed through the messdeck, he overheard that a sail freighter loaded with Haitian migrants had broken away from Ile de la Tortue and was heading northwest.

Pat climbed up to the dark bridge. Chief Landis, Tootsie Pop bobbing from his mouth, leaned over the radar. He was studying the sail freighter's course and speed, but wasn't wearing his law enforcement gear.

"You're not coming, Chief?" asked Pat, as he pulled his body armor over his head.

"Hell no, sir." Chief Landis looked up, the radar's glow illuminating his acne scars. "Trust me, I'm too old for Haitians."

Pat laughed and grabbed a forty caliber Sig Sauer pistol from the gunner's mate. "Too old? You didn't look too old when you were breaking out those moves on the dance floor in Puerto Plata."

Chief Landis grinned, and the lollipop rotated sideways like a turret gun. "Don't get me wrong, XO. I can hang with the young bucks when I need to. It's like that Toby Keith song. I'm still as good once as I ever been. Or whatever that Okie bastard says."

Laughing, Pat started toward the pilothouse door so he could load his weapon outside the skin of the ship.

"Remember, sir," said Chief Landis, his voice serious. "Bring all the life jackets you can. You never know how many people they got crammed in there."

"Roger, Chief."

Outside in the smoky humidity, Pat inserted a twelve-round magazine into his pistol and released the slide. He looked around the open-air aft deck, and the cutter suddenly seemed very small—any migrants they found would have to live in these tight quarters.

After the pre-mission brief, the interceptor was launched from the cutter's stern gate. Pat, strapped into the small boat's navigator seat and surrounded by darkness, turned the knob on the digital chart display. He zoomed the picture to a two-mile radius. A dot clearly indicated the location of the nearby sail freighter.

A few minutes later, the coxswain who was filling in for Chief Landis brought the throttle to all stop. The interceptor bobbed up and down, the waves lapping against the aluminum hull, as the crew peered into the night.

"Oh, shit."

The silhouette of a massive sail rose out of the darkness. Pat felt like he could reach out and touch it.

"Jesus, you can smell it," said Martínez from the seat behind Pat.

"Of course," said Larson, the tattooed electronics technician from Ohio. He had barely passed the French language test in order to earn a $50 monthly stipend as patrol translator. "What did you expect?"

Pat notified the cutter, which was a half mile behind them, that they were on scene with the sail freighter. He racked his microphone.

"Do it," Pat said.

The coxswain flipped on the searchlight and blue strobe. The migrant vessel was the length of a school bus, with a sail made out of a Nokia billboard. A dozen people sat on the aft deck. They shielded their faces from the spotlight.

Larson called out over the loudhailer in a swirl of broken French. Pat couldn't understand the words, but he knew Larson was identifying them as the Coast Guard and asking about the nature of the sail freighter's voyage.

Some of the migrants shouted back. One of the men pulled down his shorts and started swinging his genitals like a helicopter.

"What the fuck are they saying?" asked the coxswain.

"I don't know," said Larson. "It's goddamned Creole. I don't know Creole."

The coxswain inched the interceptor closer, careful not to startle the migrants. Pat ran his flashlight up and down the vessel, while Martínez provided cover with the M16. Pat's flashlight picked up a spherical shape just above the gunwale. He kept scanning. There were two or three more.

"You see that?" he asked.

"Yeah," said Martínez. "Cargo, maybe. Bags or something."

One of the shapes moved. Another had eyes.

"Oh, shit."

Chief Landis had been right—people were jammed into the hold. As they scrambled up to the aft deck to join the original dozen, the French and Creole shouting grew louder. Pat didn't need a translator to sense the panic.

There was a splash. And then another splash. The Haitians were jumping and falling overboard. The sail freighter rocked back and forth.

"Fuck," said Pat. This was exactly what they wanted to avoid.

The boom of the Nokia billboard swung toward the interceptor. Pat ducked. It snapped off the radar dome and Coast Guard ensign before falling into the sea with a sickening crack. Pat could barely hear the other members of the interceptor crew above the Haitians' frantic shouting.

"We have multiple people in the water!" yelled the coxswain into the radio. "Multiple people in the water. They're jumping! Get some spotlights on us!"

Within seconds, powerful white beams from the nearby cutter pierced the darkness. Pat reached behind the interceptor's seats and began throwing life jackets into the swirling black ocean. He saw a glint of light out of the corner of his eye and ducked a flying machete.

"Did you see that?" he yelled, but Larson and Martínez were too busy pulling survivors aboard to respond. Pat joined them.

"We can only take seven!" yelled the coxswain. "This boat is only rated for seven! We'll come back for the rest."

"Fuck that!" yelled Martínez, heaving a choking woman up and over the orange sponson.

Pat grabbed a wailing little girl from another woman's outstretched arms. The child wore a gold necklace spelling the word *Lovely*.

With the weight of each additional body, the interceptor sank lower into the water until the waves splashed over the gunwales. The coxswain, cursing, finally backed the interceptor out of the mass of bodies.

Thankfully, the interceptor had a jet drive and not a deadly propeller.

They made four trips back and forth between the expanding ring of survivors and the cutter. The fifth trip was for the still bodies. There were three of them, not including those who had sunk the thirty fathoms to the rocky bottom.

Larson performed mouth-to-mouth on a skinny adolescent boy who still had a pulse. After fifty compressions, salt water and vomit erupted from the child's mouth and nose. Larson didn't wipe it off his body armor, but instead held the boy's head in his lap.

Once those final three were aboard the cutter, Pat and the interceptor crew returned to the sail freighter to see if there were any migrants remaining. Pat, holding the sail freighter's tiller for balance, followed Martínez onto the wooden stern. The silence was even more disturbing than the screaming.

Pat's soaked boot landed on something soft. He looked down, and his flashlight revealed a disemboweled cat, its four paws nailed to the deck. Inside its chest cavity were extinguished candles.

"Voudou," said Martínez. "For a safe voyage."

Pat swallowed the bile that had risen to the back of his throat.

"Let's see what other surprises they have in store for us."

Pat pointed his flashlight into the hold's sloshing filth. No bodies. Only water jugs, a tire, several sandals, an Orlando Magic jersey, and trash.

Thank God, thought Pat, dropping down into the interceptor. He passed a metal gas can to Martínez, who unscrewed the cap and splashed fuel across the deck of the sail freighter.

"That should do it," said Martínez, surveying his work.

"I think so," said the coxswain.

Martínez jumped down into the interceptor, unwrapped a distress flare, set it off, and tossed it onto the floating hulk.

"Burn, baby, burn," muttered the coxswain, as orange flames leapt high into the Caribbean night.

It did. For almost three hours. But when the sun came up the next morning, the charred remains of the sail freighter were still there.

Still floating.

11

Ciego de Ávila, Cuba

"In my father's house there are many mansions," said the priest, waving a fly from his face. "If it were not so, I would have told you."

Galán tried to focus on the Gospel according to John and not the sweat streaming down his back. Khaki had been a bad choice.

"I go to prepare a place for you. And if I go and prepare a place for you, I will come again and receive you to myself."

A lone, cumulus cloud provided momentary, merciful shade for Galán, Gabriela, and the dozen other mourners. Perhaps the reprieve was a parting gift from Josefina, whose cremated remains had been deposited into her family's aboveground crypt. The Catholic Church frowned upon cremation, but el Cementerio de Ciego de Ávila had become rather crowded.

Galán looked at the mildewed marble box engraved with his maternal name: Feut. He couldn't believe he was going to leave his mother in there forever. He didn't feel like she was gone, but rather trapped, confined, a prisoner in a dark, hot cell.

She wasn't alone, though. Gabriela, sniffling at Galán's side, had insisted on putting her threadbare stuffed Mickey Mouse inside the tomb as well. Mickey had been Gabriela's prized possession ever since a childhood trip to Havana. Gustavo had purchased Mickey from a street vendor near el Parque Cervantes. Galán had been happy for Gabi until he realized his father had no money left to buy him anything.

The priest closed his Bible, signaling the commencement of eulogies. Tía Teresa was crying too much to talk, so Yunel stood in for her. He mumbled, his garish sunglasses downcast at the weeds at his feet, about how Josefina greeted each new day with a smile, despite the crosses she had to bear.

Galán didn't remember so many smiles, but maybe things had been better without him and his father.

As Yunel wrapped up, the priest looked at Galán.

We already discussed this, thought Galán, shaking his head "no" as inconspicuously as possible. He wasn't the prodigal son. He wasn't about to waltz back onto the island and wax poetic about the woman who had birthed him, fed him, clothed him, spanked him, loved him. That right had to be earned.

Seeing that there were no other takers, the priest recited one last prayer. He implored God to "bless, protect, and guide Josefina's children, Gabriela and . . . her brother."

What a petty bastard, thought Galán. He knows my name.

The mourners crossed themselves and shuffled away and out of the sun. A few nodded solemnly at Galán and Gabriela, who remained behind with their mother for just a few moments more.

"You know," said Galán, once he and Gabriela were alone, "Mami is still going to be with us. You won't be able to see her. Or hear her. But you'll be able to feel her."

Gabriela sniffled. "Are you sure?"

"Yeah, I'm sure." He wasn't, but he squeezed her hand anyway and managed a smile.

"How do you know?"

"Because for all of these years, I could never see her, and only every few months did I hear her. But I could feel her with me. Just like I could feel you with me." These weren't lies.

Gabriela wiped a tear.

"That's what family is," continued Galán. "We're always with each other because we live in each other's hearts. Even after we're dead."

"I hope so. Because I miss her so much."

Galán kissed her on the top of the head. "I know."

"And when you leave, I'm going to miss you so much, too." She buried her face in his shoulder. "It will be really hard to miss both of you at the same time."

"I know. But I promise it won't be like before. I won't disappear again. I'll come back all the time to see you."

"That would be good. Because I want my family."

"You have family," said Galán, as he watched a pigeon flutter down onto the roof of the Feut tomb. "You have Tía Teresa and Yunel. Yunel's wife . . ."

"No," said Gabriela, sitting up and looking Galán in the eye. "That's not the same. I mean real family."

Galán swallowed. The uneasy feeling came stabbing back into the pit of his stomach.

✫

The next day, Galán sat across from his aunt on a plastic-covered green love seat while Gabriela washed the dishes. Teresa tipped rich, steaming coffee into Galán's thimble-like cup. Since Galán had been too young to enjoy the beverage before departing Cuba, it was the presentation and not the sweet taste that reminded him of his childhood.

"It's good," he said, savoring the rich sweetness. "Better than how we make it in my restaurant. But you must not be able to drink it this way anymore, with the diabetes and all?"

"Of course not." Teresa laughed. "You think I want to lose my other foot? I really don't miss it. The sugar, I mean." She looked down at the scratched mahogany table and straightened the trivet. "But anyway, that gets to what I want to talk to you about."

"Oh yeah? What's that?" Galán took another sip, his cup already half empty. A clanging emanated from the kitchen as Gabriela put away a pot.

"Galán, I'm an old woman." Teresa adjusted the kerchief she wore around her gray hair. "And with my health, I don't know if this is going to work."

"If what's going to work?" He had a feeling he already knew the answer.

"This arrangement," she said, looking toward the kitchen. "If I can care for Gabriela. She needs almost constant supervision. She forgets things. I spent the other day at the doctor's—the whole day— because they were backed up. And when I came home, she hadn't even eaten anything. She was sitting in front of the television in the dark house. And I can't send her anywhere because she gets lost."

Galán stared at the hairline fracture that ran from the rim of his porcelain cup to its base.

"Oh, and then there's the sleepwalking." Teresa shook her head. "That started after you left, and it got a lot worse when your mother became sick."

Galán had never heard about the sleepwalking. There was a lot he hadn't heard about. He sighed. "So if you're saying you can't take care of her, that leaves only Yunel."

"Correct."

"And how would that work?" asked Galán.

"I don't really know," said Teresa. "Even though Yunel's marriage is a mess, he is still providing for his wife's father. That woman . . ." As Teresa's voice drifted off, she waved her hand in front of her face as if she were ridding herself of a foul smell.

"Please be honest with me," said Galán, leaning forward. "Do you think Yunel would take in Gabriela? Another mouth to feed?"

"There's really no other option. But if we could get her into one of those government homes, it would be less difficult on him."

"What? The psychiatric hospital?" As a kid, Galán and Juani had visited the one just outside of town. They had stood off to the side of the national highway and peered through the fence. Pallid figures shuffled across a yard in tan, loose-fitting tunics.

"No, not one of those," said Teresa, shaking her head.

"Okay, good. Because you heard about the patients who froze to death at la Mazorra? You know, the huge hospital in Havana?"

"What? Heavens no." She crossed herself. "But anyway, Gabi isn't unwell enough for one of those."

"So what else is there?"

"These smaller facilities. What do people call them? Day hospitals?"

"Day hospitals?" Galán had occasionally seen a small minivan pick up a group of mentally challenged adults by la Plaza Colón back in San Juan. The operation—los Gran Amigos, or something to that effect—was considered an adult day care center.

"Yeah, you know what I mean." Teresa glanced toward the kitchen again. Gabi was watering the orchids that sat on the windowsill. "Anyway, Yunel would drop her off in the mornings and pick her up in the evenings. I don't really know what they do there. Play games. Do art. I'm not sure. All I know is it means the families can live their lives."

This last comment irked Galán. He would have said something, but he realized that he had already been living his life. Unlike his mother—or even Teresa or Yunel—Galán hadn't spent a single day worrying about Gabriela's next meal. He had never had to make sure she bathed, slept, or didn't wander off. Not only that, his life had been one of American luxury.

"Think about it, Galán." Teresa winced as she pulled herself up off the couch. "I know it's not ideal. But everybody else is in Miami. You're in Puerto Rico. So Yunel and these day homes are our only option. They're Gabriela's only option."

"I'll think about it," said Galán.

Gabriela emerged from the kitchen and sat down in front of the television. The afternoon cartoons were about to begin. She smiled at Galán and patted the sofa next to her.

I'll think about it. But I'm not making any promises.

12

Off of Haiti

"There's people dead," said Pat to Larson the afternoon following the sail freighter incident, "and it seems like nobody even noticed. You would think there would have been tears."

The two were standing migrant watch on the *Strickland*'s aft deck. Pat had washed his coveralls that morning, but they already reeked of sweat and still gave off a whiff of whatever had been sloshing in the sail freighter's bilge.

"Life's hard here," said Larson, numbering toothbrushes with a marker. "Death is no stranger."

Most of the thirty migrants slept on wool blankets on the nonskid deck, but a few leaned against the taut lifelines and spoke in low voices. They looked like prisoners in their white Tyvek suits, each marked in Sharpie with an identification number.

"I suppose."

Ever since the captain had suspended the search, Pat had been thinking about the missing migrants. Were they sprawled out on the seafloor on top of centuries' worth of maritime trash, spiny lobsters scuttling across arms and legs and torsos? Or had their buoyancy left them suspended halfway toward the bottom in some sort of purgatory-like equilibrium?

A young man with a scarred face approached and indicated that he needed to relieve himself. Thankful for something to do, Pat escorted him to the makeshift toilet that emptied into the ocean through a long rubber hose. A flapping canvas tarp provided a semblance of privacy.

Out of the corner of his eye, Pat saw that the man was urinating all over the deck.

"Hey! You're missing the toilet!"

The man, laughing, didn't change his aim.

Cursing under his breath, Pat returned to the bit he had been sitting on next to Larson. When the cooks arrived with the standard fare of rice and beans, Pat divvied out the plastic spoons. He made sure each migrant only received one since the spoons would need to be collected after the meal—they made for great shanks.

With the sun dipping below the horizon and the migrants eating, Pat leaned against the pilothouse and watched the small fires burning on the brown, denuded hillsides of Tortue. He still stood behind what he had told Michaela. Haiti was beautiful in its own way.

A child approached, his large pant legs rolled up. Pat smiled, but the child didn't smile back. The boy handed Pat a seashell painted with blue, white, and green stripes.

"Thanks," said Pat, turning the sea shell in his hand.

The boy just stared.

"*Merci*," translated Larson.

"*Agwé*," said the boy, pointing at the shell and then toward the ocean. "*Agwé*."

"What the hell is *agwé*?" asked Pat.

"I have no idea," said Larson. He said something to the boy in French.

The boy shook his head and again pointed at the shell and then at the sea. "*Agwé*."

"What is he saying?" asked Pat.

"Something about voudou and the sea. I can't figure it out."

"*Agwé*." The boy made a throwing motion.

Pat tossed the shell into the sea.

The boy nodded and walked away.

Larson laughed as he pulled out a tin of wintergreen Copenhagen. "I think I get it now."

"What?" asked Pat.

Larson wiped brown spittle from the corner of his mouth. "He was just trying to get you to pay homage to one of his gods."

"Huh," said Pat. He thought for a moment. "I guess I'll take that as an honor."

"You should. Add that to your collateral duties, sir—navigator, boarding officer, property custodian, voudou priest."

Pat chuckled, but then he remembered the migrants trapped underwater and the body bags they had transferred to the Haitian Coast Guard. Maybe things would have turned out differently had the actual voudou priests done their job.

Maybe not.

✶

Pat pulled back the rack curtain, climbed under the sheets, and flipped off the fluorescent light mounted just above his face. With his dark cocoon rocking up and down in time with the swells, he tried to sleep. His mind, however, kept humming.

He and Danny were reeling in their fishing lines from the two-lane bridge, the afternoon May sun warming their necks. Danny had begun his post-deployment leave the day before, and Pat was thankful to finally have some time alone with him after the whirlwind homecoming. Pat had been waiting for this reunion for the entirety of his sophomore year of college.

As Pat checked the leech on his hook, he glanced again at the STEADFAST AND LOYAL tattoo on Danny's pale upper arm. Danny hadn't told him about it.

"I see you looking at me," said Danny. "What's up? You got a problem with my farmer's tan? It's not like we were over there on the banks of the Euphrates sunbathing and drinking mai tais."

Pat laughed. "No, it's that tattoo. I didn't know you had gotten inked up."

"Oh, yeah." Danny looked down at it, as if he were surprised that it was still there. "Me and some of the guys got it during our week back at Carson. You know me. I've never been a tattoo guy, but I figured what the hell. We earned it, right?"

"Yeah, I guess so."

"I'm just glad I didn't go first." Danny's crooked smile crept across his face. "My buddy Jimmy went first and they spelled it S-T-A-D-E-F-A-S-T. And Jimmy, like the dumbass that he is, didn't even notice."

They both laughed and swigged their Coors Lights. Danny cast, and Pat waited for the outgoing tide to pull Danny's line taut before he followed suit. They stood in silence, each reeling in slowly. Pat checked for tension with his thumb.

"Fish aren't biting," said Danny. "It's like nobody told them that yesterday was my triumphant return."

Pat had told his mom that the gigantic red, white, and blue banner that they brought to Logan was too much. It wasn't Danny's style.

"You know how the Iraqis fish?" Danny took another sip from the Coors Light. "They drop a hand grenade into the river. No joke. Maybe we should try that." He set his beer down and wiped his chin.

Pat laughed. He jerked up on his pole but felt only current.

"I'm serious. They just drop a grenade in and see what floats to the top."

"If there was anywhere in this country we could get away with that, it would be here. Live free or die trying."

Danny smiled. "You kind of have to see it to believe it. There's a lot of things over there you have to see to believe." He shook his beer can—the mountains were no longer blue. "Well, I guess we might as well call it. The fish aren't getting any hungrier."

They reeled in their lines, shouldered the cooler and tackle box, and walked to the end of the bridge. Or rather Pat walked and Danny limped with his new forward lean.

Pat backed the Chevy Blazer into the road and started heading home. They drove with the windows down, Danny drumming his fingers on the passenger door. Some part of Danny always seemed to be in motion. A finger. A knee. An eyelid.

"You want to listen to some music?" asked Pat. "You probably missed a bunch of new stuff when you were over there. I can catch you up."

"Nah, I'm good."

"You're missing out. Jason Aldean has been killing it."

"Hey, take a right on Islington," said Danny. "I want to get one more road soda."

"Oh yeah?" Pat turned the wheel, smiling. He hadn't heard his brother refer to a beer that way since before he'd joined the army. "Where at?"

"Here," said Danny.

Pat studied the intersection, but all he saw was Rod's Tire Repair and an anonymous-looking clapboard house with a sagging front porch. A '90s Cadillac and an even older, two-toned Silverado were parked outside.

"All that's here is the American Legion."

"Exactly," said Danny. "That's where we're going."

Pat had passed American Legion Post 7018 hundreds of times but had never given it a moment's thought. It was the kind of place that just existed. He parked the Blazer underneath the fluttering American and Prisoner of War flags, and the brothers walked inside.

Pat's eyes slowly adjusted to the darkness. He followed Danny toward the bar, which glowed beneath a string of Christmas lights and a neon Pabst Blue Ribbon sign. As they sat down a few stools away from a white-haired couple, "Kiss on My Lips" by Hall and Oates began to play on the jukebox—probably a selection by one of the old men playing pool.

"How you boys doing?" said the mustached barkeep. He wore a light denim shirt and dark denim pants. "Mind if I see some ID?"

"Sure thing," said Danny.

The barkeep squinted at Danny's military identification card and Pat's driver's license. "Well, I never seen you two before, but I suppose somebody's got to drink this beer and keep our register full. Plus, I like looking out for the next generation."

"We appreciate that, sir." Danny's crooked smile was back.

"So, what outfit you with?" the old man asked, his eyes lingering on the black Killed In Action remembrance bracelet on Danny's wrist.

"Fourth Infantry. Yourself?"

"First Cav. Vietnam. Sixty-nine to seventy." He looked at Pat. "How 'bout you?"

"Well, I'm not—I'm in college down the road. Over at UNH."

The old man nodded.

"He's still a young buck," said Danny. "We'll see what happens with him. He might be destined for bigger and better things."

"I see." The old man smiled. He was missing a tooth toward the back. "Well, my name's Larry. Larry Smythe. Welcome to Post 7018." He shook both of their hands. "What are you fellows drinking?"

"We'll take two High Lifes," said Danny.

"Two High Lifes it is." Larry reached into a cooler and popped off the tops with a bottle opener nailed to the wall. "So, what brings you to Portsmouth?"

"We're from here," said Danny, taking a sip. "Our family lives over by Immaculate Conception. We just wanted to come by and check the place out. Say hello. I only have a few months left on my contract, and I figure this could be a good place to spend some time later on."

"That's the truth," said Larry. "It's always good to have a community. That helped me a lot when I came back. Just having some fellows that had been there to talk to. Even if we didn't talk about our deployments, just bullshitting with somebody who had been there made a world of difference."

"Yes, sir," said Danny.

"Well," said Larry, opening a High Life for himself. "To the next generation."

Larry and Danny clinked bottles as "El Paso" by Marty Robbins began playing. Pat, unsure as to his role, if any, in the toast, nodded and drank slowly.

The little bit of sunshine that snuck through the dusty windows faded as Larry and Danny traded stories. Pat nursed his beer and listened, only recognizing a few of the dozens of acronyms that came out of their mouths—NCO, PCS, CC, 1LT. Danny's eyes no longer darted and his laugh came easy.

A group of Larry's Vietnam buddies showed up for bingo night, so the old barkeep had to step away. He gave Danny a handshake and Pat a friendly nod. Danny paid their paltry bill, and Pat took the keys—Danny's limp now had a bit of a stagger to it.

"That old man was a good dude," said Danny, nodding from the passenger seat of the Blazer. "A good dude." He produced an orange plastic pill bottle from his sweatshirt pocket and unscrewed the cap.

"What are those for?" Pat wasn't used to his brother taking medicine. His dad was the one who was always fumbling around with pill bottles. "You don't feel good?"

Danny tipped the bottle to his mouth and waved the question away with his hand.

Pat kept looking back and forth between Danny and the road.

"It's medicine," Danny finally said. "From the army docs."

"For what? Your back?"

"No, it's for my big toe." Danny shook his head. "Of course it's for my back, you moron. You ever broken your back?"

"I was just asking. I didn't know it was still bothering you." Pat tried to lighten the mood. "I thought you walked with that pole up your ass just to get sympathy from the girls."

"Jesus." Danny shook his head.

Pat tightened his grip on the steering wheel. Neither brother spoke as they turned into their neighborhood.

"You want to do something tonight?" Pat finally asked, as he parked the Blazer behind their dad's Tacoma.

Danny didn't say anything.

"There's a new bar on Daniel Street that's pretty fun. It should be hopping on a Friday. You could try out that limp for the UNH girls."

"No, I'm good." Danny unbuckled his seatbelt. "I'll probably just stay in."

"Man, old Danny would have been out there swinging from the lampposts. We could go to some of your spots if you want. Fat Belly's. State Street. We don't have to go to the new place."

"I said I'm good." Danny stepped out of the Blazer and slammed the door closed. He hunched through the glare of the headlights toward the house, leaving Pat to grab the cooler, tackle box, and fishing poles.

Pat remained behind the wheel as his brother disappeared inside. Once the front door closed, Pat wrote a text message to Danny's high school friends. The surprise party was off.

13

Ciego de Ávila, Cuba

"Hello," said Galán loudly, peering through the open front door of Yunel's concrete row house.

No answer.

Galán squeezed past a large couch and two disassembled dirt bikes and entered the kitchen. The sound of a television came from behind a closed door next to the refrigerator.

Galán knocked. "Yunel? It's Galán."

Still no answer.

Galán opened the door.

Yunel's father-in-law sat on a small cot in blue jeans buttoned at his navel and no shirt. The man, who couldn't have weighed over a hundred pounds, regarded Galán with a wary eye. An oxygen tank hummed beside him.

"Good afternoon, sir," said Galán loudly. "Yunel? Is he around?"

The old man emitted a raspy noise from his throat and pointed to his watch. He held up five fingers.

"That's fine." Galán sank into a folding chair at the foot of the cot. "I can wait."

On the television, two comedians traded inoffensive jokes at the expense of a man dressed as a giant plantain. The old man watched intently but didn't smile. Just as Galán began reading a *Granma* article about Maduro's new economic proposals in Venezuela, he heard voices on the porch.

Yunel and his wife, Lola, walked in. Neither looked particularly happy.

"I hope you don't mind that I . . ." began Galán, but Lola walked right past him into the adjacent bedroom and slammed the door.

Yunel shook his head and motioned for Galán to join him in the street.

"Let's walk and talk. I need to clear my mind of that woman." Yunel wiped his brow with a rag. "Sometimes I tell myself to just get the hell away from her before I do something I regret."

"Tell me about it," said Galán, even though he couldn't remember having ever had a real fight with Esperanza. "Women have that power."

"Exactly. They know how to get inside your brain and just fuck with you."

Galán nodded.

"So what's up? What brings you to my neighborhood?

Galán glanced at Yunel. "I had a talk with your mom earlier."

"Yeah? About what?"

"About Gabi."

Yunel wiped his forehead again but didn't say anything.

"It sounds like you're our only hope," said Galán, running his fingertips along a concrete wall emblazoned with the slogan *Con Fidel Revolución*. The C, D, and R were highlighted as a play on the acronym for Comités de Defensa de la Revolución. Citizens could go there to seek basic medical care or report on their neighbors.

"Yeah, I guess I am the only hope. That's because everybody else is in Miami." Yunel looked at Galán sideways. "Or Puerto Rico."

Galán nodded.

"And please know," continued Yunel, "that such an arrangement will not be easy. You saw how I'm living back there. You saw that old man sucking down his tanks." He shook his head. "It's bad."

"I can only imagine."

They passed the bakery where Josefina would spend entire mornings waiting for one or two loaves of bread.

"Here's the truth," said Yunel, stopping to look Galán in the eye. "Here's why I'm completely broke, why I've had it with Lola, and why this Gabriela situation is the last thing I need right now."

I'm sorry if my sister's life is a goddamned inconvenience, Galán wanted to say. But he held off. For Gabi's sake.

"I went in with some of Lola's cousins to buy a *casa particular.* You know, one of those places where the Canadians and Germans stay and pay convertible pesos. I put in everything I had. And those pieces of shit took the money and bought black-market passports and plane tickets to Ecuador." Yunel wrung out his rag, sweat dripping onto the sidewalk. "I hope they fry in the Mexican desert."

"Damn," said Galán, trying to maintain his poise. "Are you serious? Lola's cousins?"

"I know. It's crazy." Yunel put his hands on his hips and looked down the empty street before turning back to Galán. "Look, I can take Gabi. But under two conditions."

"Tell me."

"One, you need to bankroll us."

"Of course, Yunel. You know I'll do my best. I always have."

"When I say *us*, I'm talking about me, Lola, the old man, everybody."

So now my sister is your winning lottery ticket? But again, Galán held his tongue. "And two?"

"Two. She goes into one of those day hospitals."

"Teresa mentioned those. I need to visit the one here in Ciego before I leave."

"Why?"

"Why?" Galán heard the anger in his own voice, but he didn't care. "Because I need to decide if I want my sister living out the rest of her days inside one, that's why."

Yunel shook his head, seemingly unperturbed by Galán's rising temper. "Suit yourself. But it's not like you have any other option."

Galán sighed. His cousin was right. But still, he had to see the day hospital with his own eyes, even if such a visit would do nothing but further burden his conscience.

As they turned and retraced their steps, Yunel started to laugh.

"What's so funny?" asked Galán.

"I was just thinking. You know, you do have one other option. You could always put Gabi on a boat."

Galán stopped and stared at him.

Yunel laughed even harder. "Can you imagine?"

★

"Your example lives. Your ideas last."

The billboard of Che gazing into the distance cast a shadow on Galán as he stepped out of the cab. He had told his relatives that he was heading to the bus station, but he had given the taxi driver the address of the day hospital instead. With his suitcase in his hand and the sleeve of his Armani Exchange T-shirt still wet from Gabriela's good-bye tears, Galán approached the wrought-iron gate.

The guard, seated on a plastic chair, hardly looked up from his portable radio as Galán passed. Buena Fe's "Corazonero" fought to be heard through the static.

Galán followed a dirt path across a yard lined with mango trees. The hospital itself—a horseshoe-shaped, two-story concrete building—sat at the rear of the property. In its courtyard, four patients scribbled on pages ripped out of a *Finding Nemo* coloring book. They seemed oblivious to the visitor with the suitcase.

Galán entered the lobby. The walls were mustard yellow and the linoleum floor green. Galán had to admit the place looked clean.

Two female nurses in white coats lingered behind the front desk. "Can we help you?" the younger one with dyed-blonde hair asked.

"No, I'm okay," said Galán, continuing down the hall toward the sound of a television. "I'm just looking, and then I must be going."

"Sir, you need to schedule an appointment. You can schedule one with me, but we don't have openings for another week."

"That's okay," said Galán over his shoulder. He was halfway down the hall. "I'm with the Ministry for Public Health."

No response.

The deeper Galán went, the more overcome he was by a putrid potpourri of cleaning chemicals and excrement. He was rethinking his hygiene assessment when he arrived at the television room. Inside, a dozen patients, young and old, sat transfixed in front of the screen while a male nurse typed away on a flip phone. Like Yunel's father-in-law, the patients didn't seem to understand what was so funny about Mr. Plantain.

Hearing hurried footsteps behind him, Galán walked faster toward what he thought was another hallway. Instead, it was a large open room full of cots. Several patients slept, while a skinny man in a Fort Lauderdale Ban-the-Brick Classic basketball jersey and oven mitts rocked on his haunches, muttering. A woman with Down syndrome about Galán's age braided a doll's hair. The nurse sat asleep on a folding chair, that day's *Granma* spread across his lap.

Galán felt a hand on his upper arm.

"Sir, we need to see your identification," said the blonde nurse. "There are no ministry visits scheduled until the next quarter."

"The ministry does not schedule surprise inspections." Galán tried to sound sufficiently dismissive.

The nurse's fingers only dug further into his biceps. "We can sort it out at the desk." She pulled him back toward the lobby just as the security guard appeared, his baton drawn.

"No need," said Galán. "I've seen all I need to see. I will file my report from my hotel."

The nurse followed him past the security guard, through the yard, and out the front gate.

Galán turned the corner and made his way to the bus station. With the noon departure to Havana nowhere to be seen, Galán sat down on a concrete bench and watched a sanitation worker sweep the nearby sidewalk with a broom made out of twigs. Galán's mind, however, was still at the day hospital.

He pictured Gabriela filling in Nemo's face with an orange crayon. He imagined her watching Mr. Plantain, not understanding the jokes. He thought of her snoring on one of those sagging cots.

In each scene, her hair became more gray, her skin more wrinkled, her shoulders more stooped.

And then he thought about what she said as she hugged him on Teresa's porch that morning, her face buried in his shoulder.

"Please, Galán. Bring me with you. Real family is supposed to be together. Please."

Like a coward, he hadn't said anything, only that he would be back. But now he knew. Now he understood.

She only gets one life. And she deserves to live it.

But how?

14

San Juan, Puerto Rico

Pat and Galán sat across from each other on the terrace, chewing the tough *churrasco*. It was a Friday night, but they let the rest of Old San Juan party without them. Galán hadn't said much since returning to Puerto Rico, but Pat knew better than to ask a lot of questions about Cuba. Pat could tell that Galán's mind was still on the other side of the Caribbean.

As he sipped his beer and watched a distant rain squall pass over Cataño and the Bacardi distillery, Pat had an idea. He didn't have to speak loudly to be heard over the unusually quiet Chayanne song.

"I don't know what you're doing Thursday, but there's going to be this ceremony down at the Coast Guard base. Michaela will be in town, and I figured maybe you wanted to come, too."

Galán smiled for the first time in days. "For real?"

"Yeah, for real. It'll probably be boring as hell, but at least you can see where your tax dollars are going."

Galán laughed. "Tax dollars? This is Puerto Rico. There aren't too many tax dollars going your way, my friend."

"Yeah, that's right." Pat chuckled, remembering that residents of la Isla del Encanto didn't pay federal income tax. "Well, your freeloading ass should still come anyway." Pat looked over toward la Universidad Albizu, which glowed pink and purple from the psychedelic façade lighting. "It would mean a lot to me."

"Well, I'll need to think about it," said Galán smiling. "If your people see me, they might try to send me back to Cuba."

Pat laughed. "Come on! It's not going to be anything crazy. You'll like it." He sipped his beer. "You know what? I'm going to RSVP for you myself. Then you won't have any choice."

"RSVP?"

"It just means you're going to be there. It'll be good. I'm telling you."

Galán chuckled and nodded. "All right, I guess I'll be there. The *teniente* has spoken."

Pat smiled and leaned back in his chair. A breeze from the distant storm blew a dusty plastic mouse across the tile floor.

★

The next morning, Galán left Sefora in charge of la Fonda and walked east down la Avenida de la Constitución, past the capitol and the life-size statues of the US presidents who had deigned to visit the island during their times in office. He paused for a moment at Franklin Roosevelt, and studied the bronze man in his bronze wheelchair. Galán had no idea that the Americans had elected a man who couldn't walk. Or maybe the guy had survived an assassination attempt when he was in office that left his legs useless? That had to be it.

He continued on in the morning humidity, occasionally shaking his shirt loose from his sweating torso. The smell of grease drifted down from the hamburger joint that sat atop the hill to his left. Either the restaurant was open for business much earlier in the day than Galán would have expected, or the beef smoke had so completely penetrated the area that it had a permanent presence, kind of like the radiation that surrounded Chernobyl.

Chernobyl. Galán chuckled, remembering his father excitedly waving a copy of a dissident newsletter describing the nuclear disaster. Gustavo pointed to the article and gleefully predicted the imminent demise of the Soviet Union. Josefina disagreed and seemed offended when Gustavo said that the Castro brothers would be the next to fall.

Galán shook his head and kept walking. Little did any of them know.

With the lush trees of el Parque Luis Muñoz Rivera on his left, Galán studied the storefronts on the first floor of the large concrete building to his right. There it was—la Oficina de Abogados Cobián. Galán had expected the law firm to have more elegant accommodations based on the fee he was paying for his thirty-minute consultation, but he opened the glass door and walked in anyway.

"Hello," said Galán to the receptionist, a young woman with a shaved head and gold hoop earrings. "I have an appointment for ten o'clock. Betances."

"Ah, yes. I'll let Glorimar know you're here."

Galán smiled and sat down. Just as he picked up a copy of that morning's *el Vocero*, an office door opened.

"Señor Betances?"

"Yes," said Galán, standing, turning to face an attractive young woman in tight jeans, a white blouse, and a blue blazer. "You must be Ms. Cobián."

The woman laughed in a friendly way. "No, Señor Cobián is the partner. I just started here. I'm Glorimar Cancél."

"Pleased to meet you," said Galán, taking her soft hand. He didn't know what a partner was, but he would take a thirty-minute appointment with Glorimar over some old man any day.

"Please, sit," said Glorimar, leading him into her cramped but tidy office. It smelled faintly of cinnamon.

Galán eased into a leather chair across from Glorimar. Two certificates hung on the wall behind her. One was from the University of Puerto Rico School of Law in Rio Piedras, and the other was from the University of Miami.

"You're from Miami?" asked Galán. Maybe she was Cuban? This could be huge.

"No," she smiled sweetly again. "That's where I got my LLM. I'm from here. Guaynabo actually."

"Oh," said Galán. He had no idea what an LLM was. "But you're a lawyer, right?"

"Yes, yes, of course." Glorimar smiled again. "So, you mentioned you had an immigration question?"

"Yes, I do," said Galán, trying to focus. "It's about my sister. We're Cubans, and she's still there. She had been living with our mother, but our mother recently passed."

"I'm sorry to hear that."

"Thank you," said Galán, glancing at Glorimar's green Partido Independentista Puertorriqueño coffee mug. When he looked back up he realized that her eyes were almost the same color. "So, when my mother passed, my sister went to live with our aunt. But our aunt is in bad health herself, so next is my cousin."

"A quick question," said Glorimar, leaning forward. "How old is your sister?"

"Thirtysomething," said Galán. He couldn't believe he had lost track.

"So, if she's an adult, why do all of these other people matter? Why isn't she just living on her own?"

"Oh, right. She's not able to. She's different." He tapped the side of his head. "She's, I guess you would say, slow? Developmental problems? Yeah, I think that's the right term."

"Oh, okay," said Glorimar, nodding. "I'm sorry. Please, continue."

"So anyway, everything comes down to my cousin, but my cousin is struggling, too. When I was home for my mother's funeral, he said he would only take my sister in if we committed her to one of those day hospitals."

"I'm not familiar."

"They're like psychiatric institutions. You check in in the morning and check out at night."

"And?" Glorimar looked puzzled.

"And that's no life. That's no way to live."

Glorimar nodded and sipped her coffee. "So you want to know if there is some kind of visa she could get to come here?"

"Exactly."

Glorimar took a deep breath, leaned back in her chair, and stared up at the ceiling. "Cuba is complicated."

"Tell me about it."

"It's very complicated. If she were coming from anywhere else, you might have a decent chance."

Galán felt the blood rush from his face.

"She could potentially qualify for a family preference visa since she's the sibling of an adult US citizen." She looked down at Galán. "You are a citizen, right?"

"Yes."

Glorimar nodded and looked back up at the ceiling. "But those visas are almost impossible to come by in the best of circumstances, and, like I said, Cuba is extra hard."

Galán waited for something, anything, some kernel of hope.

Glorimar leaned forward, her elbows on her desk. "And honestly, a US visa is the least of your problems if Cuba won't let her leave." She thought for a moment. "Look, the way I see it, you have two options. One, you hire some great immigration lawyers. You know, ones that know this stuff better than me and Néstor Cobián. Ones who are experts on Cuba. I should tell you that they would likely charge you a lot more, too. You hire them and maybe after a few months, maybe after a year or two, you get lucky."

Galán shook his head. "My sister doesn't have the time, and I don't have the money. What is option two?"

"Well, two is just a thought between you and me as people, not as attorney and client. Two depends on how critical your sister's situation is, and only you and she know that answer. Two is that you find an alternative solution."

"An alternative solution?"

"Alternative to anything a lawyer could help you with." Glorimar looked down at her lap, her face slightly flushing. "I think you know what I mean, Señor Betances."

Galán nodded.

"I'm sorry there is nothing else I can do for you."

"Thank you," mumbled Galán, standing.

"I really am sorry. And if you change your mind and want a referral, please call me anytime. Other than that, all I can do is wish you and your sister the best."

Galán nodded again and walked slowly out of the office and into a rain squall.

☆

"So, I've been thinking," said Michaela, taking Pat's hand in hers. They were waiting for the check at la Cucina di Giuseppe, an Italian restaurant with outdoor seating on the pedestrian end of la Calle Tanca. The penne Bolognese and Montepulciano wine were as good as anything on Ninth Street in South Philly.

"I've been thinking about what you said last time I was here. When you were dropping me off at the airport. About how you feel like a part of you flies north every time my plane takes off."

"Yeah, I remember." Pat nodded. "That was rather romantic of me, if I do say so myself."

Michaela smiled. "Yes, it was. Poetic even. But what I was thinking was that maybe you're right. Maybe I should move down here."

"Are you serious?" Pat almost popped out of his chair.

"Yeah. I mean like, when else will I be able to live in paradise like this?" She motioned over her shoulder toward the old Spanish wall, the palm trees and colorful buildings of la Puntilla, and the darkening harbor. "I feel like it would be such a waste not to be able to share in this life you have."

"Yes! I know."

Beaming, she leaned over and kissed the back of his hand.

"But what about your work?" Pat asked.

"One of the ER physicians is Puerto Rican, and she has tons of connections down here. She said she might not be able to get me a job as good as the one I have at Temple because of the language barrier, but that she should be able to find me something."

"That's amazing!" Pat thought for a moment, his face clouding over. "And what about when I'm at sea?"

"Pat." Michaela frowned. "I'm a grown woman. Come on. I think I can handle myself."

"All right, all right. No prob." He held up his hands. "That's what I wanted to hear."

She smiled.

The waiter returned and handed Pat a leather-bound copy of *Orlando Furioso*. The bill and Pat's credit card were stuck between the pages—a classy touch. Pat signed the check and returned it to the waiter, who bowed.

Pat and Michaela stood. As the legs of their chairs ground against the cobblestones, several pigeons took off in flight from the bell hanging over la Capilla del Cristo.

"Oh. I have one more surprise for you," said Michaela, her bright green eyes twinkling.

"Another surprise? This better not be one of those good news, bad news deals."

"No. But let's just say it's a surprise I can only give to you back at the apartment."

"Oh, really?" Pat no longer regretted having skipped the tiramisu. "Is it something I get to unwrap?"

"You could say that." She ran her fingers up and down his forearm. "It'll be up to you how you want it."

"I like the idea of unwrapping it slowly." They had been together earlier in the day after he had picked her up from the airport. They hadn't seen each other for four weeks, so the frantic reunion was quick. "With my teeth."

"Oh my God." Michaela laughed. "You're too much."

They cut between the parked cars at the corner of Luna and San Justo. Pat, imagining what Michaela had in store for him, tried to ignore the stiffening in his jeans. He was so distracted that he hardly noticed the three people squatting in the middle of the street—probably tourists being told the myth about the Old San Juan cobblestones having been ballast on Spanish galleons.

Michaela gasped and let go of Pat's hand. She pushed her way into the group.

Before Pat could ask Michaela what she was doing, he saw the orange kitten. Pat thought it was dead until its tiny ribcage expanded with a labored breath.

"You poor baby," Michaela cooed, extending her hand toward the little head.

"For God's sake don't touch it," said Pat, moving in as the kitten's original attendants departed.

"Why?"

"Because look how dirty it is."

Michaela glanced up at him, her eyes without any trace of the seductive glint from earlier.

"I'm sure somebody will come for him," said Pat, even though he'd seen enough starving cats and dogs on the island to know that it was a lie.

"Yeah, like who? Go to the apartment and grab a towel."

"A towel? Why?"

"A towel."

So much for the surprise, thought Pat. He stood. "Well, I guess we could drop it off at the vet tomorrow. Somebody might adopt it once it's healthy."

"No," said Michaela, running the back of her index finger across the kitten's head. "I have a better idea."

15

San Juan, Puerto Rico

Galán leaned against the pink concrete wall of his building and waited for Michaela to descend the stairs from Pat's. He was glad that he wouldn't be showing up to the Coast Guard ceremony alone, but he felt foolish in his khaki suit. He'd made a mental note to get it tailored upon his return from Cuba but had forgotten. He hoped Michaela wouldn't notice that his pants were unbuttoned.

The gate to Pat's building creaked open and a slender girl in a light green dress emerged. Damn. Pat had done well for himself.

Galán cleared his throat. "So, you must be Mrs. Pat. I'm Galán. Galán Betances."

The girl turned and smiled. "I figured you were Galán." She extended her hand. "I'm Michaela. And I don't know about the 'Mrs.' part just yet. Maybe someday."

"Well, Pat would be very lucky indeed." Galán tried not to let his gaze linger on her toned legs or the outline of her panties. That would be rude under any circumstance, but Michaela was almost like family.

"Thank you." Michaela laughed. "I think he would be very lucky too. Anyway, I've heard a lot about you. It seems like Pat's always with you when I call him."

"Yes, he's a good young man to spend so much time with me," said Galán, leading the way down la Calle San Justo toward the Coast Guard base. "But don't worry, I keep the *boricuas* away from him."

106

"I appreciate that." She laughed, although not as heartily as before.

The jewelry stores and coffee shops were just opening. The cruise ships would be disgorging passengers soon.

"So, have you ever been to one of these Coast Guard events?" asked Galán, trying to change the subject.

"Yeah, a few. I'm going to warn you, though. When Pat and his friends start talking about work and their ships, it's like they're speaking a different language."

"Oh, great. I'm already speaking a different language."

"It'll be okay." Michaela smiled. "I'll do my best to translate. Or I'll just tell Pat to shut up and bring us more coffee. I think that's a girlfriend privilege."

Galán laughed and gave her an awkward high five. He could feel his face flush.

They arrived at the base front gate and gave their names to the security guard, who checked them off a list. As they continued past a pair of billowing American and Puerto Rican flags toward a white tent, Galán wondered if he would've had to show identification were it not for the presence of Michaela.

They arrived at a large white tent teeming with Coast Guardsmen in their tropical blue uniforms. Pat emerged from the throng, looking sharp in his choker whites.

"You guys made it!" He kissed Michaela on the forehead and shook Galán's hand. "See brother, I told you nobody would send you back."

"Well, there's still a lot of morning left," said Galán, laughing. He looked around, wiping sweat from his brow with a small towel. He poked Pat in the chest. "Also, I thought you were the man down here. What's going on? Where are all your medals? Why do you only have just these three?"

"Oh, I see how it is. I invite the guy to a party, and all of a sudden he's got jokes. But I'll give you this much," said Pat, smirking as he eyeballed Galán's form-fitting suit, "you do look fresh for somebody who was shopping in the kid's department at Marshalls."

"Pat!" said Michaela, giving him an admonishing look. "I think Galán looks nice."

"It's okay, Michaela. Pat's right." Galán jutted his chin toward the sector commander, who was approaching the podium. His chest was awash in a smorgasbord of medals and ribbons. "I might have to borrow that guy's sword just to get out of this suit."

There was a squeal of high-pitched feedback as the sector commander adjusted the microphone.

"All right, I have to go," said Pat quietly. "I'll meet you over there for the *mallorcas*. I heard they're better than the ones that the old Cuban guy makes at la Fonda del Ciego."

"*Cabrón*," said Galán. "I'm charging you double next time you come by."

Pat laughed and disappeared into the cluster of Coasties. Galán and Michaela found seats in the back row.

As the sector commander droned on about the drug interdiction record set over the course of the previous year, Galán tried his best to follow along. Within five minutes, however, he was lost. Michaela had been right—these guys did speak another language.

The vice commandant stepped forward next. Tall and bow-legged, he had a collection of medals bordering on the absurd. Even though Galán couldn't understand the admiral's Louisiana accent, he caught himself smiling. He loved the pageantry. The uniforms, flags, and saluting reminded him of when his family visited el Cementerio Santa Ifigenia to see the Cuban honor guard and Jose Martí's tomb.

Gabriela. Galán realized that he hadn't thought about her all morning. He felt a pang of guilt in his stomach. The feeling lingered as the ceremony closed and the band from San Juan's el Conservatorio de Música played "Semper Paratus." Galán tried to force himself back into the present for Pat's sake.

Instead of reuniting for *mallorcas*, Galán and Michaela followed Pat to the pier and across the *Strickland*'s brow. Imitating Pat, Galán rendered a solemn salute to the national ensign as he stepped aboard the cutter. He hung on every word as Pat discussed the forward deck gun, the engine room, the galley, and the bridge. He smiled when an enlisted crewmember addressed his neighbor as "sir."

On the fantail, Galán asked Michaela to take a picture of him and Pat with the colorful backdrop of Old San Juan. He insisted on three different takes and was still examining the photo when they returned to the buffet. Galán hadn't seen such a broad smile on his own face since Key West.

"Galán," said Michaela, chuckling as she handed him a coffee, "you're worse than I was with my prom pictures."

"Prom?" He sipped the coffee—not nearly sweet enough. "I've never heard of one of those."

Before Michaela could explain, Pat arrived with a plate stacked high with ham and cheese *mallorcas*. "So, what do you think, Galán? I know they kind of got into the weeds during the ceremony itself, but overall you had a good time, right? I told you it wouldn't be bad."

"It was beautiful," said Galán, smiling. He picked up a *mallorca*, but was careful not to sprinkle powdered sugar on his suit. "Very, very beautiful. I'm happy you convinced me to come."

"Me too." Pat patted Galán on the shoulder.

"But next time I only come if you are the captain. No more of being number two."

Pat laughed. "That's the plan."

Galán smiled. He didn't mention that the Coast Guard ceremony had marked his first time on a guest list.

✵

As Galán returned home by himself, he thought about Pat and Michaela. Whenever Pat had run his hand down Michaela's back or Michaela had laughed at one of Pat's jokes, Galán couldn't help but remember what he had once had with Esperanza.

Galán was seventeen. He and his father had been living in Key West ever since arriving in the United States by way of Ramón's raft. Their plan to head north to unite with Josefina's relatives in Hialeah had been torpedoed the moment Josefina and Gabriela fell into the black surf. Galán's adolescence had passed quickly but not easily.

But, for the first time in a long time, Galán had something to be excited for.

He waited on the Mallory Square park bench, the armpits of his light green button-down soaked with sweat. He was afraid that the chemistry that existed between him and Esperanza when they were waiting tables at la Bandera Cantina Mexicana would fail to extend to the outside world.

Galán checked his Timex again: 6:20. He couldn't decide if he'd rather she show up or jilt him. He had forgotten most of the conversation starters he'd brainstormed over the previous week, and he'd developed a nice pimple on his nose. No matter what happened, Darío, the cook, would find a way to tease him.

Galán was about to make the sweaty walk back to the housing project at Trumbo Point when Esperanza emerged from a throng of vacationers in a denim skirt and white tank top. When Esperanza caught sight of him, she slowed to a more casual pace and pushed some of her curly hair from her face.

Galán smiled and stood. He tried to surreptitiously smooth his pants and unstick them from his legs. His heart pounded as Esperanza approached.

"Esperanza. *Cómo estás?*"

"*Bien*, Galán." She smiled, her brown eyes twinkling from behind the cat-like eyeliner, and gave him a kiss hello on the cheek. "*Lo siento que estoy tarde, pero* is it okay if we stick to English? You know how my Spanish is. Plus, it will be good for you to practice."

"Okay," he said, forcing a laugh. "I try. But you know my good jokes are in Spanish." He averted his gaze from the hot-pink bra barely visible through the thin white fabric of her tank top. He was used to seeing her in a baggy la Bandera polo shirt.

"You know more than you think, Galán. You just need to be more confident. I can help you with that."

Flushing slightly, Galán wondered if there was a hidden meaning to Esperanza's last comment—he hoped there was—as they crossed the square to Camilo's. Galán had never been to the Cuban restaurant before, or any fancy sit-down restaurant for that matter.

The hostess sat them near the outdoor bandstand, and Galán made sure that Esperanza faced the water and the departing sunset cruises. Looking through the menu, he recognized only half of the dishes supposedly from his island—it must be nice to have such a rich assortment of ingredients to choose from.

"So, is this where you take all of your dates?" asked Esperanza. "A little taste of home?"

"No," said Galán, blushing again. "I don't have time for too many dates. Your uncle is a hard boss. But a good boss!"

She laughed. "Well, what do you recommend? The *ropa vieja*? Why would I want to eat 'old clothes'?"

"No, no. Not old clothes. It's good." He tried not to trip over his English. "It is like a beef, cut up. Not old clothes. Don't worry."

"Well, all right, if you insist. But if they bring me out some dirty laundry . . ."

They both laughed. Her dimpled face, which had more *india* in it than the girls he grew up with, mesmerized him. He couldn't remember why he'd been so nervous.

Once the food arrived, Galán resisted the urge to attack the plantains and pulled pork with his usual gusto. He ate like a gentleman, or at least how he imagined a gentleman would eat from the James Bond movies that he had seen. He set his utensils down on the table between bites and applied his napkin to the corners of his mouth. Esperanza, who cracked jokes about Darío and the rest of the crew from la Bandera, deserved as much.

After dinner, they bought ice cream from a truck painted as a cow and carried it over to the boardwalk. An eccentric Frenchman with a gang of housecats entertained the crowd by running his feline charges through a set of underwhelming acrobatics. What the cats lacked in showmanship, the impresario himself more than made up for. Esperanza laughed so hard that she had tears in her eyes, but Galán didn't understand what was so funny about the strange man asking the crowd if they would like to touch his "pussy."

Esperanza was still laughing when they found an empty bench on a quieter stretch of the boardwalk. The sun had just dipped below the horizon, and cumulus clouds burst skyward forming a blue, pink, and orange backdrop.

"I like this place," said Galán, his forearm lightly touching Esperanza's.

"What place? Key West?"

"Well, yes, Key West. But I really like this . . . How do you call it?"

"Boardwalk?" said Esperanza.

"Yes, this boardwalk."

"It's beautiful. Way different than LA."

"Do you miss it?" Galán glanced at her. "Your home?"

"Yeah, sometimes. I miss my little brother for sure. He's an idiot. He loves monster trucks and wrestling. He thinks he's Rey Mysterio." She laughed, a dab of chocolate ice cream on the corner of her mouth. "But it's okay. I go back every once in a while."

Galán looked back across the channel at Sunset Key. "That's a good thing."

"I'm sorry." She put her hand on his. "I wasn't thinking."

"It's okay." He turned to her and smiled. "That's why I like sitting here and looking at the sun go down. I feel like my mother and my sister are right there. Right over the . . . *horizonte*." He jutted his chin toward the water.

"The horizon. They're lucky."

"Lucky? Why are they lucky?"

"They're lucky to have such a good brother. Such a good son." She squeezed his hand.

Not once during the prior four years had Galán ever felt so good.

Their conversation flowed as naturally as the incoming tide. The boardwalk lights came on, and the sky darkened. As the booze cruises puttered back into their slips, Galán and Esperanza joked about the teetering, sunburned passengers and the country music that played. The boardwalk was empty by the time Esperanza fell asleep on Galán's shoulder.

He didn't want to ever move.

16

San Juan, Puerto Rico

"Galán!"

He stood up and looked over the terrace wall, shading his eyes from the afternoon sun. Even from the roof, he could tell that Yesica had changed since their date at the Isla Verde Chili's two years earlier. Back then, she still had a lot of Ciego de Ávila in her. Now, based on the designer mirrored sunglasses and tight white jeans, not so much.

Damn. I wonder if I've changed that much, too?

He descended the stairs and opened the gate. "Yesica." He gave her an air kiss on the cheek. "It's been too long. Thank you so much for coming by."

"Anything for you." Yesica fluttered her extended eyelashes.

They climbed up to the apartment and stepped out onto the terrace. Galán asked her about her recent move from Trujillo Alto to upscale Ocean Park. He nodded as she complained about the Dominican movers and described her new apartment, down to the progressive lighting and granite countertops. He couldn't focus on her story though, because his mind was five minutes ahead. Apparently she noticed.

"So what is it, Galán? I know you didn't ask me over to discuss real estate." She gave him another coquettish look. "I know what it is. You want to apologize for not calling me back after our date."

Galán forced a laugh. That awkward meal at Chili's was one of his few forays into the world of romance since Key West and

Esperanza, and he had walked away from it like he had all the others: disappointed.

Yesica smiled and raised her hands in front of her. "Galán, I have a boyfriend now. He's not as handsome as you, but still."

"You're right," said Galán. "I should have called you back. I'm sorry. That was wrong of me." He picked up his beer, but it was already empty. "But yes, I do have something I wanted to talk to you about. I understand if you don't want to, but I need to at least ask." He looked away from her toward the mountains. "I need to know about your trip here."

"My trip here? I took the low road, and it was a mess. There are three cruise ships." She gestured toward the looming exhaust stacks. "The place is crawling. I should've known better."

"No, no." Galán turned back to her. "I don't mean that trip. I mean your trip from Cuba. What was it? Five years ago? Six?"

Yesica stopped smiling.

"I know it's something you probably don't want to talk about," Galán continued, "and I'm sorry. But I need to know how you did it. I know about getting from Cuba to Florida, but I've heard those trips have become less successful these days—Coast Guard is picking up everybody. I need to know how to get someone here. To Puerto Rico. So far all I know is that they have to go through the Dominican Republic."

"I see." She looked down at her full beer can. "And who's making the trip, if you don't mind me asking? Actually, it's better I don't know."

"No, it's fine." Galán swallowed. "It's my sister." Saying it out loud made the idea of Gabriela's trip seem dauntingly real.

Yesica raised her eyebrows. "Alone?"

Galán recognized the same disappointed tone that his mother would use on him. He nodded.

"Oh Lord." Yesica shook her head.

"I know. It doesn't sound good. And it's not a done deal either. But I just need to know what options I have, and you're the only person I trust who came directly to Puerto Rico."

Yesica furrowed her brow. "I feel like if I help you, I'll somehow be responsible for whatever happens to your sister."

"No, no, no." Galán put his hand on Yesica's smooth forearm. "It's not like that. The situation for her is bad in Cuba. I don't want to go into all the details, but believe me. You remember how my sister had problems. She needs to be with me. To have a life."

Yesica looked into his eyes, seemingly searching for something—perhaps the truth.

"It would mean so much to me," Galán said, holding her gaze. He ran his fingers up her forearm. "I don't know anybody else who's made this trip. Like I said, you're the only person I can trust."

She smiled slightly and looked away toward the harbor. "I'll see what I can do. I can probably dig up the phone number for the Dominican who arranged everything for us. I never met him, but I've heard he's a bad man. I just hope nothing happens to your sister."

"Trust me," said Galán, squeezing her forearm. "So do I." He let go and turned his gaze toward the high rises in distant Condado.

They sat in silence for some time. Old San Juan sounded deceptively far away from their perch in the sky.

"You're really stressing about this," said Yesica finally. "I think it's sweet how much you care about your sister."

Galán smiled weakly.

"You need a woman, Galán." Now it was her hand on his forearm. "You need a woman to keep away the stress."

"You're probably right," said Galán, keeping his eyes on a thunderstorm drifting over the Condado lagoon. His plan was working.

"I could take away some of that stress." Yesica slid her hand down to Galán's thigh.

Galán was surprised by both the pressure in his crotch and how easily Yesica was responding to his ploy. He swallowed and looked at her. His eyes dropped to the tan line just along the top of her blouse.

"You deserve this, Galán." She stroked him slowly through his jeans.

"I want to," said Galán, more to himself than to Yesica. He hadn't expected her to take the bait so completely and quickly. "I really want to."

"Good." Yesica smiled. She gave him a gentle squeeze. "Meet me in your bedroom. I don't think you've given me a proper tour."

"But I can't." He turned away. Even though Esperanza had been so long ago, being with another woman still didn't feel right.

"You can't? I find that hard to believe. Your dick is telling me you can."

"I have a meeting this afternoon," lied Galán. "With an investor. We're thinking about opening another diner, but this time in Carolina."

Yesica removed her hand. "Fine. Suit yourself. I just hope I don't forget to give you that Dominican's number." She gathered her purse and stood.

Galán shook his head. "You don't mess around, do you?"

"No, I don't." She walked toward the door.

"Fine." He stood up also and took her hand. "If that's how it is going to be."

"Good boy." She smiled.

"But what about your boyfriend?"

"Don't worry about my boyfriend."

He followed her into the bedroom. It was hot and the air was still. Galán opened the storm shutters and turned on the box fan. When he turned back to Yesica, she was in her bra, her slight love handles pushing out above the top of her jeans. She glistened with sweat in a good way.

It's okay, Galán told himself. You're allowed to do this. But then he saw Esperanza's face.

Yesica shimmied out of her pants. She stepped toward him and lifted his shirt over his head. She leaned in and kissed him.

Galán had forgotten how a woman's mouth tasted. He put his hands on her ribs and inhaled the sweet mix of her sweat and perfume. He tried to get Esperanza out of his mind's eye.

"You don't know how long I've wanted this," she whispered into his ear.

He was allowed to do this.

"Take me any way you want," said Yesica, unfastening his belt.

He was past the point of no return. Esperanza vanished from his mind, and all he could think about was the intense pressure, the hunger he had been stifling. He pulled off his boxers and stood naked with a woman for the first time since Key West.

"Take me," said Yesica.

Galán felt the animal inside of him breaking loose. He picked Yesica up and dropped her on the bed.

A moment later, he was inside her. He wanted nothing else.

She moaned and pulled him into her deeper.

There was no point fighting it.

Several minutes later, he lay on top of her as they both caught their breath. He could no longer look her in the eyes.

"Did you?" he finally asked.

"No, Galancito. But it was still good. It was still very good."

He gave her a T-shirt to clean up with from a laundry pile that had fallen off the bed. He walked into the bathroom without looking at her or at his own reflection in the mirror. When he returned, Yesica was a naked stranger sitting up in the bed.

"Well," said Yesica, after an uncomfortable silence. "I guess you should still have time to make it to that meeting."

Galán couldn't tell if she was making fun of him, but he didn't care. He just wanted her gone.

Yesica must have sensed what he was thinking, because she got out of bed and began dressing.

"I can walk you out," said Galán, finally.

"No. It's fine."

Galán nodded. "Just let me know when you have that number."

"I will." Yesica didn't bother giving him a kiss or even smiling good-bye.

Thankful to be alone, Galán stepped into the shower. As the cool water ran down his face and shoulders, he was back in the teal Dodge Caravan on the Overseas Highway, Esperanza beside him. The seatbelt could barely contain her belly. They were headed to Miami to visit his maternal relatives in Hialeah.

"Okay," said Galán, his eyes focused on a Buick moving at a glacial pace in front of them. "I'm going to go over this one more time. Nice and slow. My aunt Rosa is married to?"

"Uncle Esteban," replied Esperanza flatly.

"Good." He smiled. "And my aunt Dolores is married to?"

"Uncle Sebastián." She rolled her eyes.

"Correct." A palm tree–shaped air freshener swung from the rearview mirror. "But everybody calls him Seba. Or so I've been told. Okay. Let's see. My uncle Leonys?"

"Aunt Carla. The white girl." Esperanza sighed. "My God, Galán. I need a break."

"A break? We haven't even gotten to the cousins yet!"

Esperanza turned up the radio. A Latin music channel came in somewhat broken, but Galán could make out Ricky Martin.

"Oh, this is that gay guy," said Galán, tapping the steering wheel with his thumbs to the beat. "What's his name? Ricky something."

"Ricky Martin. And there's nothing wrong with him being gay. We've talked about this."

"I never said there was anything wrong with him being gay. But a fact is a fact."

"People are sensitive about that stuff here." Esperanza reclined her chair and closed her eyes.

"People are too sensitive here."

"Maybe so. But if you want to move up from night manager one day, you need to learn how to talk with people who aren't Darío."

Galán shook his head as he merged into the oncoming traffic lane to pass the Buick. There was a tissue box in the sedan's rear window, and the old man gripping the steering wheel looked as though he were flying a combat mission over the Pacific.

"And you should also slow down," said Esperanza, as they crossed a spit of salt water to Summerland Key. "The speed limit's fifty-five."

Galán muttered something unintelligible.

"What?"

"Nothing. It's okay," said Galán.

"What?"

He sighed. "I just realized that it's because of the hormones and the baby." He looked over at her. "You know, why you're grumpy. I was getting upset, but now I understand." He smiled, tapping his finger to his temple. "I should be a doctor."

"Oh, my God. You're out of your mind. I'm going to take a nap. Maybe if I'm lucky I'll dream of the world's largest family tree."

Galán turned the radio down and hummed along to a Carlos Vives song. The Caravan glided across the smooth pavement, the setting sun flashing between the trees. The Latin radio station eventually devolved into static, so Galán turned the dial to a country station. He couldn't really understand the words, but he liked the laid-back melodies.

With Esperanza snoring next to him, Galán cracked the front windows for a breeze. The Caravan descended the Seven Mile Bridge, and a traffic jam at the western end of Marathon came into view. He looked at the clock on the dash—they'd be lucky to make it to Hialeah before ten.

The stoplight ahead went from green to yellow. Galán coasted through, not wanting to brake hard and wake Esperanza.

And then he saw it—a black Volkswagen Jetta stopped directly ahead of them, taillights out. Galán slammed the brakes while simultaneously checking his mirror to see if he could swerve to the right. A semitruck was there. Galán reached across Esperanza's stomach and gritted his teeth.

The Jetta began to make its left turn, but it was too late. With a sickening crunch of metal, the Caravan's hood crumpled against the trunk of the Jetta. Galán's airbag deployed, and the windshield burst into a spider web of cracks.

Esperanza didn't have an airbag. Instead, her belly and the dashboard made a sandwich out of Galan's hand.

The Caravan skidded to a stop, blocking the intersection. As Galán cleared the airbag away from his face, other drivers honked at him to move. Galán barely heard them, though, and the Caravan was too damaged to go anywhere anyway.

He looked over at Esperanza. She was grimacing. Her sunglasses had flown off, and the upper strap of her seatbelt had slipped behind her head.

"Are you okay?" he finally asked between breaths.

Esperanza looked around, sliding back up into her seat.

"Are you okay? Do you feel okay?

Esperanza reached down and felt her belly with the palm of her hand. She reached further down. When her hand reappeared, her fingertips were wet with a clear-pinkish liquid. She stared at them.

"Oh God," said Galán. "Oh, God. Oh, God." He put his hands on his head. He felt nauseous.

Kenny Chesney sang quietly in the background about drinking beers in Mexico. There was more honking.

"Hey, what the hell?" A man in a black T-shirt and gold necklace knocked on Galán's window. "You fucked up my car!"

Galán's muscles coiled.

"Galán," said Esperanza. "Don't. Please don't."

Galán swung his door open, the upper edge of it striking the man in the forehead. Galán grabbed the man with both hands by the flabby pectorals and slammed him into the mashed up trunk of the Jetta.

"I fucked up your car? I fucked up your car?" Galán screamed. "You fucked up my baby! Where were your goddamned lights? Where were they? How was I supposed to see your shit car?"

A hand ripped Galán away from the Jetta driver. It belonged to a red-faced Monroe County sheriff's deputy.

"You have to calm yourself down right now, sir!" The officer dug his fingers into Galán's shoulder while reaching for his pepper spray with his other hand. "Don't make me tell you twice."

Before Galán was able to say something he regretted, he saw Esperanza struggling to extricate herself from the Caravan. She gave him another pleading look, a pink, glistening line running down the inside of her thigh. The fight went out of him.

"*Mi mujer*," Galán's voice cracked.

"What?"

"Her." Galán said, more forcefully this time. He pointed at Esperanza. "Please help her."

The officer turned around. When he saw Esperanza's belly and her soaked crotch he released his grip on Galán and keyed the radio microphone affixed to his shoulder.

"I need an ambulance at the crash previously reported on US 1 on the west side of Marathon. I have a pregnant female with possible abdominal trauma."

Galán helped untangle Esperanza from the seatbelt. Once she was free, he wrapped his arms around her shoulders and buried his face into her neck. "I'm sorry," he said. "I'm so, so sorry."

She squeezed him back but didn't say anything.

Galán held onto her, unmoving despite the flashing lights and honking. He held onto the baby, too, praying she was okay. He didn't let go until he heard the whine of approaching sirens.

17

San Juan, Puerto Rico

"Galán's coming, right?" Michaela asked from the kitchen, her hands wet from washing the dishes after their dinner of takeout *mofongo*. She was leaving for Philadelphia the next day and had insisted on overseeing the handoff.

"Yeah, yeah, he's coming," said Pat from the hallway. He chased the kitten through the apartment, meowing. As much as he didn't want to admit it, Michaela had been right to rescue the little guy. Pat couldn't get over how the kitten had developed such an identity, such an attitude, in just a few days' time.

Just as the kitten was about to pounce from behind Pat's Coast Guard boots, Michaela scooped him up. "Are you ready to meet your new daddy?" she said, giving him a kiss on the nose.

The kitten mouthed a silent meow. His tail, patchy from the ringworm, curled up between his legs.

A thud on the patio marked Galán's arrival, and the kitten's ears shot back in alarm. Michaela, smiling mischievously, disappeared into the bedroom with the tiny orange creature still in her hands.

"There he is," said Pat, stepping onto the patio to give Galán a handshake-hug.

"You said it was urgent, so here I am." Galán looked around the terrace, his face tight with concern. "Is everything okay?"

Pat laughed. "Yes, everything is fine. There's no emergency, but there is a surprise."

"A surprise?" Galán reached back up to the ledge of the wall for his case of emergency Medallas. "I'm not big into surprises."

"Yeah? Well you might change your tune after this."

Pat motioned toward the door, and Michaela popped onto the terrace. Beaming, she held up the kitten like a baby Simba. He looked frozen with fear the way his limbs protruded stiffly into the air.

"What the hell is that?" said Galán, stepping back.

"That's your new son," said Pat, laughing. "You're the daddy."

Michaela handed the kitten over.

"I'm the daddy?" asked Galán, inspecting the kitten at arm's length. "Are you sure you want me to be the daddy? Maybe you guys should keep him, and I can be the uncle." He started to return the cat to Michaela.

"No, no," said Michaela, putting her hands behind her back. "You're the daddy. I can tell he already loves you."

"He already loves me?" Galán looked back at the little face staring up at him. He scratched the kitten's fuzzy head. "I don't know about that. He looks like he's going to piss himself."

"No way," lied Pat. "I can hear him purring from over here. You're a natural."

Galán didn't say anything, but after a moment he cradled the kitten to his chest and began scratching his fuzzy head. "I guess if you say so."

Detecting a flicker of sadness in his neighbor's eyes, Pat remembered Galán once making a vague reference to a pregnant ex-girlfriend. Maybe this was a bad idea after all.

"If you really want," said Pat, stepping forward, "I can keep him. It's no problem. You can be the uncle and take care of him when I'm on the ship."

Galán continued to scratch the kitten without looking up.

"What do you think?" asked Pat.

Galán smiled. "I think you were right all along. I think he does like me."

Sure enough, the kitten's ears were perked up like normal, and his eyes were closed. Pat actually could hear a faint purring.

Galán looked up, smiling. "Yeah, I'll be the daddy. Pat, you can be the uncle."

☆

Several nights later, Pat and Galán nursed their beers under the glow of Galán's terrace floodlights, the remnants of two strip steaks in front of them. Michaela had returned to the mainland, and the kitten scurried around the terrace, slowly adapting to his new home. The *Strickland* was getting under way the next morning, and Galán had been more adamant than usual that Pat come by for a farewell meal.

"That was good," said Pat, examining the gristle. "But what's going on? You texted me like five times today. You have a surprise for me like I had a surprise for you?"

Galán laughed. "Now you know what I meant when I said I hate surprises. And I think I was right after all." He rolled up the sleeve of his shirt. "Look at what this tiger has done to my arm. I have to drink all these beers just so I can sleep through his attacks."

"You do anything to that cat and Michaela will be on the next flight down here to beat your ass. Plus, he's from the streets. Of course he's going to tear you up."

Galán chuckled and opened another beer.

"But seriously, what's up?" Pat noticed a slight tremor in Galán's hand. "I know something's been bothering you ever since you got back from Cuba. I can see it on your face. I can see it in your shaky hand. Don't ever be a poker player because you'll lose all your money."

Galán snorted.

Pat looked at his watch. "Look, I have to be on that boat at the crack of dawn, and my bed is looking pretty damn nice right now."

Galán nodded.

"So say whatever it is you have to say, or else you're going to have to forever hold your peace. Or at least hold your peace for a few weeks until I get back."

Galán lit a cigarette, the smoke obscuring the crescent moon that hung above el Castillo San Cristóbal. "Okay, okay. You're right. I have been needing to talk to you."

Pat waited.

"It has to do with my sister."

"Yeah, I figured it was your family."

Galán exhaled another cloud of smoke. "I told you how Gabi has been living with my aunt, but my aunt isn't well. So at some point Gabi is going to have to move in with my *pendejo* cousin. And my cousin will only take her if she goes off to this hospital every day."

Pat sensed where the conversation was headed.

"It's not good, brother." Galán drummed his fingers on the table. "It's not a good situation. I need to get her out of there, out of Cuba. I need to get her here, so she can have a life."

Pat didn't say anything. He didn't want to shoot down the idea without giving Galán a chance to explain it.

"She'd have to go to the Dominican Republic first. That's where the *yolas* leave from." Galán sipped his beer. "Well, you already know that."

"Yeah, I do." Cuba to the Dominican Republic to Mona Island. Migrants attempted that journey on an almost daily basis. Pat waited for Galán to elaborate, but he didn't.

"You're sure about this?" asked Pat. "There's nobody else in Cuba? The hospital is that bad?"

Galán nodded. "I went to the hospital. It's no place for my sister. And my cousin, he's trying to do the right thing, but he doesn't love her like I do."

Pat thought for a moment. "But what about visas and stuff? Is there a legal, safe way to do this? Maybe there's some kind of humanitarian angle that you could work with the immigration people?"

Galán shook his head. "I wish. I already talked to this lawyer about that. She said I could spend tons of money and still it might never work out. Because it's Cuba."

Pat exhaled.

"I can't keep waiting for Fidel to die and Raúl to die and for everybody to die," said Galán, gritting his teeth. "Gabi's not getting any younger, you know? At some point, she deserves to live."

"I hear you." Pat saw the faces of migrants that he thought he'd forgotten. "But these are hard trips. And for a woman, they can be very hard trips. You need to think about this."

"I have."

They sat in silence. The kitten jumped up onto Galán's lap and fell asleep.

"You don't have to say anything right now," said Galán, looking down at the kitten, "but I at least need to ask. I'm not asking for me. I'm asking for her."

Pat's pulse quickened—he had thought his only job was to listen.

"You're my brother and I know you have responsibilities, but maybe there is some way you could help me, some way you could make sure your friends don't find her out there." Galán turned toward Pat. "This is my blood we're talking about."

Pat licked his lips. He started to say something but stopped.

Galán waited.

"This is a serious thing you're asking. I swore an oath to my country. And that oath is bigger than me or you." Pat finished his beer and looked at Galán. "And even if I did decide to throw that all away, I'm not sure what there is that I could really do."

Galán stroked the cat's head between the two tufted ears. "I understand. I just needed to ask."

"Look, I'm sorry, brother. I really am. But this is a big deal."

Galán nodded.

"If I get myself involved in this, I could land in jail. And even if I didn't get caught, it would still be wrong."

Galán waited, biting the inside of his cheek.

"Please think about this," said Pat. "I'm serious. These trips are no joke."

"I have thought about it."

They sat in silence. The cat repositioned himself on Galán's lap without opening his eyes.

"All I'll say for now is this," said Pat finally. "If you're really dead set on this plan, you need to do it sooner rather than later."

"Sooner? Why do you say that?"

"What was it? A year or two ago when the president announced all those changes to the relationship with Cuba? They're not our enemy anymore. Wet foot, dry foot? That's going out the window any day now."

"What do you mean?"

"If the Cuban government is no longer our enemy, then there's nothing for the Cuban people to escape. They won't get special treatment as refugees. Instead, the US government is going to start treating Cubans like Mexicans and Hondurans and everybody else. Any Cubans that make it here will have to live in the shadows with the rest of the illegal immigrants."

"Coño," said Galán, his brow furrowed. "Are you serious?"

Pat nodded and crushed his beer can. "But don't get me wrong. I still think your plan is a bad idea."

"I understand," said Galán softly.

Pat stood up and gathered his empty cans. "I should be going. I appreciate the steak. It was top notch as always."

Galán didn't look up at him, but the kitten did.

As Pat climbed over the wall and went into his apartment, he alternated between being upset that Galán would expect him to abuse his position in the Coast Guard and being honored that Galán trusted him enough to ask. But at the end of the day, it didn't matter.

Galán would have to figure out this mess on his own.

18

Sweating, Pat steered the Wrangler off of la Avenida Kennedy and into Maunabo's grid of narrow streets. Danny hadn't said a word since their lunch at el Infierno, a hillside bar with an unobstructed view of the Vieques Sound. Pat wasn't surprised.

They passed single-story, colorful concrete houses with bars over the windows. Stray dogs ducked in and out from behind sun-bleached cars parked halfway onto the sidewalks. But no sign yet of what they were looking for.

Pat had returned from his patrol to the Lesser Antilles two days earlier, just in time to unpack his seabag and pick up Danny from the airport. Danny had never been to Puerto Rico before, so he and Pat toured el Morro, watched the girls at el Escambrón beach, bar-hopped their way down la Calle San Sebastián, and barbecued with Galán. Pat had been relieved to see Danny being his old self—smiling that goofy smile, laughing, telling his dirty jokes.

Danny's lightheartedness, however, had vanished at some point during the previous night. When Pat came back to the apartment with breakfast sandwiches from Café Correa, Danny, instead of saying thanks, just asked for the vodka. Pat watched in silence as Danny, dressed in a too-big navy-blue suit, added two shots to his orange juice.

Squeezing the Wrangler past an Isuzu Rodeo on cinderblocks, Pat recognized the BORICUA SOY decal on the rear window. "I think we've already been down this street," he said, looking over at Danny. "If you have any thoughts on where to go, let me know. Otherwise, I'm going to take a right up here."

Danny studied the crumpled sheet of paper in his hand. "It's called la Iglesia de Dios Pentecostal Monte de Sion." He butchered the pronunciation. "This is Maunabo, right?"

"Yeah, this is Maunabo." Pat peeled his sweaty back from the faux-leather seat.

"Well, it's not exactly New York City," said Danny, looking up. "It can't be that hard to find. Just look for a bell tower somewhere above these houses."

"I'm looking." Pat maneuvered to avoid a pothole only to grind the tires against the opposite curb.

"We came all this goddamned way," said Danny, shaking his head. "It has to be here." He drummed his fingers against his knee out of beat with the Gyptian song that came in from the Saint Thomas radio station. "Fuck it. I'm not leaving until we find it."

Having scoured every street, Pat turned out of town in the opposite direction from which they had come. They passed the old ruins from the Columbia sugar mill and a patch of farmland. Pat was just about to turn around when he found it.

The church looked like it could have been a liquor store or an Advance Auto Parts in a previous life—definitely no steeple.

"I don't see any cemetery here," said Pat, putting the Wrangler in park.

"Neither do I. What the hell?"

"It's fine. We'll find it."

Pat stepped out into the baking sun and opened the front door of the church. A middle-aged woman was overseeing a young man on a ladder rewiring some lights.

"*Permiso*," said Pat in his best Spanglish. "I'm looking for the *cementerio*?"

The man and woman looked at each other.

"What cemetery?"

"The cemetery for members of your church."

The man and woman exchanged another look that fell somewhere between suspicion and curiosity.

"The only cemetery is the municipal one on the northside of town. That's where everybody goes. Catholics, us, even the nonbelievers."

Pat thanked her and joined Danny in the Wrangler.

"We already passed it," said Pat. "I guess it makes sense that a little place like this would only have one."

They looped through the town once more and parked next to the Cementerio Municipal. It consisted of densely packed, aboveground tombs. A few bouquets of dying flowers swayed in the hot breeze, and the midday sun reflected off of the blinding field of marble.

Danny remained in the Wrangler, his jaw clenching and unclenching.

"You good?" asked Pat softly. "You want me to come with you?"

Danny looked down at the old, tattered funeral program. "You can wait," he finally said. "It'll just be a minute." He cleared his throat and wiped his nose.

"All right. Take your time. I'll be right here."

Danny nodded, tapped the dashboard with his palm, and got out. He climbed over the rusty fence and went up and down the rows slowly. Pat felt bad watching him.

Finally, Danny stopped. He removed his suit jacket and hung it from the wing of an angel. He clasped his hands in front of him, the armpits of his white shirt soaked. He appeared to be talking to himself, or praying—Pat couldn't tell.

An older woman in a kerchief approached the Wrangler from down the street with two bags of groceries. She also stared at the *yanqui* in the cemetery, her brow furrowed.

After twenty minutes, Pat got out of the Wrangler. At the very least, he needed to stretch his legs. He walked into the cemetery with his hands in his pockets and stood next to Danny. Pat hoped his brother wasn't crying.

"You would've liked him," said Danny. "He was a crazy bastard. He had a line for everything. And always in that ridiculous accent of his."

"He sounded like a good guy from everything you told me about him."

Danny nodded. "I remember during the first few months of the deployment, every day was the same. Patrol, eat, sleep. Patrol, eat, sleep. And there was nothing to eat but MREs. And he kept talking about how all he wanted was some goddamned Po-pay-yays." Danny smiled. "He was dying for some goddamned Po-pay-yays."

Pat nodded, still looking at the dirt.

"Nobody knew what the hell he was talking about," continued Danny. "And as his squad leader, I would always give him shit about it. And he'd say, 'Sergeant Mac, when we get out of here I'm going to take you to Po-pay-yays, and it will change your life.' I would just laugh and say, 'Yunior'; his name was Junior, but it was pronounced 'Yunior.' Anyway, I'd say, 'Yunior, you just let me know where and when, and I'll be there.'" Danny wiped his face with his sleeve.

Pat put his arm around him. Danny's shoulders didn't feel as broad as they once did.

"You know what Po-pay-yays was?" asked Danny. "Popeyes. It was goddamned Popeyes. This clown was dreaming about Popeyes every night. About biscuits and thighs and wings." He laughed, shaking his head, a droplet of snot falling from his nose. "Popeyes."

Pat laughed, too.

"You know?" said Danny, "That's really what it's all about."

"What?" asked Pat. "Popeyes?"

"No, you dumbass," said Danny, smiling, his eyes pink. "It's about the people you meet. It's the people. The good ones. That's what I loved about the army. All the bullshit? All the bureaucracy? All the ridiculous orders and deployments? To hell with all that. It's the people. Just being able to know one guy like Yunior, just being able to call him your friend and know that he would always have your back no matter what crazy shit happened, made the whole thing worth it."

Danny grabbed his jacket and pulled a Popeyes bag from the inner pocket. He set the tinfoil package against the grave for PFC Vicente Rayan "Junior" Soto Camacho, beloved son and brother for all of twenty years.

"I miss you, Yunior," said Danny, biting his lower lip and tapping the marble with his palm. "I miss you every goddamned day." He turned and headed back to the Wrangler.

Pat followed at a distance.

✳

Pat woke up the next morning and saw sunlight poking through the slats in the storm shutters. Ensconced under the blanket, he closed his eyes and began to drift off. After all, his alarm still hadn't sounded.

Shit. He jumped out of bed. Danny was supposed to have woken him up at six for a ride to the airport.

He must have decided to take a cab in the early morning darkness instead.

Pat walked into the kitchen for a drink of water, thankful for the extra hour of sleep. But as he filled the glass, he noticed the living room door was still closed. Pat opened it slowly.

Danny was still asleep. The room smelled like a distillery.

"Hey. You got to get up if you're going to catch that plane. Traffic is horrible around here in the morning."

Danny groaned and rolled over. His pillow was wet with drool and sweat.

"Danny," said Pat, opening the storm shutters. "Let's go."

Danny grunted again, blocking the sunlight with his forearm. An orange pill bottle lay on its side next to the Jim Beam Red Stag. Pat picked it up and read the label. Oxycodone.

Pat sat down on the cold tile floor, his back against the rough plaster wall. Danny's eyelids fluttered from some kind of dream. Pat reached up and put his hand on Danny's sunburned forearm. Danny flinched.

Pat remembered how when they were kids and shared the same room, he would get in Danny's bed during thunderstorms. Danny had told him to get out the first time, but when he had seen how scared Pat was, he shimmied over and made room under the comforter.

"It'll be okay," Danny would say, ruffling Pat's bowl cut. "It always is. Plus, lightning strikes the highest point, and I'm taller than you."

Sometimes Pat would wake up and realize he had spent the whole night next to his brother.

"Is that you?" said Danny from the futon, his voice groggy. He reached for the pill bottle.

"Yeah, it's me. How you feeling?"

Danny took several slow breaths. "I'm sorry."

"It's all right," said Pat, his hand still on Danny's arm. "There are plenty of flights. We'll get you on the next one."

"No, not the flight. I mean I'm sorry for being this way. For being a pussy."

"Don't say that," said Pat. "That's not who you are."

Danny started to say something else, but he nodded off before he could get the words out.

"You just have to get strong again," said Pat, even though he knew Danny was asleep. "But it's okay. I can handle the lightning for a while."

Part Two

19

Ciego de Ávila, Cuba

Gabriela stirred the beans while Tía Teresa boiled the needle. The television played quietly in the living room. The Brazilian telenovela would be on any minute, and the word around the neighborhood was that the swarthy protagonist was going to have his heart broken by the blonde widow. "How handsome," Tía Teresa would say every time they showed the man without his shirt on. Gabriela felt something, too, but she didn't quite know what it was.

Gabriela carried their dinner into the living room. She set the plates onto a flimsy plastic table and waited as Teresa plunged the needle into her fleshy abdomen. Gabriela didn't understand the purpose of her aunt's insulin, but the ritual, like her own cartoons and daily lap around the park, had become routine.

"Gabi," said Teresa, as the opening credits of *Além do Tempo* began. "Do me a favor and grab us some napkins. It's bad enough we're eating in front of the television. Let's not become complete animals."

Gabriela rose from the couch. As she stepped around her aunt, her hip knocked the plates to the floor in a cascade of rice, beans, and chicken.

"Oh, Gabi, Gabi, Gabi," said Teresa, staring at the mess.

Gabriela stood frozen, her hand over her mouth.

"You need to be more careful. You're always moving too fast." Teresa looked up at Gabriela, whose face was crimson. "But it's okay. We'll clean this up and then have those bananas that are on top of the refrigerator. They should be ripe."

Gabriela scooped up the spilled dinner, careful not to distract Teresa from the dialogue on the show. In a twist, the chiseled young man broke the blonde woman's heart by revealing that he had been in love with her sister all along. Teresa didn't laugh as heartily at this development as Gabriela would have expected.

"Are you okay, Tía?" asked Gabriela when she noticed that Teresa's hands were shaking.

"I'm fine," said Teresa. "Look, that's good enough with the floor. Just bring out those bananas."

Gabriela went into the kitchen and came back out.

"We don't have any bananas, Tía. I think Yunel took them, remember?"

"Yes, yes," said Teresa, her face hard and her eyes staring into the distance. "Then bring those cookies I bought today."

Gabriela returned to the kitchen, even though she knew there were no cookies. She had eaten the whole pack that afternoon and had hoped her aunt wouldn't notice. She didn't know what to tell Teresa because she was afraid of getting in trouble.

"For the love of God, Gabi," said Teresa from the living room, "you need to bring me something to eat."

Gabi went through the cupboard and found a green plantain. She brought it to Teresa.

"No, that won't do," said Teresa, slurring her words. She was pale, and droplets of sweat poked out from her face. "Get me something, Gabi. Look above the stove."

Gabriela returned to the kitchen once again, but only found some hard cinnamon candies. She didn't take them to her aunt because Teresa always said that candy took away one's appetite, and they still hadn't had a proper dinner.

When Gabriela came back out to ask if she should cook another round of rice and beans, she found Teresa asleep on the couch. Gabi was surprised that her aunt would take a nap in the middle of the show, but she didn't want to disturb the old lady, especially after having already been yelled at.

Gabriela pulled a blanket up to her aunt's chin, sat down, and watched the last ten minutes of the telenovela. When it ended with the blonde widow walking in on her lover and her sister, Gabriela turned off the television and curled up next to Teresa. She kept her mind off of the rumbling in her belly by focusing on the chirping insects outside.

★

The mahogany clock on the wall, one of the prized heirlooms that had survived the Revolution, struck ten. Gabriela woke up, confused as to why she was on the couch. Slowly, the dinner debacle replayed itself in her mind.

Gabriela shook Teresa gently to see if she wanted to move to her bed, but her aunt didn't stir. Gabriela shook her harder. Still nothing. Beginning to panic, Gabriela backed away slowly and tried to think.

Yunel. She needed to get Yunel.

Gabriela put on her Velcro sneakers and ran the two blocks to Yunel's house. She climbed the steps and opened the door without knocking. Yunel's father-in-law was asleep on his cot, his bedroom door open. A creaking noise came from Yunel's room.

"Yunel," said Gabriela, knocking on the thin door. "It's Gabi."

No response. She could hear heavy breathing above the creaking, which had gotten faster. She opened the door.

Yunel was on top of Lola, and they were both covered in sweat. Lola screamed, and Yunel cursed, spittle flying from his mouth.

"Get out, Gabi!"

Gabriela ran to the front door and waited for her cousin. She didn't know what she had seen, but she knew she wasn't supposed to have seen it. As much as she didn't like Lola, Gabriela hoped that Yunel wasn't hurting her.

Yunel finally emerged in a pair of capris, his pot belly glistening.

"What?" he said. "What do you want? Why are you here at this hour?"

"You need to come see your mom." She stared at the floor. She hated being yelled at.

"Why?"

"I don't know," said Gabriela, her fists balled. She could feel Lola's eyes boring into her from the bedroom door.

"What do you mean, you don't know?" said Yunel, rinsing his face in the kitchen sink. "You come running over here, and you don't know?"

Even though Yunel spoke at full volume, Lola's father continued to sleep less than ten feet away. His oxygen tank clicked and hissed.

"I think she's sick," said Gabi finally.

Yunel shook his head and stepped into his sandals. He muttered something under his breath as he walked out the front door.

Gabriela followed, thankful to be outside in the darkness and away from Lola's glare.

★

The medical technician ripped off a sheet of paper, handed it to Yunel, and walked out Teresa's front door to the van that doubled as an ambulance. He turned off the portable siren and drove away down the dark street.

Teresa sat awake on the couch. She looked several years older, her hair a tangled mess. She drank from a plastic cup of mango juice that Yunel held for her.

Gabriela had the feeling that the whole fiasco was her fault, but she didn't understand why. It's not like she had tried to knock over the table. But then again, she had eaten all of the cookies.

"I'm sorry," she finally said, looking down at her lap.

"It's okay," said Yunel, tipping the cup into his mother's mouth. "It wasn't your fault. But when she takes her medicine, you have to make sure she eats. You have to promise me that."

"Okay, I promise." There were still rice and beans ground between the floor tiles. She hadn't even cleaned up right.

"You know, Gabriela," said Yunel. "Maybe it's time you come live with me."

"Live with you?" Her pulse quickened and her palms started to sweat.

"Yeah, with me and Lola. I just don't think this is working, you and my mom."

"Why isn't it working?"

"Because you can't take care of her, and she can't take care of you."

Gabriela didn't say anything, but she could feel tears building. Since Josefina died, getting used to life with just Teresa had been one of the hardest transitions of Gabriela's life, and she was just finally getting settled. And Yunel was more of a stranger than family. And Lola? She definitely wasn't family.

"Look," said Yunel, taking a sip of the mango juice himself. "I know you don't want to live with me, Gabi, but I talked about it with Galán."

"You talked about it with Galán? What did he say?" There was no way Galán would let Yunel kick her out of Teresa's house.

"He said it made sense. Especially if you could go to the day hospital."

"The day hospital?" Gabriela felt the room start spinning around her. Her doctor had mentioned that place occasionally, and Josefina would always shake her head with an emphatic no. If Gabriela's mom wasn't okay with a day hospital, why would Galán be? "I don't believe you, Yunel. I don't believe that Galán would say that."

"Well, that's what he said."

"Did he say anything else?" There was no way.

"He did say something about you going to Puerto Rico to live with him, but we both know that wouldn't work."

"He said I could live with him?" She had never thought that being together was an actual option. They had always just lived apart on two different sides of the ocean. Being with Galán was just something she dreamt about.

"You know what, forget it. I shouldn't have said anything."

"I could live with Galán? He really said that?"

Yunel put the cup on the table and ran his hands through his hair. "Yes, he did say that. But only if you promise to be really, really tough."

"Okay, but why?"

"Because you would have to go on a boat."

"I've never been on a boat." She had always wanted to see whales and dolphins in person. But no sharks. Definitely no sharks.

"Not like a boat you see on television. Not a fun boat. More like a serious boat."

"Oh." She thought for a moment. "But Galán would be there on the other side?"

"Yes. God willing."

"So when do I get to leave? I can pack my bag now!" She stood up and searched the room for the items she would bring. Her illustrated zoo encyclopedia, her pillow with the arms, her pink headband.

"No, no. Not now," said Yunel, shaking his head. "Look, I'll talk to Galán and tell him you want to go. I'm going to warn you, though, that he may have changed his mind. Or he may not be able to find a boat for you. So please, please, please don't get your hopes up."

"No, I won't," said Gabriela, beaming. She was thinking about how they could chase lizards again, assuming Puerto Rico had lizards.

Yunel bent forward, his head in his hands. "God, I shouldn't have said anything."

"No, it's so good that you did!"

Gabriela hugged Yunel and Teresa, who was still dazed. Neither of them hugged her back. Gabriela couldn't remember the last time she had been so happy.

20

San Juan, Puerto Rico

"You really have been at sea, haven't you?" said Galán, laughing.

Pat smiled sheepishly, but stole another glance at the girl on the other side of the alley bar. Even though she seemed lost in the music, she smiled back at him. Pat turned away from her toned midriff, his face flushing.

Because it was Pat's birthday, Galán had reluctantly agreed to hit the town. Ever since the terrace discussion about Gabriela, Galán had been more preoccupied and serious than usual. But a birthday was a special occasion according to Galán, and special occasions demanded proper celebrations. So here they were, working through a six-pack of Medalla and eating *pastelillos* as the sun set over the Atlantic and couples of all ages danced salsa.

"Betances! *Qué es lo que hay*?" A portly man wearing a Gucci fanny pack appeared from the direction of la Calle Norzagaray. He held a bottle of Buchanan's whiskey.

"Quique!" said Galán, standing. He shook the man's hand and hugged the woman with copper-dyed hair at his side.

Quique, laughing, said something in Spanish that Pat didn't understand.

"Well here I am," said Galán in English. He put his arm around Pat. "It's my friend's birthday today."

"*Felicidades*!" the couple said in unison. Quique removed the cap from the Buchanan's and took a swig. "A birthday shot!" He handed the bottle to Pat.

"Why not?" said Pat, laughing. He took a long pull. His eyes watered as he handed the bottle to Galán.

"No, no. I'm too old for that." Galán shook his head. "That's a young man's game. And everybody knows a young man can do two!"

Pat laughed and took another, shorter pull. He handed the bottle back to a laughing Quique. The couple disappeared into the gyrating crowd.

As Pat finished his beer to wash away any remaining traces of the Scotch, his eyes returned to the girl. He had the sense she was dancing just for him.

"Hey," said Galán. "I still see you looking."

Pat laughed and pulled the last *pastelillo* from the greasy brown bag. As he searched for the little cup of mayoketchup, his elbow sent a fresh, unopened beer rolling down the cobblestones. He collected the can and was wiping the dirt from it with his polo shirt when he noticed a shadow in front of him.

It was the girl.

She wore a yellow button-down shirt tied off above the belly button and tight, low-riding jeans. Pat couldn't tell if she was nineteen or thirty.

"My friends and I are going to another bar down the street," she said, smiling. "Maybe you want to come?"

Pat swallowed.

"It's not a difficult question." She smiled a little more, this time with her eyes.

Pat looked at Galán and then back at the girl. "We have nothing better to do, I guess."

"*Qué bueno.*"

Her name was Maribel, and her floral scent made Pat feel weak in the knees. He didn't even bother trying to remember her friends' names.

Pat and Galán followed the girls west down la Calle San Sebastián. Galán shook his head and gave Pat a look—something in between disapproval and amazement.

They entered a karaoke bar that Pat had never noticed before. The bartender, a young guy with a shaved head, nearly jumped over the counter to hug Maribel. Her two friends didn't rate nearly as enthusiastic a greeting.

"This is my friend Patrick," said Maribel to the giddy bartender. "And Galán."

The bartender replied to her in Spanish, pursing his lips momentarily toward Pat.

Maribel nodded, laughing. "He says he doesn't know if you can handle *pitorro*. Real *pitorro*."

"I guess there's only one way to find out." Pat stared at the bartender for a moment longer than was polite. Who was this guy to question him?

The bartender reached down and produced a clear, unlabeled bottle full of a dingy liquid and fruit slices. Maribel explained how Puerto Ricans had been making the homemade moonshine for centuries as she filled six plastic cups. "It's strong," she said, handing the first one to Pat, "like you."

They raised their glasses and each took a shot. And then another. The *pitorro* burned Pat's throat, but he was too distracted to care.

"So, what do you two think?" asked Maribel. "Do you like this bar?"

Pat could tell she was just including Galán to be polite, and it made him feel bad. But not too bad.

"I'm all about karaoke bars," he said. "Because people only sing karaoke when they're hammered. So you know it's always going to be a good time. Especially when it's your birthday."

"It's your birthday?" asked the shortest girl.

Pat nodded.

The girls giggled and exchanged a look that Pat couldn't interpret. The *pitorro* bottle reappeared, and they all did another shot. Well, except for Galán, who just watched. He reminded Pat of the Cistercian monks who ran his high school when they would chaperone the mixers with Saint Cecilia's. Pat had pitied the monks then, and he pitied Galán now.

The *pitorro* kicked in, and Pat's face became numb and his tongue loose. Maribel no longer intimidated him. Instead, Pat wanted to tell her his life's story without the chapters about Michaela. Before he had the chance, though, the three girls went up to sing.

Maribel, doing her best Natti Natasha impression, kept her eyes on Pat from start to finish.

After the song ended, they finished their beers and went back into the street. Pat didn't know where they were going, but Maribel did.

Galán grabbed him by the shoulder. "I think we should go home."

"Go home? It's early."

"I'm telling you this is a bad idea."

"It's fine," said Pat, putting his arm around Galán. "We're just having a good time. Hey, it's my birthday, right?"

Galán just shook his head. The girls were half a block ahead.

Pat let go of him. "You're worrying too much."

"Fine," said Galán, stopping. "I get it—you're a grown man. But I'm done here." He started to turn back toward his apartment. "Just remember Michaela."

Michaela. Pat felt a pang of guilt as he watched Galán weave between the young revelers.

But why should he feel bad? He wasn't doing anything wrong.

Pat caught up with the girls in a dark bar with *reggaetón* and smoke machines. A psychedelic light display spun across the walls and ceiling, making Pat even dizzier.

Now Maribel was holding his hand. Pat had no idea how long that had been happening.

A shot of something clear appeared. Pat didn't know what it was, but he drank it anyway. A vague sense of unease came over him as the night proceeded faster and faster—he felt like he was on a runaway train.

Pat found himself on the dance floor with Maribel, his face the only white one in the crowd. He could feel her chest against his and her hands behind his neck. His hands were on her waist, and then they dropped lower.

Pat was back at the bar. This time it was a beer. He looked down and saw that his shirt was soaked in sweat.

He was on the dance floor again. Now Maribel, if it was Maribel, had her back to him and was grinding against his crotch. He moved with the music and let his hands slide up under her shirt, his fingers running against the fabric of her bra.

Back at the bar. Tequila. Pat tried to say something, but the words wouldn't come out.

A dark room. Pat sat on a wooden bench, his back against a plaster wall. He felt something wet on his face, and realized it was a girl's mouth. He liked it. He also liked the way her hand was undoing his belt.

★

Pat opened his eyes. Sunlight streamed in through the open window of his living room. He was on the futon and not in his bed. Strange. He rolled over to look for his phone, and the room began to spin. He closed his eyes and waited for the vertigo to pass.

When he finally opened his eyes again, he saw that he had missed six text messages from Michaela. He didn't have the energy to read them. All he could focus on was the invisible vice crushing his head and the desert in his mouth. He lay still until he could no longer stand his thirst and his own foul breath.

Pat shuffled into the kitchen, holding onto the wall for support. He filled a glass with water and fought off the urge to vomit. He felt hot and realized that he was still in his jeans and stained shirt.

Slowly, the night before replayed itself in his mind, or at least the snapshots that he remembered. Drinking beers at the alley bar with Galán. Doing a shot with the couple from la Fonda. The karaoke bar. Maribel.

Maribel.

Sweat beaded on his face and dribbled down from his armpits. His heart accelerated. Pat did a sweep of the apartment but thankfully didn't find her.

But then he remembered Maribel, or whoever it was, kissing him in that dark room at that last cave-like bar. He remembered her messing with his belt. He remembered her unwrapping a blue condom wrapper.

Everything after that was black.

★

Galán had spent all morning at la Fonda del Ciego trying to wake up. When his phone finally buzzed in the pocket of his white guayabera, he knew it was Pat. Galán, tempted to let his neighbor stew in his own uncertainty and guilt, finally responded to Pat's third text message.

"Come to la Fonda."

Within minutes, Pat burst through the front door, his face pale and clammy. Galán sat him at a booth away from the other diners and signaled for Sefora to bring over two *cafés con leche*.

Pat stirred in a packet of sugar, erasing the heart that had been drawn into the foam with espresso.

"Big night," said Galán finally.

Pat couldn't tell if it was a statement or a question. "Do you know what happened?"

"You messed up. As soon as that girl arrived, you were done with me. But that doesn't matter. What matters is you also forgot about Michaela."

Pat swallowed. He couldn't look Galán in the eye, so he watched the WAPA morning news instead. There had been a shooting in Caguas.

"So, anyway," continued Galán, "I was mad. Very mad. But as I was walking home, I realized I shouldn't have left you no matter how much of an asshole you were being. I turned back and saw you go into that *reggaetón* bar. I walked in but couldn't find you in the crowd. Well, I know the bartender there, Wilson. He's a good guy . . ."

Pat couldn't care less about Wilson.

"So I told Wilson that my friend, a *yanqui*, had just come in with some girls. Since you were the only white guy that has been there probably ever, I figured he would be able to spot you."

"So, what happened?" Pat finally shifted his gaze back to Galán.

"So, I told him you were drunk and that that girl was going to be a problem."

"And?"

"So Wilson called me an hour later. I had barely been asleep. And he says he thought you were with some girl in his storeroom, and that I should come get you."

"Did you?"

"Of course I did." Galán smiled. "What kind of question is that?"

"What were we doing?"

Galán raised his eyebrows and looked down at his coffee. "I think you know what you were doing."

"I honestly don't."

Galán looked Pat in the eyes. "You were inside her."

Pat felt his stomach turn.

"Look," said Galán, "If it makes you feel any better, after all the *pitorro* you drank, I don't think you were able to do a whole lot of damage."

Pat nodded. He hoped to God he had worn that condom that had magically materialized.

"Look, what is that expression you people use?" asked Galán. "The water has passed under the bridge? What happened, happened. All you can control is the future."

Pat nodded, his mind racing.

"But just don't try that shit again, okay?"

"I won't," mumbled Pat.

"Good, because I don't like getting caught up in that kind of stuff. I'm too old for it. And it hurts me to see you looking the way you do right now. Not to mention that it's wrong by Michaela, and she's my friend, too."

"I know. And I'm sorry."

Pat stood and walked out of la Fonda without paying for his coffee or saying good-bye.

★

Later that evening, Pat sat on his roof and watched the mountains across the harbor grow darker. Normally he would have had a beer, but now the Medallas in the fridge seemed to be taunting him: drink me and see what happens.

He looked down at the contact list on his phone. Michaela's face looked up at him, her lips pursed in an exaggerated kiss. He remembered her texting him that picture during his first liberty of Officer Candidate School. She had waited for him for all those months. She was still waiting for him.

His finger hovered over the screen. She had the right to know. She had the right to decide who she loved. Plus, how would he be able to hold her, kiss her, make her laugh, knowing that he had gone behind her back? He had friends that could compartmentalize these encounters, but not him. He had to tell her.

Pat pressed CALL. Michaela answered on the second ring.

"Hello?" The cheerfulness in her voice told him that she had forgiven him for being incommunicado the night before.

"It's me. What are you up to?"

"I'm just about to get on the train to go in for a night shift. Why?"

Pat tried to steady his breathing. "Do you have a minute?"

"I guess. Why? What is it? You never call me like this."

He didn't know what to say.

"Pat, you know you can't propose to me over the phone." She laughed.

Just get it over with. He took a deep breath. "I think I might have had sex with a girl last night. It was really dumb. I'm really sorry . . ." He sputtered on as if he were back in the confessional for his first Sacrament of Penance. He was afraid to give her the chance to respond, afraid to hear her cry.

But when he finally stopped, there was nothing.

"Hello? Hello? Michaela?"

She had hung up.

Even though the night had gone black, Pat didn't move. At some point he heard Galán's terrace door open and the faint chords of a Marc Anthony song ring out from the portable speaker. But the secret was a secret no more, and a kind of relief came over his exhausted conscience.

Just as Pat was about to go inside to force himself to eat, his phone rang.

"How could you do that?" Michaela's voice was cold yet surprisingly steady. "How could you do that to me?"

"I was drunk. I'm sorry. I'm so sorry. It's no excuse—"

"I can't believe this. I always thought you were too good for this, and now you're just like everybody else. There's nothing special about you."

"I'm sorry."

"And to think I was just about to quit this job, throw away everything I've worked for, to come live with you down on your fantasy island."

"I know." Pat didn't know what else to say.

"I was going to go work in some strange hospital in a language I don't even understand? I knew that was a bad idea the minute I mentioned it to you. But now, to top it all off, you would just be chasing skanks while I'm in the ER."

Pat didn't take the bait, but rather waited for her to hopefully calm down.

Michaela sighed. "You remember how I told you about my parents and their divorce?"

"Yes." Pat and Michaela had only spoken about it a few times, and her cryptic answers had kept him from pressing for details.

"Well, my dad was a cheater. And my mom caught him once early on, and he did your whole sob story routine. She bought it. And then it happened again. And again. And always the same routine."

Pat didn't say anything.

"And when she finally had enough, he hired some bigshot law-yers to screw her and me and my sisters out of everything."

"I'm sorry," said Pat. "I didn't know all that."

"So, yes, I get it that what you did was dumb. And that you were drunk. And that you feel bad. But I'm sorry, Pat. I love you, but I don't trust you. And life is too short to spend with someone you don't trust."

Say something, he thought. Anything. Don't let her go like this.

"I love you," he finally stammered. "I love you so much. Please don't do this."

No response.

She had hung up.

21

Santurce, Puerto Rico

Galán hustled down the sun-drenched sidewalk of el Barrio Obrero. As in so much of metropolitan San Juan, concrete stretched in every direction. The heat shimmered off of it in waves.

He finally found Bar Punta Cana squeezed between a laundromat and a unisex Venezuelan barbershop. A nylon Dominican flag and a poster of a curvy woman's silhouette hung next to the door. A black trash bag was duct taped over a broken window.

Galán stepped inside. Despite the neon Presidente and Medalla signs glowing on the far wall, Galán had to blink several times before his eyes adjusted to the darkness. Romeo Santos's "Hilito" played over the speaker system. There were no customers.

"Can I help you?"

Galán squinted in the direction of the bar. "I'm looking for Adonis."

"Oh yeah?" The voice belonged to a young man in camouflage pants and a baggy Ecko Unltd T-shirt who had emerged from behind the bar. As the bartender approached, Galán noticed a scar running from his chin to his lip. "And who are you?"

"G—Gregorio," said Galán.

"What?"

"Gregorio. Gregorio Betances." Why he used his real last name he didn't know, but he wasn't sure if using a fake first name was a good idea either. He hadn't thought about it until now.

"And what does Gregorio Betances want from Adonis?"

"To discuss some things out west." It sounded stupid, but it was what Yesica had told him to say.

The bartender grunted, and slouched his way across the buffed concrete floor. He checked Galán's waistband, legs, crotch, and ankles. He even reached up and under Galán's shirt, running his palms over his clammy chest.

"Efraín," said the bartender, apparently satisfied. "Keep an eye on this guy while I talk to the chief."

Another young man emerged from the direction of the empty dance floor. He wore skinny jeans, a bejeweled T-shirt, and a flat-brim Chicago Bulls hat. He leaned against a cigarette machine, folded his arms, and watched Galán. The bartender disappeared behind a clear, plastic curtain.

Galán's heart pounded, and he was tempted to walk out the door. These were the kind of guys that he had always avoided—guys who carried guns, guys who understood how to use violence to their advantage. Instead of running, though, he pictured Gabriela arriving at the day hospital, a coloring book page and a soiled cot waiting for her.

The bartender reappeared. "He will see you now."

Galán dipped through the curtain and into a narrow cinderblock space. He squeezed between a freezer and a tower of Presidente cases, his shoulder knocking a framed icon of la Señora de la Altagracia askew. At the end of the passageway was a door from under which crept a line of fluorescent light.

Galán knocked.

No answer.

He knocked again, waited a moment, and entered.

A middle-aged man with gray, close-cropped hair sat behind a folding table. He stared at Galán through rimless reading glasses and wore a sleeveless T-shirt, his muscles surprisingly taut. A gold necklace with Jesus's bearded face hung from his neck, and a Figaro-link gold bracelet dangled from his wrist.

"Adonis?" said Galán tentatively.

"Yes." Adonis dragged the word out in a way that suggested Galán was wasting his time.

"Adonis, I'd like to discuss some things out west."

"Yes." Adonis neither moved nor blinked.

Galán didn't know how to begin. He was afraid he might violate some unwritten rule if he was too direct. He thought for a moment. "I need to get somebody here."

Adonis nodded, and his lips curled into a sneer.

"I need to get somebody here. A Cuban. I was told you could help me."

Adonis emitted a half-laugh, half-snort. "I'm not in the business of helping. I'm in the business of transportation."

Galán waited for Adonis to say something more, but the man only stared. "Understood," Galán finally replied.

"How old is the traveler?"

"About thirty."

"Male or female?"

"Female."

Adonis appeared to be intrigued by that piece of information. "And will she be needing me to secure a Dominican visa?"

"Yes." Yesica had told Galán about Adonis's contact inside the Dominican Republic's Tourism Ministry. With Adonis's help, his clients only had to present themselves at the Dominican embassy in Havana to have the highly sought-after visa glued into their Cuban passports. At that point, they could "legally" fly to Santo Domingo and begin their journey in earnest.

"You know this service of mine affects the price, right?" said Adonis. "My competitors don't offer this." He tilted his head as if the other human smugglers were sitting next to him at the tiny table.

"Yes. I understand that this is a special service that only you offer."

"And the voyage from the Dominican Republic? Will this woman be traveling coach or first class?"

"Excuse me?" asked Galán.

"I offer two different . . . packages, you could say." The angle of Adonis's lips changed, and his sneer became a smirk. "At two different prices."

"And the difference?" Yesica hadn't said anything about two different rates.

"Look, something you need to understand is that I'm not in the boat. I'm just a facilitator. So, before I tell you about the two packages, keep that . . . fine print . . . in mind."

"Okay," said Galán, even though he didn't understand.

"First class means I can almost, *almost*, mind you," said Adonis, holding up a long finger, "almost guarantee that your person will arrive in one piece. The journey is usually quick and carried out by one of our better captains on one of our better boats. Your woman will also travel in a smaller group, which is a considerable perk. For an additional fee, I can guarantee that your woman passenger will not be . . . harmed . . . along the way."

"Okay." Galán's mouth felt dry, and his knee shook. He hoped Adonis couldn't see it. "And coach?"

"Coach is the more popular fare. Your traveler will most likely arrive, but then again these are not our most seasoned captains, and these are not our finest vessels. And with regards to protection? Well, sometimes things happen . . ." He smiled broadly, revealing two gold teeth.

Yesica had said that the man had a vile reputation.

Galán broke eye contact and shifted his gaze to an out of date Presidente calendar—a woman in a string bikini straddled a supersized beer bottle. "And the prices?"

"Three thousand."

Galán felt something cold pour into his stomach. "Three thousand?"

"Supply and demand." Adonis maintained his marble-like posture.

"And coach?"

"That was coach."

Galán swallowed. Sweat ran down his chest where the bartender's cold palms had just been.

"For first class," said Adonis, "it is four thousand."

"Oh, four thousand Dominican pesos," With the exchange rate, the cost now made sense.

Adonis chuckled. "Dominican pesos?"

"Yeah."

Adonis's face was suddenly serious again. "Where are you right now?"

Galán didn't understand.

"Where are you right now?" This time louder.

Galán looked around. A string of ants carried grains of rice from a Chinese food takeout container. "Bar Punta Cana?"

Adonis shook his head.

"Puerto Rico?"

"The United fucking States," said Adonis, pounding the table with his fist as he enunciated each syllable. A cigarette butt fell from an ashtray to the floor. "That's the whole reason you're doing this, right? To get this woman to the United States?" Adonis leaned forward. "Therefore, it would make sense that if I do business in the United States, I get paid in green dollars. Yes or no?"

Galán felt like he was back in Ciego de Ávila, the Fortuño twins throwing his baseball back and forth over his head. He wanted to put his hands around Adonis's leathery neck and squeeze until the man's gold teeth popped out. Instead, Galán just nodded and waited for the rage to dissipate from Adonis's eyes.

Galán cleared his throat. "Well, this has been very helpful. Let me think about your offer."

"Fine. But just remember that inflation is a part of every economy."

"I will." Galán bowed his head slightly and immediately hated himself for making even this subtle sign of respect. As he showed himself out of the makeshift office and bar, he was overcome by the desire to take a shower.

22

Naval Station Guantánamo Bay, Cuba

Pat stretched on the pier in the predawn darkness. The *Strickland* was getting under way at nine, so he wanted to squeeze in one more jog before his world shrank to 154 feet of steel. Exercise and beer had always helped him clear his mind.

He took a right onto Céspedes Avenue. The road, named after the Cuban War of Independence hero, rose to meet the coming dawn. It felt good to move, to breathe, to sweat. Except for a few Jamaican and Filipino contractors on their way to work, the morning was still. Even Camp Delta, up on the hill to Pat's left, seemed dead. Pat wondered what time reveille was for the Naval Station's guests from the war on terror.

The road finally leveled off above Girl Scout Beach. Pat took out his headphones and walked to the edge of the cliff. A ferry crossed the harbor, leaving a V-shaped wake in the gunmetal gray water. The sky was still a dark purple beyond the scrub-covered mountains to the west. It was easy to forget about the manmade border of cacti and landmines that separated this strange rental property from the rest of Cuba.

Pat heard a rustling to his right. He turned and saw a banana rat's head poking out of the underbrush. It studied Pat with a flinty eye before scurrying across the road. Pat tried to take a picture, but the well-fed varmint was gone before he could unlock his phone. He realized it didn't matter. Who was he going to send the picture to?

As Pat pictured Michaela's smiling eyes and heard her innocent laugh, he felt a tearing in his stomach. Maybe she would give him another chance someday. Maybe not. He took a deep breath—he had no choice but to move forward.

Turning his attention to the harbor and coastline, Pat opened his phone again and this time did take a picture. He couldn't fully capture the raw beauty of the vista, but Galán might appreciate the effort just the same.

Pat put his headphones in and began running back down the hill to the *Strickland*. The barely visible sun had already raised the temperature a few degrees, and his sweat flowed more freely than before. His thoughts, too. As the balls of his feet bounced off the pavement, he realized something.

He realized that all he had anymore were his two brothers.

☆

The following afternoon, Pat and the interceptor crew trailed an overloaded migrant chug across the Old Bahama Channel. The chug consisted of an inflatable dinghy further buoyed by four tire bladders, and it trailed a spinnaker of blue smoke from a fifteen-horsepower outboard.

A man in a light blue button-down shirt with a white collar poured gasoline into the engine. The stock-broker-looking *balsero* had told Petty Officer Martínez that he and his seven compatriots had been under way for three days. He didn't seem concerned, however, that the chug was headed northeast toward the Bahamas, or that the mountains of Cuba were still visible over the southern horizon.

"Are these guys serious about staying out here?" said Chief Landis, clutching in and clutching out so as to not overshoot the slow-moving target. "They look like hammered dog shit. I mean, damn."

One woman had vomited over the side twice in the last hour, and another man had yet to move more than an eyelid, let alone emerge from the shade of an umbrella.

Pat turned to Martínez. "You sure they understood you?"

"Yeah. I told them we have food, water, even a shower. But they just said they love America. The fat guy said that Obama is a great friend."

Larson chuckled. "Well that's where they messed up."

"And I was like, 'Bro, I don't care. We both know how this ends.'"

Pat shook his head. They had no choice.

Sure enough, the radio buzzed fifteen minutes later. The Command Center in Miami had finally approved the plan. They'd be out of the baking sun soon.

The interceptor crew didn't say anything to each other. Instead, Pat adjusted his compression shorts and finished his Gatorade while Chief Landis unwrapped another Tootsie Pop. Martínez put his hat on over his barely-within-regulations fauxhawk. Larson applied sunscreen to his tattooed arms before pulling on Latex gloves.

Pat felt bad about removing the pistol from his thigh holster, but for the plan to work, they had to sell it.

Chief Landis turned the interceptor away from the chug in a slow, gentle loop. He brought the boat to a stop about a hundred yards away.

The migrants craned their necks. Even the man under the umbrella turned to look over his shoulder.

Chief Landis snapped his helmet chinstrap beneath his razor-burned jaw. "Ready?"

"Yup." Pat closed his eyes and inhaled. You have to do this. They will die out here, otherwise.

Chief Landis slammed the throttle forward. Pat opened his eyes as the bow leapt out of the water, pointing directly for the chug.

The migrants stared slack-jawed as the interceptor bore down on them. Fifty yards. Thirty yards. Ten yards.

Chief Landis turned hard to port and pulled back on the throttle. The interceptor's wake soaked the migrants, and the umbrella flipped over into the sea.

"*Manos arriba!*" yelled Martínez, pointing his pepper spray at the shouting migrants. "*No se muevan!*"

Pat aimed his pistol just above the migrants' heads, his finger outside the trigger guard. He saw a look of terror on an old man's face but reminded himself of the nasty inbound weather—there was no alternative.

The side of the interceptor made contact with the chug. Larson began pulling the Cubans aboard, and Martínez sat them along the deck as well as on top of the padded engine hatch. They waited with their hands interlaced on their heads.

The last migrant aboard the chug was a scrawny teenager in a wifebeater and oversized swim trunks. He picked up a clear jug full of yellow liquid and began drinking.

"Hey! Drop that!" yelled Pat.

Martínez looked up from distributing life preservers and yelled something in Spanish.

The boy didn't seem to listen, but he did sink to his knees. His eyes rolled back in his head, and the jug spilled onto his chest.

"It's gasoline!" Larson leapt onto the chug, almost swamping it in the process, and caught the kid before he fell into the gentle waves.

Pat jumped aboard as well. The chug reeked of gasoline and moved beneath him like a waterbed, a waterbed covered in discarded sandals, soda bottles, and food wrappers. Pat grabbed the boy's ankles and helped Larson raise him into stern of the interceptor.

"Is he breathing?" asked Chief Landis.

Pat leapt back into the interceptor and positioned the boy between his legs as if they were riding a toboggan. He leaned over and put his ear to the boy's mouth. He could feel shallow, hot breaths. "Yeah, he's breathing."

Chief Landis slammed the throttle forward.

Pat kept the boy upright so as to prevent him from choking on his own vomit. He held the back of the boy's head against his body armor to keep it from bouncing.

Don't die on me. Please don't die.

★

San Juan, Puerto Rico

Galán woke up in a pool of sweat. He had forgotten to shut the terrace windows, and the morning humidity had overpowered the wall-mounted air conditioner. He peeled away his blanket and stumbled into the bathroom. As he vomited into the toilet, he remembered the twelve-pack of Medalla and the third of a bottle of Ron de Barrilito that he polished off the night before.

He flushed the toilet and sat against the bathroom wall, shivering in the heat. When he closed his eyes, he was in Adonis's cinder-block office. The old man was beckoning for Galán to hand over the money, his gold teeth flashing in a Cheshire grin.

Galán opened his eyes and stared at the mildewed ceiling. Just make a decision and live with it. He wiped his forehead and stood. Steadying himself with one hand on the sink, he brushed his teeth.

The orange kitten walked in and rubbed itself against Galán's clammy leg. The cat hopped onto the edge of the tub and stared expectantly, his tail swishing back and forth.

Galán rinsed out his mouth and turned to his diminutive roommate.

"What would you do?"

23

Windward Passage

Pat joined Martínez behind the pilothouse for migrant watch. The eight Cubans they had interdicted the day before lay sprawled out between the box-like engine room air intakes. All except the brother of the young man who drank the gasoline—he sat by himself, legs crossed, staring through the black nylon mesh at the horizon. His brother hadn't swallowed enough to warrant an airlift and was instead recovering on the fantail.

"That kid said this was their fourth time," said Martínez, spitting sunflower seeds into a cup. "The first time they got scared and turned back. The second time they got stranded on some cay in the Bahamas. And the third time Station Fort Lauderdale stopped them just outside the surf." He shook his head and turned to Pat. "He said they were so close they could see people partying on a hotel balcony."

"Damn." Pat laughed softly. "That sucks."

"Yeah, poor son of a bitch. I mean what do you tell a kid like that?"

"I have no idea."

Pat stood in silence, his sweaty back pressed against the superstructure. Black smoke billowed out of the port side exhaust as the number one engine came online. The number two engine went quiet. There was no mission other than kill time until the Citizenship and Immigration Services agent arrived to complete the manifestation of fear interviews.

The gentle, steady vibrations of the engine running at idle speed had a somnolent effect, and Pat caught himself drifting off. He paced from one side of the ship to the other. He wanted to look at his watch, but he knew that he would be disappointed by what he would find. He couldn't wait to go below, get out of his stinking boots and filthy coveralls, and take a shower. Maybe before he racked out he could even read a chapter of that Whitey Bulger biography that his mom had mailed him.

He leaned over the starboard rail and looked aft. The wake stretched like a white ribbon toward the clear horizon. The threat of the previous day's foul weather had not materialized.

"Ayyy!"

The shrill scream came from behind the opposite air intake. Pat darted over and almost tripped on a woman scuttling sideways across the deck. Her white Tyvek suit was splattered with crimson. Still screaming, she pointed at the young man of Fort Lauderdale fame—he was slumped over in the fetal position.

Pat dropped to his knees and rolled the boy onto his back. The crotch and legs of the boy's suit were soaked with blood. Pat pulled apart the fabric and uncovered a stab wound. The small yet rough incision near the femoral artery quickly disappeared under the pulsing blood.

Martínez banged on the pilothouse window. "Pipe the corpsman up here! I got a goddamned kid bleeding out!"

The rest of the migrants hovered around Pat and the boy.

"Al piso!" Martínez yelled, pulling them back one by one. "Get down!"

Pat balled up the sopping crotch of the boy's Tyvek suit and pushed it against the wound. Everything was so wet and so red. He was overcome by a memory of doing dishes at his grandmother's house, his hands submerged in the warm water

The boy's dark mustache contrasted with his paling skin. He opened his eyes briefly, his pupils pressing against the edges of the brown irises. Pat stared back at him. He wanted to say something, anything, to quell the boy's panic.

Pat didn't know how much time had passed before he felt a hand on his shoulder. What sounded like distant yelling grew louder. The hand gripped Pat tighter until it finally yanked him back toward the lifelines that ringed the deck. A turnbuckle cut into Pat's back, but he hardly felt it.

Petty Officer Bartlett knelt over the kid with a gun bag full of compresses and bandages. He must have been eating dinner when Martínez sounded the alarm, because he was still wearing his brown nonregulation Top-Siders. He tore open the kid's suit and stuck his gloved fingers inside the wound. The pulsing stopped.

Pat closed his eyes and leaned his head against the taut lifeline. He sat there motionless while the chaos of screaming migrants and shouting Coast Guardsmen raged around him. He wished he were anywhere else.

✯

San Juan, Puerto Rico

It wasn't until it was too dark to read that Galán closed his thick accounting notebook and rose from the desk in the diner's back office. For the second time that week, he had been an hour late to work. If he wouldn't tolerate a bus boy showing up hungover, how could he tolerate the same behavior in himself? The silver lining to spending the afternoon and evening paying his taxes to the commonwealth was that the forms and calculations distracted him from Adonis.

As Galán headed home, he skipped his nightly visit to the grocery store and instead bought what he knew would be an underwhelming pastrami sandwich from Subway. They didn't sell alcohol there.

Seated across from the orange kitten and with the enormous sub in hand, Galán thought about his father. He thought about the rum and the cans of Bucanero. He thought about the yelling and screaming, and the sound of flesh on flesh. He remembered the tears, the mumbled apologies, the meager gifts provided as penance.

Gustavo Betances had seen things in Angola. Almost nobody remembered that war, but Gustavo did, despite how hard he must have tried to forget. Galán didn't know what happened on the other side of the Atlantic, but he knew that it had ruined his father.

Whether he said so or not, Gustavo always had Angola. It was his curse and his crutch. It was what kept Josefina sticking around for as long as she did. She could blame the bruises and lacerations on the war and not the man.

But me, thought Galán, I haven't seen shit. I have no excuse for being weak, for being a drunk. I'm just imagining what might happen on a *yola* in the Mona Passage.

★

Windward Passage

The cool salt spray landed on Pat's face and arms, which were still stained a reddish ocher from the young man's blood. The adrenaline of orchestrating the medevac by Jayhawk helicopter had worn off. Glad to finally be away from the rest of the crew and migrants, Pat sat beneath the twenty-five-millimeter bow cannon and watched the western sky turn orange.

Pat heard footsteps and turned. Chief Landis was leaning over the rail of the deck above.

"You got room down there for one more? If I didn't get off that messdeck I was going to wring that nonrate's neck and hang him from the jack staff. Damn, that kid's a dumbass."

Pat laughed and moved over. Chief Landis sat on the grate-metal deck and produced a tin of Skoal.

"I thought you gave that up?" asked Pat.

"I did," said Chief Landis, putting a pinch in his lower lip. "But sometimes you need a little pick-me-up. So I jacked this out of Bartlett's locker." He wiped some black flakes from the corner of his mouth. "So, how you doing? That whole mess was kind of fucked up, huh?"

"I'm all right. It just caught me by surprise. I've heard of that shit happening, but still."

"I know," said Chief Landis, spitting into an empty water bottle. "You know how he did it?"

Pat shook his head.

"He broke off a piece of that cofferdam. All he needed was a little jagged piece of steel no bigger than his pinkie."

"It's just hard to imagine," said Pat.

"Hard to imagine? You ever seen my deckies doing their freshwater washdowns? Dumbasses. Of course that shit was rusted."

"No, I mean it's hard to imagine doing that to yourself because you're so desperate to get away from somewhere."

"Oh." Chief Landis deposited another slug of brown spit into the bottle. "Yeah, it's pretty messed up."

"You think he's going to make it?"

"I don't know. If he does, he's going to be in for a rude awakening. He didn't wager that we'd fly his ass to the Bahamas."

"That's a good point," said Pat. "No dry foot." Since the kid hadn't made it to American soil, he would be going back to Cuba after the Bahamian doctors stitched him up.

"It won't be all bad," said Chief Landis, smiling. "He might get some ass thanks to that scar."

Pat laughed. "He'll have to come up with a better story, though."

"Yeah, you're probably right." Chief Landis held up the tin of Skoal. "You want some?"

"Yeah, why not?" Pat took a pinch of the moist, shredded tobacco and placed it between his gums and his lip, fumbling a small clump onto his lap in the process.

Chief Landis chuckled. "I guess you don't dip too much neither?"

"How could you tell?"

"Here, have the rest of it, then," said Chief Landis, handing Pat the tin. "Life's more fun when you have a habit or two. Plus, I know the combo to Bartlett's locker. 1790."

"For real?"

"What? You didn't know he was hard for the Guard?"

Pat laughed. "1790."

They sat in silence for some time, the horizon rising and falling. If he focused on the sunset, Pat could quiet the afternoon's events which replayed in his head. After several minutes, the last crescent of the sun dipped below the darkening sea. No green flash.

Chief Landis sighed and stood. "Well, that rack is calling my name. Typical that I got midwatch after a day like today." He was about to pull himself up to the deck above when he paused. "Oh, and I guess you'll be wanting this."

"Thanks," said Pat, taking Chief Landis's warm spit bottle. "You shouldn't have."

"For you, sir, the world."

"I appreciate it, Chief. Sweet dreams."

Chief Landis chuckled as he walked away. "Some titties would be nice."

Pat smiled, the nicotine finally kicking in. His head felt light and his mind smooth. Turning to his left, Pat could still see the mountains of Cuba in the hazy distance. Somewhere beyond was Galán's sister.

As Pat thought about Galán's plan, he began to appreciate what was at stake for Galán's sister. He began to understand the desperation that had pushed Galán toward such a harebrained scheme. And no, it wasn't the nicotine that was causing Pat to reconsider—it was the memories of one young man drinking gasoline and another stabbing himself with a broken piece of steel.

24

San Juan, Puerto Rico

Pat pressed the Tyvek suit into the wound, his hands disappearing into the pooling blood. The artery pulsed against his fingers. He couldn't believe this was happening again.

"Check him for shock," said a voice from over his shoulder. "Keep him awake. Talk to him."

Pat tried to talk, but his tongue wasn't forming words. He felt like he had a rag in his mouth. As the blood seeped past his wrists, he wondered where the corpsman was.

"Look at him," said the voice, more persistently. "You're starting to lose him. Make a tourniquet."

Pat wanted to, but he had to maintain pressure on the wound. His heart pounded. He looked up to see if the Cuban boy was conscious.

Except it wasn't the Cuban boy. It was Danny. He was pale and sweaty like he had been the morning he missed his flight out of Puerto Rico. His eyes were vacant.

"Goddamnit!" said the voice behind Pat. "You're losing him. Do something!"

Pat wanted to ask Danny how he had gotten there, why he had stabbed himself. But his tongue just wouldn't comply.

Danny smiled weakly. "Just don't forget, Patty. Just don't forget."

Pat didn't understand. Don't forget what? He had no idea.

"Come on, McAllister! Do something!"

To hell with it. It didn't matter why Danny was there or what he was saying. All that mattered was that Pat loved him and wouldn't

169

let him slip away like this. He applied more pressure and concentrated on his tongue. No matter how hard he tried, though, the words wouldn't come.

Pat woke up with a gasp, facedown on the wet bed. He was gripping his balled up sheets and pressing them into his mattress. He slowly caught his breath and realized he was in his apartment. Danny was in New Hampshire. They were okay.

Pat unclenched his fists and rolled onto his back. He checked the time on his phone—it wasn't even midnight. He lay in the dark and stared at the ceiling.

Screw it. He scrolled through his contacts until he found Michaela. He had no idea what he was going to say, but he didn't care. He just needed to hear her voice, even if he knew it would be without its loving softness. He just needed to know that he existed in her world.

He pressed the CALL button and waited. The phone rang twice before going to voicemail. Pat hung up before the beep. As he lay there, he suddenly became aware of the thousands of miles of ocean that separated him from Michaela, from Danny, from his parents. He felt tiny, and so did his island of Puerto Rico.

Pat closed his eyes and tried to quiet his racing mind. He couldn't. Instead, he thought about Galán. He wondered how often his neighbor woke up alone in the dark missing Cuba, or his sister, or his mother. And for Galán, the miles really did matter.

Well, I guess we have each other.

✯

San Lorenzo, Puerto Rico

Galán brought the beers and the plate of mofongo to the table. Outside on the denuded plateau, Puerto Rican flags flew from the roll bars of immaculate Jeep Wranglers and Suzuki Samurais. Inside, the *salsero* Willie Colón blared at an unholy level.

Yesica had invited him to spend the afternoon at this mountaintop bar popular with the *chinchorreo* crowd, and he had felt compelled to accept because of what she had done for him, for Gabriela.

He didn't mind how she looked in her backless dress, either. She hadn't mentioned her boyfriend, and Galán sensed that this afternoon might end in a similar fashion as their last encounter.

"Enjoy," said Galán, pushing the plate of mashed plantains toward her. She smiled, and they began to eat.

As much as Galán tried to focus on the music and panoramic views of central Puerto Rico, Adonis kept creeping back into his thoughts. He considered ordering a bottle of Ron de Barrilito to take off the edge, but he didn't trust himself.

"You want to dance?" asked Yesica, pushing the plate of mofongo back toward him. Her eyes had a seductive sparkle. "I didn't come all the way up this mountain just for the food."

"Why not?" said Galán, sipping his beer. "But I'm a little bit out of practice."

"Are you saying you want me to lead?" Yesica's eyes flashed.

"No, no," said Galán, laughing. "I may be a bad dancer, but I will always be a man." As soon as the words came out of his mouth, though, he remembered his recent amorous performance with her, abridged as it was. His face flushed.

They squeezed onto the dance floor just as Joe Arroyo's "Rebelión" began playing. Galán needed a moment to get the timing down, but soon enough he and Yesica were stepping in perfect unison across the wooden planks. The last time that Galán had truly danced had been in Key West with Esperanza, and he felt a twinge.

"Rebelión" was followed by a dirty *reggaetón* throwback much to the delight of a group of preteens gathered around the jukebox. Galán and Yesica came to rest as the aggressive lyrics reverberated off the thatched roof. Yesica extended her face toward Galán's, but he only kissed her lightly on the forehead before retreating to the table. He didn't have to look at her to know that she was no longer smiling.

Something didn't feel right about going farther with Yesica when there was so much uncertainty back in Ciego de Ávila. It seemed wrong, like eating meat on Good Friday. Plus, his attraction to her was purely physical. There was none of that chemistry that he had shared with Esperanza, the kind of bond where they could read each other's thoughts and sense each other's emotions, no matter how hidden they were.

Yesica went to the bar to order another Medalla for him and a Redd's for herself. A younger man in tight-fitting pants and a shirt unbuttoned past his sternum started talking to her, not bothering to take off his oversized sunglasses. Yesica welcomed the attention, or at least pretended to.

Galán didn't care, though. His mind was back in Key West.

He and Esperanza were seated on a bench at the Greyhound station. A few leathery drifters and single mothers with small children loitered around them. The trip to the Marathon emergency room had confirmed what they already knew. Tears gave way to days of silence, until Esperanza announced that she wanted to go home, that she needed to go home, if only for a little while. The Greyhound would take her to the airport in Miami. From there, she had a one-way ticket to Los Angeles.

Galán still didn't understand why Esperanza needed to leave, but he knew that there were some things a man could never understand. He put his arm around her and kissed her on the top of her head. She leaned into him, and they watched the buses come and go and the old people suck down their cigarettes. There was no reason anymore to avoid the smoke.

"You need to tell me as soon as you get to Miami," said Galán. "And then you need to tell me as soon as you land in Los Angeles." Any conversation was better than silence.

"Okay."

"You know I'll be waiting for you whenever you come back. Or I can go to Los Angeles." He paused, waiting for a response. "I can introduce your family to *ropa vieja*." He hoped she would laugh, or at least smile.

A bus approached their departure bay. It slowed to a stop in front of them, its air brakes whining. The uneasiness in Galán's stomach intensified. The doors opened, and the southbound travelers spilled out and huddled around the luggage bins.

"You know I love you more than anything," said Galán, squeezing her, trying to freeze the moment so that he would always remember how her shoulder felt under the soft cotton shirt.

"I know." She was looking at the bus, but Galán knew that her thoughts were elsewhere. He wondered if he were in them.

"Eleven thirty to Miami," said the oncoming driver, his short-sleeve button-down shirt yellowed under the armpits. He took one last drag on his cigarette. "Have your tickets ready and ensure your personal belongings make it into underside storage."

They stood. Galán grabbed Esperanza's bags and gave them to a balding porter. Esperanza showed her wrinkled ticket to the driver, who ripped off his portion and returned the stub. She turned toward Galán and hugged him.

"Once we take your ticket, you have to board," said the driver, his pink brow beaded with sweat.

Galán held Esperanza tight against his chest. This is just temporary, he told himself. This isn't forever.

"All right, we got to go," said the driver.

Galán opened his eyes as the last passenger in line schlepped an oxygen tank aboard.

Esperanza leaned back and looked up at Galán. "I'll always love you, too. Always. I promise."

Galán forced a smile. "Then we'll see each other soon, right?"

Esperanza didn't say anything. She kissed him and boarded the bus without looking back.

Galán waited for the bus to disappear before finally making the sweaty walk back to la Bandera. He entered the dimly lit storeroom with a Budweiser, a stack of blank paper, and a marker. He sat down on a stool and thought.

"Complete set of baby accessories," he finally wrote. "Crib. Clothing. Diaper bag. Toys. $150."

He put the marker down and sipped his beer, examining his work. It would do. He proceeded to finish the rest of the fliers that he would hang from telephone poles around town—the town that he needed to escape. He didn't know where he would go, but he couldn't stay in Key West. The incomplete past would always be there.

Galán dropped the fliers on the floor and finished his beer. He stood and stretched his stiff back, taking one more look at the two neat piles of baby gear leaning against the opposite wall. Only the larger stack was for sale. He figured nobody would want items already monogrammed with the name "Gabriela."

☆

San Juan, Puerto Rico

The moored ship was quiet. With the exception of the two-man duty section, the rest of the crew had gone home the moment liberty was granted—it wasn't like the captain could pay overtime. Life for the executive officer, on the other hand, wasn't so simple. Pat had purchases to approve, evaluations to write, and training records to certify.

Pat leaned back in his chair and closed his eyes. The only way the paperwork stopped was if he stopped. He dozed off until the patter of rain on the deck above woke him.

Pat looked at his watch. It was almost 5:00. Good enough for government work. Just as he was about to log off his computer, he received a new email from the shoreside command center. It was an updated patrol schedule for the six San Juan–based cutters.

Pat entered the password to open the classified spreadsheet. He scrolled down to the *Strickland*'s section and scoured it for any changes to port call locations or dates. The last thing he wanted to do was rebook pier space and fuel through the lethargic Russian husbanding agent in Miami. Saint Thomas was still there. As was Saint Croix. Good. Even their in-port maintenance periods were intact.

Pat stood and took off his heavy uniform blouse. He was undoing his rigger's belt when a thought crossed his mind. A crazy thought, but a thought nonetheless.

Pat sat, logged on, and opened the document once more. He compared the *Strickland*'s schedule with those of the other five cutters—different colored boxes indicated when the ships would be under way and where they would be patrolling. He kept looking.

There it was. Several weeks out. A three-day stretch when the Mona Passage would be open. *Strickland* would be the last cutter out there before the gap in coverage.

Pat wrote down the dates on a scrap of paper.

25

When Pat landed on the terrace the following evening, Galán was bent over a mess of papers and a laptop computer from the floppy disc era. A tangle of wires snaked through the barred window into the apartment, and the sleeping kitten served as a paperweight.

"What in the world is going on here?" asked Pat. "You getting into the stock market?"

"No, no, I'm just working on some stuff." Galán removed a pair of green reading glasses and deposited the kitten on the floor. He gathered the papers together. "I didn't know you were coming over."

For the first time since meeting Galán, Pat sensed he was intruding. He approached the table nonetheless and glanced at Galán's notebook. There were phone numbers and dollar amounts written in a neat print, as well as names and dates. Pat saw "Cuba" and "RD" and "PR."

"So, it's really happening?"

Galán sighed and gave up trying to hide the evidence. "I don't know. I think so. I'm just putting it all down on paper to make sure I understand how it would work."

Pat nodded and turned. He looked out over the plaza, his hands on his hips. "You know, I've seen some things these past couple of patrols, and I've been doing some thinking. About you. About your sister. About what really matters." He turned back around and licked his lips. "I think I can help you."

Galán looked up at him but didn't say anything.

176

Pat reached into his back pocket and pulled out a folded piece of paper. He held it out to Galán, who started to reach for it before changing his mind.

"No, I can't take that." Galán shook his head. "Hell, I don't even know what that is. And I don't want to know. I'm sorry I even told you about the mess with Gabriela. That was wrong of me. I should never have put you in that situation."

Pat unfolded the scrap of paper and slid it under the computer so it wouldn't blow away.

Galán regarded it as if it were contaminated. "Take it back. I'm serious. I don't want it."

"Too bad." Pat pointed to the sheet. "You see those dates? That's when Mona will be open. That's your window. That's when you have to do it."

Galán squinted at Pat with his brow furrowed. "Why? Why are you doing this? I told you I changed my mind about getting you involved."

"You know why I'm doing this. You said it yourself. It's about blood. Nothing comes before blood."

Galán blinked.

"If the roles were reversed," said Pat, leaning on the table, "if you could do something that would change my brother's life, I'd damn sure expect you to do it."

Galán nodded and slowly reached for the paper. "Thank you." He studied the information before looking back up. "Thank you, really. I don't know what else to say."

"You don't have to say anything." Pat pulled out a chair and sat down. "Just get your sister here in one piece."

☆

Santurce, Puerto Rico

Galán walked past the weaves hanging in the window of the Venezuelan barbershop, the bulging traveler's neck wallet bouncing against his chest. He looked up and down the shimmering white concrete of la Calle Delgado before stepping into the darkness of Bar Punta Cana.

Galán blinked as his eyes adjusted. The same surly bartender from his first visit appeared. His Jordan sweat suit seemed like an odd summer choice.

"I'm here for Adonis," said Galán.

The bartender grunted before frisking Galán for wires and weapons. He fingered the neck wallet.

"The fuck is this?"

"As I said, I'm here for Adonis."

The bartender shook his head and shuffled down the narrow passageway to his boss's office.

Galán waited while an older woman with a stooped back mopped the concrete floor. She didn't make eye contact with him.

A minute later, the bartender reappeared. He motioned for Galán to enter.

The office hadn't changed. Even the takeout containers were the same—a family-sized carton of General Tso's chicken accompanied by not one but two boxes of fried rice. A regiment of ants marched up and down the cinderblock wall armed with their share of the feast. They were perhaps the most well-fed ants in all of Puerto Rico.

"So," said Adonis, his hands clasped in front of him, "have we come to a decision?"

"We have." Galán pulled the neck wallet out from under his shirt. He extracted a piece of paper and put it on the desk. "Here is my sister's visa information."

"Good," said Adonis without examining it. "She can pick it up at the embassy at the end of the month. And so what is it going to be? Coach or first class?"

"First class."

"Good. In this economy of budget travelers, it's been hard to fill the first-class seats." He took a bite of the General Tso's, sauce dripping down the front of his black SALSA, PLENA, BOMBA, RUMBA T-shirt.

"And how much today?" asked Galán, opening the envelope.

"Three today. One later."

"I have a proposition." Galán hoped his voice didn't sound as nasally to Adonis as it sounded to him. "I'm thinking two today and one later."

Adonis set down his chopsticks and smiled. "Well, that wouldn't be first class, then? Would it?" He wiped his mouth. "Let me tell you something. It is very, very much in your interest to not make this, should we say . . . difficult? And while it is very much in your interest, it is even more in your sister's interest."

"I understand. But you wouldn't just be getting the money."

Adonis laughed so hard that he induced a coughing fit. Grains of rice flew from his mouth. Galán prayed that the smugglers who would actually carry out Gabriela's journey weren't this loathsome, but he didn't have much faith.

"You Cubans are something else," said Adonis once he had composed himself. "Please, explain to me why you think you should get a discount. I want to hear this." He drummed the table with his fingers, the extra-long fingernail on his pinkie making a disconcerting sound.

Galán opened the fat envelope. On top of the bills was Pat's scrap of paper. Galán unfolded it and held it up. "I think this will be useful to you and your captains."

"What the hell is that?"

"This is when the Mona Passage will be clear."

"I don't know what you're talking about. Clear? What do you mean clear?"

"No Coast Guard," said Galán. "Your captains will have a straight shot."

Adonis leaned forward and studied Galán with a new interest. "First of all, where would somebody like you get that kind of information? And second, how do I know you aren't bullshitting me just to get a discount?"

"I got it from a friend of a friend." Galán had told himself he would keep Pat out of this. "A guy in the Coast Guard. I don't know his name. But how do you know I'm not bullshitting you? My sister is going to be in that boat. Why would I lie to you? Why would I give you bad information when it's my sister who's at risk? I trust this information."

Adonis leaned back in his chair and rubbed his jaw. For the first time in either of their meetings, he broke eye contact with Galán. He bit the inside of his cheek before looking back. "You really are something else, worm."

"Look," said Galán. "If you don't trust this information or don't want my business, I understand. I can always go to Don Gerónimo. I've heard he's good, too." Yesica had said that Don Gerónimo was the cheaper, less reliable version of Adonis.

Adonis shook his head and snorted. "Give me that goddamned paper." He studied it, his brow furrowed, before looking back up at Galán. "You know what? I don't think you're smart enough to fuck me. Give me the two thousand dollars. You have yourself a deal."

Galán opened the neck wallet again and extracted the bills. He had to concentrate to keep his shaky fingers from dropping the money.

★

The *Strickland* rocked against the pier at Sector San Juan. Pat felt like they had just returned from their last patrol, yet here they were, three weeks later, about to do it all over again.

He nodded at the quartermaster.

"Now, set the special sea detail," said the quartermaster, wincing from the feedback. He moved the microphone away from his mouth. "*Strickland* will be getting under way in three zero minutes. All stations report manned and ready."

Pat picked up a clipboard from the console and looked at the checklist. Nobody had switched the electrical load from the shore tie to the generators, and the trash cans were still full. The mooring lines hadn't even been singled up.

He thrust the clipboard at Tim, who was trying to unwrap a Starburst with his tongue. "Carnival Glory is coming in at 13:00," said Pat. "You ever been jammed up with a cruise ship in restricted waters?"

Tim didn't say anything.

"Well, neither have I. And I'd like to keep it that way. Drive this checklist so we can get the hell out of here."

"Aye, sir." Tim rarely called his roommate "sir."

"And get that shit out of your mouth."

Pat stepped out onto the forward deck. The heat and humidity felt good after the air conditioning, but within minutes he was sweating. The thick blue fabric of his uniform didn't breathe. He looked down onto the pier where Larson was chatting with a friend from the sector armory, the electrical shore tie in one hand and a thermos of coffee in the other.

"Hey, Larson," said Pat, leaning over the rail. "We don't have time for smoking and joking. Let's go."

Larson squinted up at him before shuffling toward the brow.

Pat glanced up at the mast. The call sign still wasn't hoisted, and the radar antenna wasn't rotating. He shook his head and walked back into the pilothouse.

Tim and the Operations Department petty officers stood by the chart table laughing. One of them took a pull on an e-cigarette before emitting an enormous cloud of purple water vapor. The other made thrusting motions with his pelvis.

Pat grabbed the clipboard from Tim and held it up. "We're supposed to be under way in twenty minutes, and nobody's done shit. Everybody's just dicking around."

They stared at him.

"Well get it right!" He smacked the clipboard onto the Plexiglas-covered table and exited the pilothouse, slamming the door behind him.

Pat paced under the shade of the aft deck's awning. He took off his ball cap and wiped the sweat from his brow. He could see his reflection in the silver lieutenant junior grade bar.

He took a deep breath.

You need to relax. These guys may be behind on the getting under way checklist, but they didn't give classified patrol schedules to their neighbors. That shit is on you.

The ship's whistle sounded. Pat put his ball cap back on and looked up the hill toward Galán's apartment.

Make it be worth it, brother.

Part Three

26

Havana, Cuba

The doors of the *camello* swung open, and Gabriela and Yunel stepped down onto the hot pavement. The air was thick with diesel fumes from the afternoon rush hour. Gabriela wasn't used to being surrounded by people in every direction, so she stood close to her cousin.

Yunel craned his neck to the left and right, his brow furrowed. He finally nodded, picked up Gabriela's backpack, and took off across the four-lane street. Gabriela hustled after him.

Neither spoke as they picked their way down the opposite sidewalk. Gabriela wasn't entirely sure where they were going, but she hoped they would get there soon. The daylong trip from Ciego de Ávila had left her exhausted. And Yunel had said that this was the easy leg of the journey.

They took a left on la Avenida Paseo and passed the mansions of el Vedado. The palatial homes had been subdivided into apartments, and lines of drying laundry flapped softly in the ocean breeze. Gabriela tried to linger in the shade of the mature trees that lined the street, but Yunel was walking too fast.

As she skipped ahead to catch up, Gabriela noticed a group of children playing with a litter of dachshund puppies next to a dry fountain. For the first time since saying good-bye to Tía Teresa, Gabriela smiled.

Several blocks later, Yunel finally stopped. He looked up at the stone building before them with his hands on his hips. Gabriela brushed the hair out of her eyes and repositioned her blistered foot in her sandal.

"Excuse me, sir," said Yunel to a toothless old man who was shuffling past. "Is this the old Gómez building?"

"It is, young man." The words came out garbled through his flapping gums, and he continued sliding down the pavement in his patent leather shoes.

"Let's go," said Yunel to Gabriela.

They passed under an archway into a dark lobby and climbed a wide spiral staircase. The entryway reminded Gabriela of a dusty, dark version of the castle where Cinderella had to wash the stairs for her evil stepmother. There were no talking mice, but a pair of pigeons did coo from an overhead beam.

Gabriela followed Yunel down a third floor hallway. Down below was an interior courtyard, empty save for a rusted bedframe. Gabriela was trying to make eye contact with a skinny black cat prowling on the opposite railing when she walked into Yunel.

"Damn," he said. "Try to look where you're going. That's the third time you've done that."

"I'm sorry." Her voice cracked.

Yunel shook his head and turned back to the iron gate in front of him. He stood there, head inclined and eyes closed. "Yes, this is it. This is definitely it." He reached through the gate and knocked on the wooden door.

There were footsteps, and the door opened. A tall man with a goatee stood before them in a wifebeater and tight jean shorts rolled just above the knee. He studied Gabriela and then Yunel until a smile spread across his face.

"Wow, Yunel," he said, opening the gate. "You look like shit."

"Speak for yourself, bro." The two embraced. Yunel pointed to Gabriela. "This is my cousin Gabi. She's the one I was telling you about. The one making the trip."

The tall man nodded before leaning in for a kiss on the cheek. "They call me Ricardo. Your cousin and I spent a summer here in la Habana many years ago. He's a crazy bastard. But I'm sure you knew that."

Gabriela nodded. She didn't like bad words and just wanted something to drink.

"Well," said Ricardo, looking back at Yunel. "Come in. This is your house now."

"Thank you, brother." Yunel patted his friend on the shoulder. "I appreciate it. But don't worry, we shouldn't be here too long. Today's Monday? We go to the Dominican embassy tomorrow, and then Gabi leaves Thursday. Maybe I can stick around for the weekend, though, and we can check in on those Uribe sisters. What do you think of that?"

Thursday, thought Gabriela. The word turned in her head as if she had never heard it before.

As the reality of her departure dawned on her, Gabriela realized that she would never have another weekend in Cuba. She remembered all those Sundays going to Mass with her mother and Teresa. She remembered the movies she would watch before bed on Sunday nights. When she was living with Teresa, her aunt would sometimes give her a cup of ice cream. Strawberry was her favorite.

She took a deep breath.

It's okay. Galán will be there on the other side.

☆

Mayagüez, Puerto Rico

Pat looked down at the pier from the bridge wing of the *Strickland*. The three-hundred-foot stretch of concrete, illuminated by towering stadium lights, had grown ever more familiar over the past several months—the college town on Puerto Rico's west coast was the most convenient place to drop off smugglers apprehended in the Mona Passage.

The Venezuelans who had been nabbed three nights earlier emerged onto the deck below and shuffled across the brow and onto the pier. Their Coast Guard–issued sandals slapped against the concrete and the legs of their baggy Tyvek suits made swooshing noises. Two rotund Customs and Border Protection agents escorted them to a waiting van, while a third agent photographed the bales of cocaine stacked in the bed of an unmarked government truck.

The detainees looked remarkably unconcerned, thought Pat, given their reversal of fortune. One of them even smiled at Petty Officer Martínez, who was busy talking to the fuel contractor. Martínez nodded in acknowledgment.

In a few days, Pat would be on his roof drinking coffee made his way and listening to the potted plants rustle in the breeze. The Venezuelans would just be getting cavity checked at the federal correctional facility in Guaynabo.

Home. Pat couldn't wait to get home. Thanks to the drug interdiction as well as a successful multi-day search for a surfer off of Rincón, the patrol had been both productive and exhausting. Between the seemingly nonstop operations and the unforgiving watch rotation, Pat hadn't slept for more than three hours at a time.

But before Pat became too excited about the buffalo chicken pizza he would eat on his first night back—accompanied by a few cold Medallas and no Coasties—he remembered something else. He remembered that he would be tucking into his bachelor's banquet just as Galán's sister was setting sail for an unguarded Mona Island.

Pat felt a cold liquid run through his gut. Galán's sister. He hadn't thought about her since before they caught the Venezuelans. He'd been too busy with the evidence log, witness statements, and case package. He took a deep breath and waited for his nerves to settle. If he was this anxious, he could only imagine how Galán was doing on the other side of the island.

The captain appeared, pulling Pat back into the moment. "XO, are you good to drive us out of here?"

"Yes, sir," said Pat. "Definitely." He readjusted his ball cap and followed his boss into the pilothouse.

As Pat checked the trackline on the electronic chart, he was thankful that at least he and Galán should have some closure soon.

One way or the other.

☆

Havana, Cuba

The next morning, Gabriela, Yunel, and Ricardo descended la Avenida Paseo toward the Atlantic. Steam rose from the pavement, and the Hotel Riviera stood tall before the sparkling sea. An empty tanker, its bulbous bow poking above the waterline, moved silently in the distance.

"This is all we truly have," said Ricardo, gesturing down the Malecón. The sea wall and the adjacent boulevard curved east past weather-beaten colonial buildings toward the lighthouse and stone ramparts of el Castillo de los Tres Reyes Magos, better known as el Morro, like its Puerto Rican counterpart. "They can take everything else, but they can't take this."

Gabriela didn't know who "they" were, but her eyes feasted on the enchanting waterfront nevertheless.

"What do you think, Gabi?" asked Ricardo. "It's beautiful, right?"

"It is. I like it so, so much."

"Just wait until you get to the United States." Ricardo laughed. "Then you'll see beautiful."

Gabriela stopped smiling and felt a fluttering in her stomach. She remembered the dream from the night before. She was splashing frantically in the black water from that morning so many years ago, struggling to keep her head afloat. This time her mother was nowhere to be found.

Gabriela tried to slow down her breathing by focusing on two teenagers laughing and holding hands on the stone wall. It'll be okay. Galán will be there. It'll be okay.

Gabriela repeated that mantra as they walked west along the water away from the old city. The morning traffic sped past on their left. The modern Chinese cars emitted high-pitched whines, while the old American sedans rumbled by heavily.

"You said your appointment is at 11:00?" asked Ricardo.

"Yes," said Yunel. "Apparently all we have to do is show up. My cousin in Puerto Rico has connections." He made a face that Gabriela couldn't decipher.

Ricardo rubbed his thumb against his forefinger and middle finger. "Money talks, my friend."

Yunel nodded.

They kept walking, and the road dipped into a tunnel beneath the Almendares River. Gabriela liked the tunnel's coolness, but she didn't like the rushing force of the passing cars. She walked faster to escape the amplified engine noise. Yunel and Ricardo hustled to keep up.

They emerged into Miramar and passed the Avenida de las Américas monument. The sun reflected off of the marble fountain, and a seabird groomed itself on one of the muse's heads. They kept walking and found themselves dwarfed on either side by pristine mansions. Unlike many of the homes in el Vedado, these ones hadn't been left to Mother Nature.

Gabriela's eyes grew wide.

"These are embassies," said Ricardo. "Important people from other countries live here."

Gabriela nodded. She loved the different flags and perfectly manicured lawns. "I want to live in an embassy," she said quietly. Maybe there were embassies where Galán lived.

They kept walking, but slower than before. The climbing sun had burnt away the morning haze. Gabriela tried to find her shadow, but there were only little patches of black beneath her sandaled feet.

"We should be getting close," said Yunel, looking at his folded map. Sweat dripped from the tip of his nose and onto the glossy paper. "Number ninety-two."

"Ninety-two," said Ricardo, scanning the buildings that lined the opposite side of the street. "There. I think that's it. Ninety-two." He pointed at a white Spanish colonial building. A blue-and-red flag snapped from a tall flagpole. The grass was cut in even rows, and the bushes were squared.

They approached the wiry security guard who smoked a cigarette inside his sidewalk cubicle.

"We have an appointment," said Yunel. "At 10:00. For a visa."

"Name?" asked the guard, the cigarette poking out the side of his mouth. He pulled out a clipboard.

"Betances," said Yunel. "Gabriela Betances."

The guard examined his list. "Here you are." He pushed a button, and the gate made a buzzing noise and opened. Ricardo and Yunel exchanged another look that Gabriela couldn't interpret.

They followed a path toward the building and stepped into an air-conditioned waiting room. Yunel entered Gabriela's information into a ledger, and they sat down. Gabriela didn't know whether to feel better or worse when she noticed that the other people waiting also looked nervous.

The sweat dried from Gabriela's skin, her wet clothing becoming cold. Gabriela thumbed through her Cuban passport. She understood that small blue booklet had been an ordeal to obtain. Luckily for Gabriela, however, her mother had initiated the process two years earlier, right when her health had begun to decline.

"Betances," said a shrill voice from behind the counter where they had signed in. Yunel stood up and motioned for Gabriela to follow him.

"We're Betances," said Yunel to an austere woman with short hair.

"Are you Gabriela Betances?" the woman asked Yunel in a strange accent, her eyebrows raised.

"She is." Yunel nodded at Gabriela.

"Well, then you can take a seat in the waiting area, sir." She motioned toward the empty chairs next to Ricardo.

"But, my cousin . . ." Yunel struggled to find the right words.

"You can take a seat in the waiting area."

Yunel looked at Gabriela before walking away. Gabriela sat down across from the grumpy woman.

"Ms. Betances, where are you going in the Dominican Republic?"

Gabriela didn't say anything. Her heart was beating too hard.

"Ms. Betances, I asked you a question."

"Santo Domingo," said Gabriela, barely audible. Yunel had rehearsed this with her the night before in Ricardo's apartment.

"And the nature of your trip?"

"The nature?"

"Business or pleasure?"

Gabriela didn't really know what the lady meant even though Yunel had tried to explain it. "Pleasure?"

"And where will you be staying?"

"With family."

The lady looked up at her. Gabriela didn't know what was wrong. She felt like the lady's eyes were boring holes into her brain.

"With family?" the lady finally repeated.

"Yes."

"Where do they live?"

Yunel said she needed to answer this question quickly. "Santo Domingo Este."

The lady continued to study her. "Please wait a moment." She rose and conferred with an older woman in the back of the office who was sipping a small cup of coffee. The younger woman showed her Gabriela's passport. They both looked over at Gabriela before turning back to their conversation. The younger woman shook her head and rolled her eyes.

Just as Gabriela was going to retreat to Yunel, the younger woman returned to the window. The woman peeled a glossy visa from its backing and stuck it onto one of the many empty pages in Gabriela's passport. "This is good for thirty days." She handed the booklet to Gabriela without making eye contact. "Enjoy your trip."

☆

Mona Passage

Pat climbed the ladder to the dark bridge. He set down his coffee mug next to the throttles and looked at the radar display. The only green blip on the otherwise black screen was jagged Desecheo Island five nautical miles to the north. The *Strickland* was all alone.

"You hear the news, sir?" said Tim, who was leaning against the captain's chair. For once, he wasn't eating Cheetos.

"No," said Pat, plotting the cutter's position on a paper chart. "What news?"

"We're getting extended."

"We're getting extended?" The words didn't register at first.

"Yeah," said Tim, gathering his empty water bottle and sweatshirt. "Captain just called up."

"How long?" Pat tried to sound calm.

"Five days."

"Five days?" Pat regretted how forcefully the words came out of his mouth.

"What's wrong, sir?" said the engineer from the gun console. "You got a hot date? Hey, if she's got a sister, put in a good word for me. Hell, I'll even take a mom."

"Five days?" repeated Pat, his hands gripping the edge of the chart table. "Did captain say why?"

"He said it was because Mona was going to be gapped. I guess they can't gap it anymore with wet foot, dry foot on the chopping block." Tim laughed. "The migrants be running."

Pat stared at the digital anemometer, but his mind was churning too much to think about the wind speed and direction. "Whatever. Five days it is. Let me do a round outside, and then I'll relieve you."

Out on the bridge wing, Pat leaned on the rail, his fingers crunching down on a fine residue of salt. The nighttime humidity fogged his glasses, but he didn't bother wiping them.

Five days. How could he have been stupid enough to think that Sector San Juan would really leave Mona unguarded? Like they wouldn't have noticed that the cutter schedule was screwed up? Stupid. Stupid, stupid, stupid.

He stood straight and exhaled. He had to tell Galán before Gabriela set sail. The problem was that cell phone use wasn't authorized, and even if it were, there wouldn't be any service. And emails were monitored.

Goddamnit, he thought, staring into the foggy darkness.

☆

Havana, Cuba

Gabriela waited in the departures terminal at el Aeropuerto José Martí with her passport and ticket clutched against her chest. Long lines of travelers snaked away from the undermanned ticket windows and security checkpoints. Her empty hand trembled.

"Gabi, you need to be strong for me, okay?" said Yunel, putting his hands on her shoulders. He smiled, but even Gabriela could tell he was forcing it. "When you get nervous, just think how happy Galán will be to see you. You two will be a family again, just like you've always wanted. You're so close. Just do what the men tell you, and everything will be okay. But you need to be tough."

She stared at the little green alligator on his white sneakers and swallowed.

"You have to go now, okay," said Yunel. "You have to get in that line and put your bag through that machine. You have to go now, or else the airplane is going to leave without you."

Gabriela wanted the plane to leave without her. She wanted to get back on the bus to Ciego de Ávila and go back to her life with Tía Teresa.

"Now, Gabi. It's time."

She didn't say anything.

Yunel, no longer smiling, pushed her toward the end of the security line. Gabriela felt like she was in a strange dream. He waited with her until the line split.

"Only ticketed passengers beyond this point," said a beige-uniformed young woman.

Yunel nodded and turned to Gabriela. "You can do this, Gabi. You can do this." He kissed her on the forehead and walked away.

The line continued inching forward. Just as Gabriela was about to duck under the rope and escape, she pictured Galán. Yunel was right—they'd be a family again, just like they were always supposed to be. She just had to be tough. She just had to be tough for Galán.

She picked up her bag and walked toward the man slapping the handheld metal detector against his palm.

27

San Juan, Puerto Rico

Galán shut the windows of his apartment to silence the breeze. The kitten looked at him with his fuzzy ears angled backward—Galán never closed the windows during the day.

"Can you hear me, Yunel?" said Galán into the cell phone. Yesica had taught him how to dial a combination of country codes, area codes, and other codes to sidestep the most onerous long distance fees. "Yunel? Are you there? It sounds like you're a thousand goddamned miles away."

"That's because I am."

Galán couldn't tell if Yunel was laughing, as the connection was just as muffled as it had been several Christmases ago. Galán remembered every word of that trans-Caribbean conversation. Little did he know that he would never hear his mother's voice again.

"Anyway," continued Yunel, "it's done. At least my part is. I saw her go through the security machine and everything. She was on Cubana seventy-eight."

"Yeah, I know. Cubana seventy-eight to Santo Domingo." Galán verified his handwritten itinerary and wiped the sweat from his brow. "How was she when she left?"

"Scared. Shit, I would have been, too. But she did it. Walked right through the damned machine. I waited at José Martí for an hour in case she changed her mind, but she didn't come back out."

Galán swallowed. He didn't know how he felt. "Thank you. I know it wasn't easy."

"No, it wasn't. But like you said, we had no choice."

"Yeah, I know." Galán had tried to reassure himself of that the night before. By the twelfth Medalla, he had more or less succeeded.

"So, I guess she's in your hands now, cousin." Yunel's voice echoed as if he were on the far side of a cave.

"No, not yet." Galán wiped his face again. "Now she's in God's hands."

Yunel started to say something, but the call failed. Galán tossed the cell phone onto his mattress and sat motionless. Rivulets of sweat dripped from his nose and chin.

In his mind, he was sitting next to Gabriela at thirty thousand feet, the claw of Haiti visible through the airplane's window. He held her hand to keep her from getting nervous and pointed out different clouds. There, beyond the wingtip, was a turtle. Below that was a horseshoe. Up ahead, a boot.

Galán didn't move until he felt the kitten pawing his knee.

★

Santo Domingo, Dominican Republic

The Econoline van struggled past a cluster of motorbikes and onto la Autopista Siete. A green plastic rosary swung from the rearview mirror, and the wipers fought weakly against the afternoon rain. The interior smelled of cigarettes and lemon air fresheners.

Gabriela stared out the window at the passing countryside and tin-roofed neighborhoods, squinting to keep her eyelid from twitching. If it weren't for all of the motorbikes, modern cars, and advertising signage, she could have still been in Cuba. When she noticed the driver, a young man with a perfect lineup and a gold chain, looking at her through the rearview mirror, she looked down at her lap.

In the rows between her and the driver were four other Cubans who had been on her flight—a young newlywed couple and two male cousins about her age. They whispered amongst themselves in voices too low for Gabriela to understand. She wondered if they were going on the boat, too. It would be nice to have some friends, but the driver made her too nervous to talk.

An hour later, the driver pulled the van off the highway and into an Esso gas station. A young boy begged for change, and water dripped from the edges of the pumping area's overhang. The driver got out without saying a word and disappeared inside the building.

Gabriela licked her lips and leaned forward. "Excuse me," she said quietly to the other four passengers.

They kept talking.

"Excuse me," she said a little louder, this time with her arms on their seatback.

The four heads turned.

"Are you all going on the boat, too?"

They stared at her before one of the cousins laughed. "No. We just came here for a little vacation."

"Oh. That sounds nice. I'm supposed to be going on a boat."

The married couple smirked, and the two cousins looked at each other and shook their heads. "Are you messing with us?" asked the other cousin, turning back to Gabriela. "Or are you just retarded?"

Everybody laughed but Gabriela. She sunk back into her seat, bowed her head, and squeezed her hands together to keep them from trembling. She remembered how she felt in elementary school when the other kids would torment her during recess on days Galán wasn't around. They would chase her and call her "little monkey."

She bit her lip and tried to imagine that Galán was sitting next to her.

★

Mona Passage

Pat stood below the gun mount on the *Strickland*'s heaving bow, staring at his phone, waiting for the NO SERVICE icon to disappear. The pitching was strong enough to lift him off his feet were it not for his grip on the rail. Stomach churning, he looked out at the pink horizon to restore his equilibrium. He'd never been sea sick before.

The *Strickland* was only two miles west of Aguada. Pat could see the beaches and green hills smattered with civilization.

"Come on," he muttered to himself. He held the phone close to his body in case he was in view of any of the ship's closed-circuit cameras. He didn't need a bunch of questions when he went back inside.

Finally, a lone bar appeared in the upper corner of the screen. He already had Galán's number pulled up. He tapped the CALL icon and wedged himself between the gun mount and superstructure. After two rings, Galán answered.

"Hey! It's me, Pat. I can't talk long."

"What?" asked Galán. "Pat? Is that you? Why are you calling me? Are you home?"

"It's me! Pat! Listen!" He was almost shouting.

"Hello? Pat? Hello? I can't hear a word you're saying."

"You have to call it off!"

"What? Hello? Pat?"

"You have to call it off?"

"Huh? Pat?"

"Goddamnit." Pat ended the call and began typing a text message, afraid that he would lose service any moment. "Cancel it. Not a good time for her." He hit SEND. After a minute of hesitation, the message went through.

Pat took a deep breath and put his phone into his cargo pocket. He watched the swells roll toward him from some storm beyond the horizon until the pitching became too much. Just as he was about to head back inside, he noticed a shadow looming over his shoulder.

"XO? What are you doing out here?" It was Petty Officer Bartlett in an I GOT BOURBON-FACED ON SHIT STREET tank top. He was setting up for a workout on the forward deck.

"What am I doing out here?" said Pat, stammering. He tried to think. "Just checking the bosun hole. I heard there might be some water intrusion down there."

"With your cell phone?"

Pat hoped Bartlett couldn't see him swallow. How long had he been up there watching? "It's dark down in that bilge. Goddamned Tim lost my flashlight."

"Oh, right." Bartlett smiled. "It's okay, sir. You can trust me."

"Trust you with what?"

"Trust me that I won't tell nobody about those nudies you just got." Bartlett's smile widened, a lecherous gleam in his eye. "As long as you share the wealth."

Pat felt some of the tension dissipate from his shoulders and chest. He smiled and shook his head. "I don't think you want to see your mom like that."

"Damn, sir!" said Bartlett, grinning wildly. "That's fucked up!"

Pat forced a laugh and made his way toward the amidships hatch. As soon as he was past Bartlett, his smile disappeared.

☆

Samaná, Dominican Republic

The van snaked its way into the northeastern Dominican town of Samaná just as night fell. The rain had settled into an ambivalent patter, and nobody spoke. The occasional orange streetlight illuminated closed businesses and shuttered homes. Those people who hadn't retired for the day huddled under cover or waded across the partially flooded streets.

The driver turned the van into the Motel el Dorado parking lot and killed the engine. A neon sign bathed the wet pavement in pink. "Wait here," he said, looking at his charges through the rearview mirror. He stepped out and darted toward the closet-like lobby.

Inside the van, the couple and the cousins broke out in conversation. Gabriela tried to listen, but they spoke too fast about subjects she didn't understand. All she wanted to know was where they were and what they were doing, but she didn't want to be made fun of again. After several minutes, she finally tapped the skinnier cousin on his bony shoulder. "What is this place?"

He shook his head at her before turning to the rest of the group. "Is she for real?"

The young wife sniggered. Gabriela wanted to hit her.

"This is the safe house," said the young husband. He was the only one who didn't laugh.

"Thank you." Gabriela wanted to ask more, but she knew it was no use. Plus, all she could think about was her bladder. She had needed to use a bathroom ever since being questioned by the muscular Dominican customs agent at the airport.

The lobby door opened and the driver emerged. With him was an overweight, middle-aged man in a straw hat. The fat man slammed open the sliding door and stuck his head into the van, his eyes lingering on each face. "Let's go," he finally said. "First floor. Number six."

The passengers spilled out with their small bundles of possessions. Gabriela got out last, her eyes searching the fat man's face for any clues as to what was going on.

"The hell?" said the fat man. "What do I look like, your doorman?"

Gabriela put her head down and scuttled after the others. The kid driver opened the hotel room door, and Gabriela was overcome by the stench of sweat and body odor. The driver pushed her over the threshold into the dark room, and she stumbled over somebody's bare foot. A dozen shadowy figures were crammed on and around the two beds in front of a muted television. Gabriela sensed that those awake were staring at her.

"Move," said a voice behind her.

Gabriela found an open patch of carpet in front of the air conditioner. She stepped over sprawled-out limbs and sat down against the humming unit, clutching her backpack between her knees. She didn't dare speak, but instead prayed to la Virgen de la Caridad just like her mother taught her. Picturing the little copper statue they kept above the sink in their Ciego de Ávila home, she told la Virgen that she was scared and asked to be reunited with Galán as soon as possible. When she finished, she made an almost imperceptible sign of the cross.

Looking around the dark room and feeling the pressure in her bladder and the aching in her head, Gabriela had a hard time believing that so much of her journey still remained.

☆

Santurce, Puerto Rico

Galán got out of the cab and jogged to the front door of Bar Punta Cana. He went inside and hustled over to a female bartender who was finishing her lunch. There were no patrons, but he could smell the hookah from the night before.

"What do you want?" she asked, eyeing him warily from beneath false lashes. She didn't appear to be used to customers in such a hurry for their midday drink.

"I need to speak to the owner. To Adonis."

"Sorry." She ran her long fingernails through her hair. "He's not around today."

"Where is he?"

"I don't know." Her brow furrowed. "Who are you?"

"I'm a friend." Galán knew it didn't sound believable. "Can you give me his number?"

"If you were a friend, you'd have his number. So no, you can't have it." She rose from her barstool and threw away the remnants of her meal.

"Fine. Don't give me his number. But can you call him for me?"

"Call him for you? And tell him what?"

"That I need to talk to him about business."

"What business?" She rinsed her hands in the sink. Two butterflies were tattooed on the small of her back.

Galán looked around the bar. The little bit of light that had managed to penetrate the building bounced off of glassware and mirrors. There appeared to be no one else around, but he lowered his voice anyway. "A trip from the Dominican Republic."

"Oh, I don't mess with that," she said, shaking her head. "I don't want anything to do with that. What are you? Police?"

"No. I'm not police."

She studied him. "I didn't think so."

"So, when can I see him? When will he be back? This is important."

"I don't know." She sunk back onto her barstool.

"How do you not know?" said Galán, his voice rising. "Isn't he the goddamned owner?"

"Exactly," she said, opening a stubby brown bottle of Malta India. "He comes and goes on his own schedule."

Galán shook his head.

"Look. Try him at the gym tomorrow. I shouldn't be telling you that, but you seem like a nice guy."

"What gym?"

"Sixto Escobar in Bayamón. He has fighters there."

"Sixto Escobar in Bayamón," said Galán, nodding. "Thank you." He turned and started walking away.

"Just don't tell him it was me that told you."

Galán didn't respond, but kept repeating "Sixto Escobar in Bayamón. Sixto Escobar in Bayamón." According to the handwritten itinerary, he and Adonis should have just enough time to keep Gabriela in the Dominican Republic until they could come up with an alternate plan.

28

Samaná, Dominican Republic

Gabriela sat against the sputtering air conditioner. On her right, a young couple took turns rocking a baby and whispering to each other in a language Gabriela didn't recognize. On her left, a young man who looked as if he were the kid driver's brother napped in the room's only chair, a machete across his lap. Gabriela had thought earlier that his eyes seemed too old for his face.

Shifting her weight, Gabriela grimaced. Her mouth felt like sandpaper, and her abdomen was cramping after all of the hours of having to urinate. She didn't know if she was allowed to get up, and she was too afraid to wake the *machetero*.

"When do they let us use the bathroom?" she asked the young foreign couple.

The man just shrugged his shoulders and continued bouncing the baby on his knee.

"The bathroom. You know, to pee?"

"You! Quiet!" The *machetero* was suddenly awake. He pointed his blade at Gabriela. "You have something to say, you say it to me."

Gabriela braced against the air conditioner and nodded. She could feel the other eyes in the room staring. It reminded her of when she was supposed to recite "los Pollitos" in elementary school. She couldn't remember a single line, a single word. The teacher kept her standing at the front of the class as the other students snickered and mimicked her stutter. It wasn't until she met Galán outside for lunch that she stopped crying.

Galán. She was starting to worry that Yunel had lied to her. She didn't have a lot of confidence that these men, these kids, were going to get her to her brother. They didn't seem like the kind of people he would trust. She felt like a trapped animal, but before the tears began to flow, something else did.

She looked down at the puddle between her legs, and the father next to her signaled to the *machetero*.

"Disgusting bitch," said the *machetero*, standing. He wrenched Gabriela from the ground by her sweatshirt and dragged her across the carpet. She bounced off of the others, eliciting curses. The *machetero* pulled her into the bathroom and dumped her into the rust-stained bathtub. He turned on the shower.

The cold water took Gabriela's breath away. She fumbled with the knob before finally shutting it off.

The *machetero* shook his head and left her soaking in the tub.

Gabriela shivered, the water dripping from her clothing and running down the drain in lazy rivulets. She didn't see any towels. Finally, she sat up and removed her shirt and wrung it out. She was putting it back on when a man she hadn't seen before entered.

The man, whose bald head shone under the bathroom's lone bulb, regarded her briefly before unzipping his fly and urinating into the toilet. He didn't put himself away or flush, but instead turned to Gabriela with his hands on his hips.

Gabriela tried to keep her gaze on her soaked sweatpants. She was still shaking, but no longer just because of the cold.

The man looked over his shoulder through the ajar door. With his sandaled foot, he pushed it closed. He held a stubby finger to his pursed lips, a smile spreading. He approached.

Gabriela wasn't entirely sure what was happening, but she knew it wasn't good. When she felt his fleshy thing bump against her forehead, she looked up. She screamed, raised her wet foot out of the tub, and kicked him. The man fell onto the toilet, and his head bounced against the sink. His face darkened, but before he could get up, the door swung open.

The *machetero* stood there with his blade by his side.

"What the fuck is going on in here?" he said, looking from Gabriela, crying with her shirt partly off, to the bald man splayed on top of the dirty toilet, his pants around his thighs. He pointed his blade at the bald man's face. "What did you do?"

"Nothing," said the bald man, his hands up in front of him. "This whore came on to me. I was just trying to take a piss."

The *machetero* closed the door and locked it. He secured the handle of the blade under his belt. "Really? This retard bitch came onto you?"

The man nodded. Now he was shaking.

"For some reason, I find that hard to believe."

The *machetero* stepped forward and punched the man in the jaw before grabbing him by the back of the shirt and jamming his shiny head into the toilet. After a brief struggle, the *machetero* flushed the toilet, and the bald man choked. When the *machetero* finally let go, the bald man pulled his head out of the water and fell back onto the floor, gasping.

The *machetero* turned to Gabriela, who was so stunned that she was no longer crying. "Put your goddamned shirt on."

She did, albeit backward. The *machetero* dragged her out of the bathroom by the arm. This time, nobody made any noise when she bounced off of them in the darkness.

Gabriela, too scared to pray, shivered and dripped against the air conditioner until the sun came up.

★

Bayamón, Puerto Rico

A mural of the bantamweight Sixto Escobar stared down from the gym's cinderblock exterior. Puerto Rico's first world champion leaned forward, his gloves just below his unafraid chin. He made eye contact with all of the aspiring pugilists and hangers-on who stepped through the door below him.

Once inside the gym, Galán leaned against a vending machine and tried to inconspicuously survey the crowd. A dozen boxers of all sizes toiled under the fluorescent lights. In the elevated ring, a middleweight worked the mitts with a bald trainer in sagging shorts. Galán could feel the compressions, and sweat shot into the air with each blow. Still, the teenager wasn't even breathing hard.

"Follow the jab!" shouted an old man in a New York Yankees hat leaning on the apron. "Don't hold back!"

An electronic bell dinged, and all activity ceased. Galán scanned the room once more, and this time he found Adonis.

The Dominican was leaning against the opposite wall in his customary sleeveless T-shirt, one foot propped up behind him. He returned Galán's stare.

The bell rang again and the thwack of leather on leather began anew. Galán weaved between a boy skipping rope and a girl shadowboxing in front of a sweat-splattered mirror. He apologized to the two contenders, but they were too focused to respond.

"I didn't know you were in the fight game," said a smirking Adonis.

Galán didn't say anything until he was within whispering distance. "We need to talk."

"Then talk."

"Not here. You know what it's about."

"Too bad," said Adonis, "I'm working. You see that kid on the mitts. That kid is an animal. He's going to fuck everybody up. All the way to light heavyweight." He looked at Galán, the corner of his lip creeping up. "Too bad you're a broke Cuban or else you could make a little money off him."

The kid unleashed another combination.

"He looks like a strong fighter. But really, we have to talk."

After regarding Galán as if he were inspecting a dead fly on a windowsill, Adonis finally peeled himself from the wall. Galán followed, as did a fat man in a Miami Marlins jersey. The threesome stepped into a musty locker room, just as a skinny little kid was getting out of the communal shower.

"Move it," said Adonis to the boy.

The kid, without making eye contact, quickly threw on some jeans and darted through the door in bare feet.

"Well?" said Adonis, turning to Galán.

"You remember what I told you? That it would be clear?" said Galán. "Well, it's not clear."

"What's not clear?"

"Mona Passage. The Coast Guard is out there. They weren't supposed to be, but they are."

Adonis stared at him, his expression unchanging. "And?"

"You need to call your partners and call it off. At least for now."

Adonis laughed. He looked to the fat man who was leaning against a locker. "You believe this fucking cocksucker? Telling me how to run my business?"

The fat man snorted.

Adonis looked back at Galán. "Who cares?"

"What?"

"Who cares if there's Coast Guard out there? They're always out there, but they're a bunch of dumbasses, too. And even if they do manage to catch this load, to hell with it. I already got half the money. The other half?" He shrugged. "It's the price of doing business."

Galán didn't say anything.

"There's no shortage of Dominicans, Cubans, and Haitians who are dying to make this trip. I appreciate your concerns, but business is good." Adonis made for the door.

"If you don't care," said Galán, his voice about to break, "then why did you give me a discount?" As soon as the words came out of his mouth, he knew he had made a mistake.

"That's a good fucking question, worm," said Adonis, turning back to Galán. "I had almost forgot about our little deal. I thought you were giving me a sure thing, but now it looks like I was wrong." He took another step forward, and the fat man closed his WhatsApp conversation. "Now it looks like you owe me a thousand dollars."

"That information was good," said Galán through gritted teeth. "I can't control what the Coast Guard does. But I'm telling you, you need to call your people in the Dominican Republic."

"I don't take orders from your kind," said Adonis, inches from Galán's face. "And even if I was a little bitch that was scared of the

Coast Guard, that round has been chambered. The safety's off." He paused, thinking for a moment. "But what I want to know is where you got your information since it was so goddamned good."

"I told you. I got it from a guy in the Coast Guard. A friend of a friend."

"I said I want to know who."

Galán swallowed, unable to hold Adonis's stare. His eyes darted from the showers to a moldy glove on the floor to a pair of purple trunks hanging from a locker. He tried to think of something to say that wouldn't compromise Pat.

"I said I want to fucking know who."

Galán could smell Adonis's foul breath. The fat man in the corner lifted up his jersey as well as his sagging belly to reveal a matte black pistol.

"Why?" asked Galán, finally looking Adonis in the eye. "What difference does it make?"

"Maybe I want to do some research of my own. See if this really was an honest mistake or if you were just bullshitting me." Adonis shook his head. "I should have known. Never trust a worm."

"I'm telling you, I don't know the guy personally. He's just some white boy who comes to my restaurant. One of my waiters sells him coke on the side, and he got me the information in exchange. Maybe the white boy made it up, but I didn't. Why would I bullshit you when it's my sister in that boat?"

Adonis screwed up his face as he contemplated the lie. "Coast Guard doing coke? Your little altar boy ass has friends that deal?"

"I know. I don't like it, but it's true." Galán thought his eyeballs were going to fall out of his skull, but he didn't look away. Just then, the door to the locker room flew open. It was the same boy who had been evicted.

"Didn't I tell you to leave?" yelled Adonis.

"It's Esmilin," said the boy breathlessly. "They think he broke his hand sparring."

"Son of a bitch," said Adonis, pushing past Galán. "I'm coming." When he reached the door, he paused and turned.

"Don't think I'm going to forget that money."

Galán kept his mouth shut.

Adonis opened the door but turned back a second time. "And one other thing, worm. You need to surround yourself with better people."

★

Mona Passage

The *Strickland* was two days into the extension, and all was quiet. The crew had been able to catch up on rest, and Pat was even able to schedule some much needed damage control training. The only problem was how the crew performed during that afternoon's drill. If there really had been a fire in the generator space, they would have lost the ship.

Pat looked at his shipmates, his hands on his hips. They stood around him in firefighting ensembles, roasting beneath the midday sun. "There's no other way to put it. That was straight up piss poor."

A few faces held his stare. Others looked down at the deck or over his shoulder at the sea.

"We're leaving charged hoses unattended. We have no standard phraseology. Nobody knows who the hell is on air . . ." Pat shook his head. "That was just shitty all around." He thought for a moment. "We really should do this again. But what's the point? We're just wasting each other's time." He waved them away. "Go. Get out of here. I'm sure there's a movie on the messdeck that needs watching."

The crew dispersed and began stowing the helmets, extinguishers, and box fans. Everybody except Chief Landis. He just stared at Pat before shaking his head and going back into the pilothouse.

To hell with him, thought Pat. To hell with all of them. He emptied a water bottle onto his head and moved into the shade, trying to collect his thoughts. He knew he should go below and respond to his mom's email, but he didn't know what to say.

How was he supposed to react to the news that Danny wasn't just on pills anymore? How was he supposed to respond when he heard that his brother had taken the Blazer out for a joyride with his blood-alcohol concentration through the roof? Was he supposed to just say that it would all work out? That Danny would finally find peace in prison?

Pat sat down on a mooring bit and stared at the ridges in the nonskid deck. His mom had been right. The army had fixed Danny's back, but that wasn't all that was broken. Danny had been crumbling before Pat's very eyes. And instead of worrying about Danny—his brother who would take a lightning bolt for him—Pat had been worrying about his other brother, and his other brother's sister.

29

Samaná, Dominican Republic

The gauzy morning light had just begun to illuminate Motel el Dorado's room number six when the fat man burst through the door. Gabriela jumped—she didn't know what day it was, let alone the schedule of her guards' comings and goings. As her nerves settled, her stomach began to grumble. Sadly, the fat man didn't have the usual bags of potato chips and cartons of apple juice. Instead, he surveyed the waiting migrants from the doorframe.

"All you Cubans," he said, a toothpick bouncing off his lower lip, "drink, piss, shit. Whatever. We leave in fifteen minutes." He paused. "Quickly!"

The *machetero* stood and snapped open black garbage bags. "You get one and only one. It will be wet out there."

Gabriela's desire to escape the foul hotel room was suddenly overcome by a fear of setting sail with the Dominican smugglers. She remembered again the dream she had in Havana of splashing around in the heaving black water. Her pulse quickened, but she had no choice. Like Yunel said, she had to listen to the men. The men would bring her to Galán.

Gabriela stood, knees shaking, and waited to use the filthy bathroom. When it was finally her turn, she had to hold her breath. The finicky toilet had finally succumbed after days of abuse.

After she finished, Gabriela rejoined her compatriots by the van. The kid driver was back, and he counted the migrants out loud—fifteen—before opening the sliding door. The van sank deeper onto

212

its shocks as each person climbed aboard. Gabriela found a seat in the back and watched through the dirty window as the fat man and scrawny *machetero* mounted an idling motorbike. Looking around the van, she realized that it was the non-Spanish speakers who had remained behind in the motel room. She still didn't know what country they were from.

Unlike the ride from the airport, only a few minutes passed before the kid driver pulled off to the side of a dirt road in the middle of a scrubby forest. The fat man and the *machetero* dismounted and led the group single-file into the brush. Plastic bottles, wrappers, and aluminum cans were scattered about the path. A hundred meters later the trail opened onto a rocky, desolate beach, where the migrants waited in silence.

The sound of the waves reminded Gabriela of the last morning her family had been together, but the wind dried her tears before they could roll down her face.

⋆

San Juan, Puerto Rico

After lying in a state of semiconsciousness, Galán gave up on trying to sleep. His head pounded from the Medallas, and he couldn't stop thinking about where Gabriela might be. He tried to distract himself by watching the morning news on WAPA, but the thought of his sister being alone and scared, her well-being in the hands of criminals, was too much.

As the sun climbed above the neighboring terraces, the morning's first rays of light penetrated the apartment and illuminated the statue of la Virgen de la Caridad. Galán, turning off the television, stared at la Virgen and the three plaster fishermen in the rowboat at her feet. He realized what he needed to do just as the light shifted and the shrine fell back into the shadows.

After showering and donning a clean guayabera, Galán descended the stairs and crossed over to la Plaza de la Barandilla. He passed the municipal garbage workers sweeping up litter in their neon-green shirts and strode through a flock of cooing pigeons. He climbed the two front steps of la Parroquia de San Francisco and opened the deceptively light wooden door.

His intuition had been correct, as there was indeed a morning Mass. At the lectern, a priest, his brown Capuchin hood hanging over the back of his cassock, delivered a subdued homily to a small congregation of elderly, frail women. Galán heard the words but didn't listen. Instead, he breathed slowly and tried to let the surrounding atmosphere, perhaps the presence of God, soak into him. Eventually, he began to pray.

Galán started with a Hail Mary, since that was what he said every night in front of the votive candle. When he finished, he was at a loss for words until he remembered what his mother had taught him in Ciego de Ávila. "Just talk to God like you would to me or Gabi." A one-way conversation, and perhaps nobody was listening, but Galán could still do it.

"Please," he said, surprised at how easily the words flowed. "Please protect her. Please get her here. Please don't let anything happen to her. I promise I will do whatever it takes to repay You if You can just get her here. Please." He listed off all of the ways he would make good on such a debt.

Feeling a hand on his shoulder, Galán looked up, startled. It was the priest, no longer wearing his liturgical robes, but rather a black shirt and Roman collar. The Mass had ended. Galán realized he had fallen asleep before Communion with his forehead on the back of the hard wooden pew in front of him.

"Are you all right?" the priest asked, sitting down next to him.

"With the help of God, I hope so." Galán shared his burden, omitting only the details involving Adonis and Pat.

The priest sighed and looked toward the altar. A crucifix hung in front of a wall painted with three windows opening up to a bucolic landscape. He turned back to Galán.

"You seem like a man of faith," said the priest, his Roman collar pushing gently into his neck with each breath.

"I think so," said Galán. "I hope so."

The priest smiled, his crow's feet deepening. "Well, that's what matters. As it sounds like you already know, the sea can be a frightful place. And that is why Jesus and the Virgin Mary are so often invoked out there, so often seen out there. Their dominion doesn't just stop at land's end."

Galán nodded. Just having somebody acknowledge the pressure that had been suffocating him for the last several weeks helped him breathe easier.

"And I have a feeling," continued the priest, "that this sister of yours is not an insignificant soul in the eyes of Jesus and Mary. I have a feeling that they care about what happens to her."

Galán nodded again. The priest was right. Gabriela was the only truly innocent soul he'd ever known.

"The Lord doesn't make things easy for us. He doesn't send us constant signs. If he did, there would be no struggle in belief. So, it is natural that you are suffering right now. But suffering can be alleviated by prayer. And suffering can be alleviated by putting your trust in God."

Galán nodded again and wiped his nose.

"Have you put your trust in God?" asked the priest.

Galán looked at the back of the pew in front of him. "I guess so." He looked back at the priest. "I don't see what other option I have."

☆

Samaná, Dominican Republic

After what felt like hours of sitting on a rock by the water's edge, Gabriela heard a commotion behind her. The other migrants were standing, and the kid driver directed them down the rickety wooden pier that extended past the surf.

"Wait out there for the captain."

Gabriela followed the other migrants to the end of the pier, where she gingerly sat down on the wet boards. Back on the beach, another young man had joined the kid driver and the *machetero*. This boy wore camouflage pants and a blue Armada Nacional T-shirt, and a black rifle hung from his shoulder. He accepted an envelope from the fat man and walked away, his rifle swinging from side to side.

The fat man and his lieutenants ambled up the pier, the wooden boards creaking. The fat man dropped his own garbage bag and studied the faces of his passengers.

"All right," he said in his baritone. "Before we go, we need to get some things straight. First, I'm the captain. That means what I say is what happens. And if you disagree? Just remember, it's a big ocean." His greasy face broke into a gap-toothed smile.

"Second. If we get stopped, there is no captain. I'm just one of you pieces of shit. Understood?"

A few of the migrants nodded. Gabriela didn't. She couldn't follow his logic.

"And finally, the journey may take a night, or it may take two or three. I know what I'm doing, and I don't take suggestions." He paused. "Any questions?"

Nothing.

"Good." He stepped into a long, low-slung wooden *yola* with a single 150-horsepower outboard motor. *Mi Jeva* was written along the side in faded white paint, and the bow rose upward into a sharp point. The fat man sat down on the rear bench by the tiller, and the stern squatted beneath his heft. He motioned for the migrants to join him.

Gabriela thought the boat would be much larger, but she followed the group aboard nonetheless and found a seat next to the rail. She had no choice now but to remain with the others. How would Galán feel if they arrived without her?

With all of the migrants seated, the *machetero* stepped aboard. He acknowledged neither the migrants nor the fat man as he made his way to the bow. Gabriela didn't dare look him in the eye.

The fat man yanked the ignition cord on the outboard motor. It sputtered briefly but died. He yanked the cord again, and this time the motor caught, emitting a puff of blue smoke.

"And we're off," he said, untying the stern line and tossing it to the kid driver who remained on the pier.

The kid driver caught the line and pushed the *yola* out to sea with his impeccably white sneaker.

Gabriela didn't jump.

★

The fat man guided *Mi Jeva* across the Samaná Bay and past Miches. He kept the *yola* far enough from shore that it was clear of surf and shoals, but close enough that it blended in with the normal traffic of recreational boaters and fishermen. As the sun set behind the *yola*'s bubbling wake, Gabriela could make out the beachside cabanas and bars of Punta Cana. The scene reminded her of a day trip her family had made to Varadero on Cuba's northern coast.

Gabriela remembered how her uncle had saved for months to pay the toll for the tourist bridge, and how crossing it was like crossing into a different country. The hotels were modern and freshly painted, the roads were smooth and well-marked, and the sand was white. There was no trash anywhere, and the cars seemed like they were out of some futuristic movie. She remembered that Galán had found a starfish and had named him Pepe. He would have been their first and only pet, but he dried out on the car ride home.

Gabriela blinked away a tear and shifted her sore backside on the wooden bench.

The afternoon twilight eventually evaporated into blackness, and all that remained of the Dominican Republic was a smattering of lights on the horizon. Gabriela watched them slowly fade into nothingness.

As the ocean expanded around her, Gabriela felt even more trapped and alone than she had back at Motel el Dorado. All she wanted was to be back in Teresa's house. Her aunt was probably clearing the dishes and getting ready to put in her curlers for the night.

The steady whine of the outboard motor suddenly went quiet. Gabriela turned. The silhouette of the fat man rose up in the darkness, and he urinated over the side.

"I suggest you all do the same," he said into the wind. "From here on out, I don't plan on stopping."

The passengers stirred, men supporting women as they squatted over the rail. There was the occasional sound of flatulence. Gabriela looked from face to face for someone to help her. Finally, an older woman grudgingly held Gabriela by the shoulder so she too could relieve herself.

Gabriela had yet to sit down when the motor came back to life. She secured herself to her bench as best she could as the gentle rocking morphed into a pronounced pitching. Within minutes her sweatpants were soaked from the salt spray, and she peeled them away from her skin to keep from getting too cold.

According to a man seated near her, they were finally in the Mona Passage. The ocean currents that wrapped around Hispaniola and Puerto Rico collided here, causing a washing machine–like effect.

A retching noise came from somewhere up forward. A young man leaned over the side, the wind whipping his vomit into the faces of several of the other migrants, two of whom began to vomit themselves. The inboard victim had no choice but to launch the contents of his stomach between his legs and into the gasoline and oil that sloshed around the *yola*'s deck.

Gabriela, watching the filth run back toward her feet, felt her own stomach turn. She looked out at the dark horizon and swallowed. Her breathing had quickened again, and she tried to think of something calming. She tried to picture Galán's apartment, her future home, which she had never seen before. She tried to imagine how safe she would feel going to sleep that first night under the same roof as her brother.

Her breathing slowed.

You just have to get there, she told herself, staring into the darkness beyond the *yola*'s bouncing bow. You just have to get to the other side of this water. The water has to stop somewhere, and that's where you have to get.

30

Mona Passage

Pat leaned against the console and stared out into the blackness of the Mona Passage. He had ninety minutes left until he could hit the rack, and only three watches after that before the *Strickland* would pull into San Juan. Pat didn't want to get his hopes up, but maybe Galán had called the whole thing off. Or maybe the *yola* had darted past the *Strickland* in the dead of night, disgorging its passengers on Mona or the Puerto Rican mainland. Maybe in a few days this mess would be nothing more than a bad memory.

Pat looked over his shoulder. The quartermaster was still behind the gun console, absentmindedly panning the infrared camera back and forth across the horizon for *yolas*. There was nothing to see, however, but the occasional whitecap.

"Why don't you shut the camera down for a little bit?" said Pat, sipping the dregs of his tepid coffee.

"Shut it down, sir?" said the quartermaster. "Don't the captain's night orders say we're in the threat vector? I thought it was supposed to be the migrant five hundred out here?" He laughed at his own joke.

"Yeah, he did. But you're just going to burn out the sensors." It sounded reasonable enough, thought Pat, assuming the quartermaster didn't know more about the camera than he did. "You can keep checking, but only do a sweep every fifteen minutes."

"Roger, sir." The quartermaster flipped the power switch and covered the console with its canvas hood. He finished his can of

Monster and tossed it into the wastebasket. "You mind if I go out for a quick smoke?"

Normally Pat would say no, not on watch, but he knew a cigarette cherry was visible for miles on a moonless night. It couldn't hurt.

☆

 As the *yola* crashed across the dark sea, salt spray soaked the huddled migrants. Gabriela had been shivering for hours, and the cold was all she could think about. She barely noticed when the boat eased to a stop.

The *machetero* clambered to the stern and conferred with the fat man. They looked up toward the sky, Gabriela following their gaze. Against the backdrop of stars and a faint band of the Milky Way, a blinking white light moved in a lazy arc.

Just a few moments of looking into the night sky, combined with the side-to-side rocking of the adrift boat, caused Gabriela's stomach to turn. She thrust her head between her knees and vomited into the shallow slop. Voices rose in protest, but the others were too exhausted to get overly upset. Somebody did grab her by the collar and throw her against the rail of the *yola*, bruising her sternum, but it was too late. She only dry heaved into the black waves.

By the time Gabriela sat back up, the rest of the *yola*'s occupants had noticed the flashing white light.

"That's an American spy plane," said a man one row ahead. "It's over. I knew it would end like this."

"No way," said one of the cousins from the airport van ride. "Why would the military or the police fly with their lights on? That's some kind of passenger plane. Or maybe a satellite."

"A satellite? What the hell do you know about satellites?"

"Enough!" yelled the fat man.

Nobody spoke. The *machetero* climbed back to his spot on the bow, his blade clanging against a wooden bench as he moved.

"Now we sit and wait," said the fat man finally. "They can't see us if we leave no wake."

Gabriela put her face in her hands. She didn't care what the flashing light was. She just wanted to keep moving so that the seasickness would go away, so that they would get to the other side of the water. She just wanted it to be over.

★

Fifteen minutes remained before watch relief, and Pat could hear the oncoming bridge team bumping around on the messdeck below. The familiar sound of the coffee pot being changed and the toaster being charged had a Pavlovian effect, and Pat was suddenly overcome with weariness.

Pat closed his eyes, the blackness of the horizon giving way to the darker blackness of his eyelids. He rested like that for several seconds until he heard a faint transmission from the radio. He opened his eyes and turned the volume knob to the right.

"Cutter *Strickland*, this is Maddog Six," said the communications officer from the airplane providing aerial coverage of the Mona Passage. "We're approaching bingo here. Anything you want us to check out before we return to base? We can't stray too far from your position on account of fuel."

"Maddog Six, Cutter *Strickland*," said Pat into the handheld microphone. "Negative. We don't have any contacts visually or on radar." The only light he could see through the pilothouse windows was the Mona tower to starboard, and the radar display was completely black with the exception of sea clutter.

"Good copy," said the voice from thousands of feet overhead. "We'll do one more sweep before going wheels down in Aguadilla."

"Roger. Have a safe trip home. *Strickland* out." Pat racked the microphone and rubbed his eyes.

The quartermaster came back into the pilothouse along with a whoosh of humid air. "I miss anything, sir?"

"Nothing," said Pat, glancing back at the quartermaster's dark silhouette, "but that must have been one hell of a smoke break." He brightened the electronic chart display—they were approaching the edge of the navigational box that the captain had uploaded before going to sleep. Pat switched the cutter out of autopilot and grabbed the miniature helm lever. "Coming around."

"Aye," said the quartermaster, reaching for the overhead grab rail.

Pat pushed the helm to a rudder angle of thirty degrees starboard, and the flashing light on Mona drifted across the front windows of the pilothouse. As the cutter momentarily went beam to the swells, it rocked heavily from side to side. Pat gripped the wooden rail affixed to the console and chuckled as dishware clattered off the messdeck tables below. He knew by the particular sequence of curse words which engineer had lost his bowl of Lucky Charms.

A few minutes later, the radio crackled again. "Cutter *Strickland*, Maddog Six."

"This is Cutter *Strickland*," said Pat, wondering what they wanted now. The aircrew should have been on their final approach to Aguadilla with nothing on their minds other than which breakfast sandwich they would order at the Boquerón Bakery. Or maybe they would get *quesitos*? The thought of the sweet, crunchy fried dough made Pat's stomach grumble.

"Cutter *Strickland*, Maddog Six." The aircraft's communications officer sounded as if he were debating whether to use a pitching wedge or a nine iron. "We got something on our surface radar. Small contact. We're going to drop down to get a better look."

Pat's pulse quickened. You've got to be kidding me. There was no way.

"*Strickland*, Maddog Six. Did you copy my last?"

Pat swallowed and licked his lips. "Affirmative. You can pass latitude and longitude when you have it. We'll be standing by for intercept if it doesn't check out."

"Roger."

Pat racked the microphone. "No way," he said again, this time out loud.

31

Mona Passage

After an hour of bobbing in the confused chop with no further airplane sightings, the fat man finally twisted the *yola*'s throttle. The boat surged forward and the bow rose, levitating those crammed onto the forward-most bench. Gabriela, her stomach now empty, was thankful to be moving again, and the rushing air dried the sweat from her clammy face.

Two rows in front of Gabriela, the *machetero* reached into a garbage bag and handed out tins of Vienna sausage. Gabriela wasn't hungry, but she had learned over the previous week to not refuse food. After discarding the razor-sharp lid over the *yola*'s side, Gabriela dumped the slippery pieces of pork into her mouth. She had been told to conserve her water bottle for as long as possible, but the saltiness was too much.

As the *yola* bounced forward toward the ever-advancing horizon, Gabriela once again lost track of the passage of time. Instead, she just focused on surviving each moment. The only breaks in the relentless pounding came when the fat man would check his handheld GPS—obscuring its green glow with his ample belly—and slightly adjust course. Gabriela was convinced by now that this man and her brother couldn't possibly be friends, even if Yunel had said to trust this unfriendly ogre.

The unceasing wind, sea spray, and engine noise dulled Gabriela's senses until she retreated into a state of semiconsciousness—the ride was too rough for her to sleep. She gripped the wood rail with one hand and the bench with the other as her mind traveled back and forth between foggy recreations of Ciego de Ávila and Galán's mysterious home.

It felt good to finally be far, far away from the Mona Passage.

✶

Pat held the sound-powered phone to his ear, his knees shaking. As he waited for the captain to wake up, he thought about how he could stall so as to give the *yola* a head start to Mona Island.

But that's crazy, he tried to reassure himself. These migrant ventures happen almost every day. It's not Galán's sister out there. There's no way.

"Yeah?" The captain's hoarse voice brought Pat back to the moment.

"Good morning, sir." Pat tried to keep his voice steady. "It's XO on the bridge. The plane spotted a target fifteen miles west of us. It looks like a *yola* with about a dozen people aboard."

There was silence as the captain digested the information, his mind perhaps still trapped in a dream. "Did the *yola* counter-detect the plane?"

"I'm not sure. It's heading southeast toward Mona."

"Roger, XO. I'll be right up. Set the bill."

Pat hung up the phone.

"Should I do it, sir?" asked the quartermaster. He was standing expectantly next to the alarm panel with the microphone in his hand.

Pat didn't say anything. His thoughts were racing in different directions. What if he really ended up interdicting Galán's sister? How would he tell his neighbor? What if she somehow got hurt in the pursuit? What if she or one of the smugglers knew about him?

"Sir, should I do it?" asked the quartermaster, louder this time.

"Yeah," said Pat, trying to bring himself back to reality. "Go ahead."

The quartermaster flipped a switch and a shrill siren rang throughout the dark, sleeping ship. "Now set the migrant bill, set the migrant bill. There will be a small boat brief on the bridge in zero five minutes. Now set the migrant bill."

As soon as the quartermaster put the microphone back into its holster, doors and hatches opened and closed in the bowels of the ship. Pat bent forward and checked the *yola*'s most recent position on the electronic chart. If he came to port thirty degrees, the *Strickland* would cut off the migrant vessel well before Mona.

Just as Pat put his hand on the rudder lever to make the turn, Galán's shrine with the votive candle and two photographs flickered across his mind. Pat let go. By maintaining course and speed, the gap between the *Strickland* and *yola* would only widen.

Pat put his hands in his pockets and looked into the darkness behind him to see if anybody was watching him. The quartermaster was distracted with the gun camera and the engineer was getting the offline engine warmed up. Otherwise, the pilothouse was empty.

Every minute helped.

☆

From directly overhead, a roar disturbed Gabriela's reverie. She jumped from the shock, and her foot stomped into the filth below. Nastiness sprayed against her leg and the legs of the man in front of her. Against the celestial patchwork, Gabriela saw the black silhouette of a large airplane flying at a low altitude. It lumbered toward the horizon before circling back. This time its lights weren't on.

The *yola* accelerated, and Gabriela lurched backward. Luckily for her, she didn't fall off her bench into the foul mess like some of her fellow passengers. As she pulled herself upright, the fat man began yelling instructions at the *machetero*, who had removed his knife from his belt. Gabriela couldn't make out what they were saying, because just then the airplane came roaring back for a second pass. Gabriela thought that if she jumped, she could touch the plane's dark belly.

Gabriela's nausea returned, so she lowered her eyes to the horizon. For the first time, it wasn't completely dark. Instead, directly beyond the bow, a white light flashed. Maybe that was where the water ended. Digging her fingernails into the *yola*'s soft wood, Gabriela willed the flashing light closer.

☆

San Juan, Puerto Rico

The air conditioner hummed in Galán's bedroom. He lay sprawled beneath his sheets, his face twitching. The orange kitten slept between his legs.

Behind his closed eyes, he was back at Varadero, where the tourists spent their convertible pesos. He stood in the clear water fifty feet from the white sandy beach, and the sun beat down on his bare shoulders. He heard shouting. He turned and saw a girl standing in the water, holding out a starfish.

It was Gabriela.

Overcome with happiness, Galán tried to yell to his sister, but the words wouldn't come out. His tongue rebelled against his brain, and his lungs seemed incapable of generating the breath necessary to make any kind of sound. Galán continued wading, but he wasn't getting any closer to Gabriela, who continued smiling at him with her starfish.

Feeling like he was in quicksand, Galán looked down at his feet through the clear water. He concentrated so hard on synchronizing his steps that he began to sweat. Right. Then left. Then right. But within seconds, he was all tangled up again. He looked up toward Gabriela, but she was no longer holding the starfish. Instead, she had in her arms the orange kitten. He looked terrified of being dropped into the water.

Galán heard a voice from the beach. He turned and saw Pat in his white dress uniform. Pat was sitting on the sand drinking a Medalla, waving at Galán. Galán wanted to tell Pat to stand up, that the sand would dirty his uniform, but again no words came. Pat lifted his beer in a toast.

Galán, still struggling against the thick, heavy ocean, turned back toward Gabriela. She was gone, though. All he saw was the kitten running across the surface of the water toward the beach.

"Gabi! Gabi!" he tried to yell. But yet again, the words wouldn't come.

Galán woke up, a hoarse wind emanating from his lungs. The orange kitten scampered across the bedsheets, overcome by a nocturnal burst of energy. Galán finally stopped struggling when he realized where he was.

Galán reached for his phone but ended up knocking an empty bottle of Ron de Barrilito from the bedside table. It landed heavily on the floor but didn't break. The kitten shot from the room and sought cover under the couch.

Galán waited for his heart to stop pounding. He held the phone above his face and tapped its screen with his finger, the brightness casting a murky white glow. It was just after four in the morning.

Still no word.

32

Mona Passage

"Ready in the boat!" yelled Chief Landis.

"Ready in the boat, aye!" responded Fireman Jackson from the *Strickland*'s aft deck, yellow hard hat perched precariously on his shaved head. He leaned down and pulled the quick-release cable, sending the interceptor sliding backward into the cutter's violent wake.

"Dude, you shot last time," said Wallace over the crew communication system. "It's my turn, and we all know it."

"Yeah, I shot last time," said Martínez. "That's because the last time you shot, it took four slugs before you hit that Mercury outboard. The days of taking turns are over. Am I right or am I right?"

"Shut. The. Fuck. Up," said Chief Landis, pointing the bow toward the *yola*'s last reported position. "You two are worse than my goddamned kids." He pushed the throttle forward, the roar of the engine mixing with the rushing wind.

"Come on, XO," said Martínez, undeterred. "You agree that I'm shooting, right?"

Pat said nothing. He was too focused on times, speeds, and distances. His stalling tactic on the bridge had only lasted a few minutes since Tim—his relief—had quickly noticed Pat's supposedly honest mistake. The young ensign had the cutter thrashing through the swells toward the *yola* before Pat had even donned his bulletproof vest. Whatever head start Pat had given the migrants quickly diminished.

Pat glanced down at the electronic chart and wiped away the beads of salt water. It was hard to read the screen with all of the jolting, but he finally managed to put the cursor in the right place.

Only two miles to intercept.

Pat dimmed the display and gripped the handle welded to his seat. His pulse quickened. Not good.

"Now listen up," said Chief Landis. "The plan is to get as close as we can before going overt. Have your weapons drawn when I say so . . ."

Pat wasn't listening. Instead, he was too focused on trying to harness his racing, disjointed thoughts—thoughts fueled by anxiety, exhaustion, and caffeine. He started mouthing the words of the Our Father. Rather than pray for safety, though, he asked God something else.

Please. Please don't let it be her.

★

The *yola* slowed for the first time since being buzzed by the airplane. Gabriela stared at the white light that flashed just above the dark horizon and tried to figure out how much farther they had to go. She couldn't tell.

"You, with the red hat," said the captain from the stern. "Come back here."

Gabriela pressed herself against the rail to allow a corpulent, middle-aged male migrant to clamber past. She turned and watched as the captain made room on the bench next to him. The overweight migrant sat, and he and the captain looked like two unhappy brothers squeezed onto a love seat. The captain grabbed the migrant's hand and jammed it onto the tiller's throttle grip.

"Whatever I say," said the captain, "you do. And don't screw it up. Because if the Americans arrive, you're the captain." He removed a red ball cap from the migrant's bald head and tossed it into the heaving sea. "Do you understand me?"

The conscript nodded.

"Good," said the captain. "Now aim for that goddamned light."

The other man nodded again. He pushed his glasses up his wet nose and twisted the throttle.

Gabriela didn't understand the change, but she didn't care either. She turned back toward the white light in the distance that marked the finish line of her journey and pictured Galán standing below its powerful beam. Maybe his kitten would be with him, she thought, as she wiped salt water from her eyes. Maybe this would all be over soon. For the first time since leaving Havana, Gabriela allowed herself to believe.

★

Chief Landis kept the bow pointed into the waves and the engine at idle speed. The interceptor bobbed up and down as the swells passed below the aluminum hull. Pat scanned the horizon through a night-vision scope, hoping not to see anything. If he did, he certainly wasn't going to speak up.

"Got 'em," said Wallace, rendering Pat's resolution moot. "Off to starboard. Maybe five hundred yards. Tracking toward Mona."

Pat felt a sinking sensation in his stomach. Of course, he thought. The one time you don't want to find a boat, you find it immediately. Like a reverse Murphy's Law. He aimed his scope off to the right, and sure enough, there it was. The low-slung *yola* barely poked above the waves, but its ghostly rooster tail of prop wash was impossible to miss through the green lens.

"Vector me in," said Chief Landis. As a coxswain, he wasn't authorized to use night vision.

"Come five degrees to starboard," said Wallace.

Chief Landis turned the bow slightly to the right and came up in speed.

"Good. Hold that."

Chief Landis continued to push the throttle forward.

"Five more to starboard," said Wallace. "Perfect."

The slow breathing technique Pat had used before high school football games did little to slow his racing heart.

"I see it now," said Chief Landis, pushing the throttle the rest of the way forward. "Hold on back there because I'm about to show you how an old man drives."

Pat slapped himself across the cheek.

"You okay up there, XO?" asked Martínez.

Pat didn't say anything to Martínez, but he did have some words for himself: stop being a bitch and do your job. Galan's sister wasn't going to be on this particular *yola*, and even if she were, it wasn't his problem. He'd only given Galán patrol dates—he'd never made any promises.

The pounding in Pat's chest subsided.

"I'm moving in," said Chief Landis, turning the helm.

Pat wiped his protective goggles and stared into the darkness. The *yola* was nothing but a black silhouette bouncing across a dark gray horizon.

"Cutter *Strickland*," said Pat, keying his microphone. "We're on scene with the target of interest. Position is as follows. One eight decimal one zero degrees north. Zero six seven decimal zero five degrees west. How copy?"

"Good copy. *Strickland* standing by."

Cutting the distance to fifty yards, Chief Landis moved the darkened interceptor into pursuit position just outside the *yola*'s wake. Since they were headed into the seas, the ride became even more turbulent, and salt spray shot over the bow. Pat could tell that they hadn't been counter-detected because the overloaded *yola* continued to crash forward through the waves in a straight, unconcerned line.

"I think it's about that time," said Chief Landis, reaching his free hand to the instrument panel on his console.

"Do it, Chief," said Pat, verifying that his thigh holster hadn't slid around his soaked leg. Wallace tightened his helmet chinstrap, and Martínez examined his shotgun.

They were ready.

With the flip of a switch, their small patch of ocean flashed blue and rang loud with the high-pitched wail of the siren.

*

Gabriela gripped the wooden gunwale so hard her forearm ached. It was all she could do to keep from being ejected. She had no idea who the men were in the other boat with the flashing lights and loud siren, but she knew that they were trying to stop the *yola*. They weren't having any success though, as the new fat man at the tiller kept *Mi Jeva* surging ahead.

"If anybody moves, you slice their ass!" yelled the captain to the *machetero*. His words were barely audible over the rushing wind and screaming engines. "You know how this goes!"

The *machetero* nodded.

In the faint, predawn light, Gabriela could see the panic in the eyes of her fellow passengers. Their fear caused the pounding beneath her soaked T-shirt to grow even stronger. Desperate for escape, Gabriela willed closer the flashing white light and flat black landmass that rose above the sea.

"They're going to kill us!" yelled a woman in the row behind Gabriela, struggling to be heard over the engines and the wind. "For the love of God, please stop! The Americans are going to kill us!"

Gabriela turned and looked past the woman toward the powerful orange boat. Some of the men aboard held long black guns.

"Those pussies aren't going to do shit!" yelled the captain, his eyes fixed on Mona's flashing light. "So shut the fuck up and don't move unless you want the knife!"

The woman, still wailing, made the sign of the cross. The *machetero* climbed over a bench, shoving several of the migrants out of his way, and punched her in the temple without warning. She slumped forward, and the man traveling with her yelled in protest. The *machetero* punched him as well. Blood poured from the man's nose.

Gabriela looked away, careful to avoid the *machetero*'s attention. She didn't know if she was more scared of him or the men in the orange boat with the guns. Or the swirling black water. She squeezed her eyes closed and tried to survive each individual second until she could reach the other side of her living nightmare.

★

Pat heard the cutter hailing them over the radio. "Go ahead," he said, blocking the wind from his microphone.

Tim was barely audible. "District Seven has granted a statement of no objection for warning shots and disabling fire."

They were a go. Pat checked the electronic chart once more—the shoal water off of Mona was quickly approaching. Based on the remaining distance and the speed of the two boats, they had ten minutes before they would run aground—just enough time to compel compliance.

"You ready back there, Martínez?" asked Chief Landis, his voice calm.

"Been ready, Chief." Martínez loaded the last of the pyrotechnic rounds into the shotgun.

Chief Landis nudged the throttle forward, bringing the interceptor parallel with the overmatched *yola*. Every flash of the blue strobe light illuminated a dozen staring faces.

Martínez shouldered the shotgun and sighted in. "On target."

"Batteries release."

There were two quick pops, and the pyrotechnic rounds exploded into little golden fireworks just off the *yola*'s bow. The rickety wooden boat didn't stop, though, but merely swerved away in a serpentine pattern. Chief Landis turned the helm hard to port and crossed the *yola*'s wake.

Pat switched on a handheld spotlight. If he could identify the *yola* operator, the prosecutors in Puerto Rico could press human-smuggling charges. Pat narrowed his search to two large men sitting near the tiller. He would need to do better, however, if the government was going to meet the "beyond a reasonable doubt" burden of proof.

"XO, we're not about to tear the bottom off this boat, are we?" asked Chief Landis. "Mona is getting pretty goddamned close."

Pat zoomed in the display on the electronic chart. Just as he was moving the cursor to verify how much safe water they had, the *yola* slowed to a stop.

Chief Landis pulled back on the throttle, keeping a distance between the two boats.

"What the hell is this?" asked Martínez.

"They got machetes!" yelled Wallace. "Somebody's waving one around."

A metallic glint flashed in the air above the migrants. Pat didn't bother drawing his pistol. The handgun wouldn't be accurate from that distance, and the *machetero* was surrounded by innocent people. The floodlight was more useful.

Martínez yelled over the loudhailer in Spanish for the man with the machete to throw his weapon into the water. The man didn't listen, though, as the blade remained suspended overhead. With all of the engines puttering at idle speed, Pat could hear the terrified screaming.

"Listen up," said Chief Landis, moving his goggles from his eyes to the front of his helmet. "I'm going to make an approach. Nobody goddamn shoot unless I say so."

Pat fixed the floodlight on the *yola* as Chief Landis slowly drew the interceptor closer. Wallace and Martínez aimed their guns.

The outboard migrants shielded their faces from Pat's blinding light. All except one. It was a woman's face, and she stared right back at him.

"You've got to be kidding me," said Pat.

"What's that, sir?" asked Chief Landis. "Are you good with the plan or not?"

Pat didn't respond. All he could focus on was the female migrant with the graying hair and agape mouth. And vacant looking eyes. For the second time that night, he pictured the photograph next to the votive candle on Galán's dresser.

The face was older, but it was her.

Pat closed his eyes. Maybe his mind was playing tricks on him. After all, he hadn't slept in twenty-four hours. But when he opened them, Gabriela was still there, not more than ten yards away.

Suddenly, the machete came slashing down into the crowd. A body went overboard, and the *yola* lurched forward, motor whining.

Chief Landis gunned the interceptor in response, slamming Pat against the back of his seat.

"XO, call the cutter!" yelled Chief Landis. "Person in the water!"

Pat wasn't listening. All he could see in his mind's eye was Gabriela's stunned face.

"Christ! Wallace, you do it!"

"Roger."

Chief Landis maneuvered the interceptor toward the floating bulk, and Martínez pulled the soaked body aboard. Salt water and blood poured onto the deck and ran out through the scuppers. The left side of the man's face flopped from his temple to his chin like uncooked skirt steak. He moaned, pushing the skin uselessly against his jaw.

Pat didn't say anything. Or do anything. He felt like he was watching a strange movie.

"Strap him in," said Chief Landis. "And bandage his face back on. Quickly!" He didn't wait for Martínez and Wallace to secure the migrant in the extra seat before coming back up to full speed.

"Sir!" yelled Wallace, shaking Pat by the shoulder strap of his body armor. "I need the first aid kit!"

Pat turned and stared at him blankly.

"It's in your seat!" He shook Pat again before slapping his helmet.

The reverberation in Pat's skull brought him back to reality. He undid his seatbelt, stood, and extracted the green medical kit from under the cushion. His hands shook.

In less than a minute, Wallace bandaged the man's face, but blood still poured out of the seams. The migrant continued moaning but managed to stay upright as Martínez strapped an orange life jacket around his sopping torso.

Thanks to Chief Landis's aggressive driving, they were already back alongside the *yola*, Pat looked down at the digital chart—less than half a mile separated the two boats from the rocky cliffs of Mona. The squat, smooth plateau had taken on a green, three-dimensional, textured appearance in the burgeoning dawn.

"Martínez, get the rifle ready for disabling fire," said Chief Landis, his voice shaking. "These motherfuckers aren't making it. No fucking way."

Pat felt like the only thing keeping his pounding heart from shooting out of his chest was his body armor. Two well-placed rounds from Martínez's M16 into the *yola*'s outboard would ensure that the *machetero* would spend years behind the concertina wire in Guaynabo. He deserved that fate.

But then Pat pictured Gabriela's face. And Galán's. His neighbor pleaded with him. "Don't do it, Pat. Please, please don't do it."

Pat shook his head.

"On target," said Martínez, staring through the rifle's iron sights.

"No," said Pat, breaking his silence. "No! Avast!" He could see Galán nodding with encouragement.

"What?" said Chief Landis. "The beach is right there!"

Pat tried to come up with a reason. He needed to tell them something. Something believable. "We're not doing it," he said, buying time. "No disabling fire."

"What the fuck?" said Chief Landis. "Martínez, tell me when you're on target."

"There's too many people," said Pat. "We'll hit a migrant."

"It's an easy shot! It's flat-ass calm!"

Chief Landis had a point. They were now in Mona's protective lee and the sea state was like rolling glass.

"Martínez!" yelled Chief Landis, loud enough to be heard without the headsets. "You still on target?"

"We're not doing it!" yelled Pat.

Chief Landis ignored him. "Martínez, are you on target or are you not on target? Talk to me!"

Martínez had been looking back and forth between Pat and Chief Landis. They both outranked him. He muttered something under his breath and sighted back in, salt water dripping from the rifle barrel. "On target."

"Who's the mission commander on here?" said Pat. "I'm the mission commander. And we're not doing it!"

"Batteries release, Martínez!" said Chief Landis.

"Do not shoot, Martínez!" said Pat.

Martínez disengaged the safety and placed his gloved finger on the trigger. The beach was so close that Pat could make out the breaking surf. The *yola* was only fifteen feet away from the interceptor, and the migrants and *machetero* stared.

So did Gabriela.

Without realizing what he was doing, Pat reached forward across Chief Landis's lap and yanked the red kill switch out of the console. The engine went dead, and the interceptor's stern lifted as it was overtaken by its own wake. The *yola* broke ahead, its occupants watching in apparent disbelief.

Chief Landis, who had been too focused on positioning the interceptor for disabling fire to notice what Pat had done, frantically checked the gauges on the console. The fuel state, battery condition, and engine temperature were all fine.

"What the hell is going on here?"

Wallace pointed at the red kill switch sitting impotently on the deck.

Chief Landis looked up at Pat, who held his stare.

"Un-fucking-real," said Chief Landis before picking up the kill switch and plugging it back in.

By the time he had the engine running, though, the *yola* was bouncing into the surf.

In one motion, Chief Landis ripped off his helmet, goggles, and headset and slammed them against the deck. The plastic headset broke in two, and one of the foam earpieces bounced into the water.

Wallace unfastened his seatbelt and removed his helmet. Martínez pulled out a cigarette and lit it with a shaking hand. The bleeding migrant in the aft seat moaned, his face upturned to the bluish-gray sky.

The *yola* made landfall and slid to a stop in the sand. The occupants spilled out and darted into the undergrowth and palm trees.

Wet foot. Dry foot.

Chief Landis shook his head and turned to Pat with his piercing blue eyes. "You're going to have to answer for this, McAllister. I swear to God you will."

Pat said nothing, staring past Chief Landis toward the beach.

The migrants were already gone.

Pat unbuckled his helmet, tossed it to the deck, and took a drink of water. To hell with Chief Landis, he thought. To hell with all of them. And to hell with the consequences.

You know what you did and why you did it.

33

Mona Island, Puerto Rico

Gabriela huddled with the others beneath a canopy of palm fronds and watched the day break. The young married couple cried softly. The two male cousins tried to convince an older man that they really had done it, that this deserted island was a part of Puerto Rico and thus a part of the United States. The woman whose husband had been slashed and jettisoned sat apart from the group, her frozen face bruised and her eyeball bloody. The *machetero* and captain squatted on their heels and spoke in hushed voices.

Despite all the conversations, Gabriela could only focus on her parched throat. The seasickness had worsened her dehydration, and she looked from person to person for a jug of water. Of those few people that still had one, none were willing to share with the strange woman who was traveling alone. Only one man even deigned to make an excuse, saying that he wasn't sure how long it would be until the lone park ranger would rescue them.

After an hour of resting, the *machetero* stood and walked to the edge of the beach, where he buried his blade in the sand. He and the captain then stripped themselves of their outer clothing and buried those soggy items as well. They were refugees, for now at least, just like Gabriela.

The captain stood in front of the group in Adidas basketball shorts and soiled V-neck undershirt, his hands on his hips. "Unless you want to die in this jungle," he said, his voice less angry than before, "the journey continues. It's time to move. Let's go."

Gabriela and the others stood. Her joints ached, but the stiffness didn't compare to the pain in her tailbone or the chafing between her legs. She walked gingerly to minimize the rubbing of her soaked and salty sweatpants against her raw skin.

The group penetrated the forest and found a sandy path marked by discarded packages of food, empty bottles of water, and soiled clothing. They followed it beneath chirping green parrots until they came face to face with a towering rock wall.

The *machetero* found a slippery foothold and began climbing. The others followed. Refusing to die of dehydration in that beautiful jungle, Gabriela inched upward hand over hand until blood trickled from her palms and down her wrists. From her girlhood experiences climbing the ceiba tree in front of the Catholic church, she knew better than to look down.

Just when Gabriela thought her shoulders would give out, she reached a crevice in the rock face. She pulled herself in and rested on her hands and knees, trying to catch her breath.

"Let's go, woman," said one of the male cousins below. "You're not the only one dangling from this wall."

Gabriela stood, still panting. Using the wet rock surfaces to her left and right for support, she continued the climb, her hands leaving bloody prints. Instead of thinking about her desperate thirst, Gabriela focused on a seabird that circled in the blue sliver of sky, its wings undulating in the whistling breeze.

Gabriela finally emerged from the crevice and collapsed like the others onto a field of rustling waist-high grass. Her legs and arms shook. She waited for the pain to recede from her spent muscles as the morning sun and brisk breeze dried her skin and clothing.

Upon hearing the sound of a plastic bottle being opened, Gabriela sat up. The captain gulped loudly before dumping the remaining water over his head. Gabriela thought he was crazy until she saw that he had a second bottle tucked into his pocket. She stuck out her hand because her mouth was too dry to speak. The captain only smiled. For the second time since leaving Cuba, Gabriela wanted to inflict pain on another person. She laid back down and cried.

Where was Galán? He was supposed to be here. He would have given her water.

Gabriela closed her eyes and dreamt that Galán was filling glass after glass of water and lining them up on Tía Teresa's kitchen table. Every time Gabriela reached for one, he would push her hand back and smile like the fat man.

"And now," said a raspy voice, waking Gabriela. "What do we do now?"

She looked and saw that it was the imposter captain speaking, his eyes bloodshot. His bald head was red from the climbing sun.

"Now," said the real captain, reclining on his elbows. "Now, we wait to get found."

Get found, thought Gabriela. That would be nice. But what was nicer was water. She closed her eyes and returned to her dream. She reached for another full, sweating glass, only to have her hand pushed away by Galán. He smiled a strange smile. She wanted to ask him why he was hurting her like this, but her mouth was too dry to speak.

☆

San Juan, Puerto Rico

Galán felt a tugging on his nose. He opened his eyes to find the kitten gently biting him. Galán picked up his roommate by the scruff of the neck and deposited him on the floor.

Sunlight pierced through the slats in the storm shutters. His head pounding, Galán staggered into the kitchen and filled a glass with water. There were more empty beer cans in the trash than he remembered.

According to the microwave clock, it was five past nine.

Galán checked his phone—he had six missed calls from Sefora. Galán remembered that he had the only key to la Fonda del Ciego.

Shit.

Still cursing, Galán showered and dressed. The kitten, intrigued by Galán's frantic movements, watched him from underneath a pile of laundry on the closet floor. As Galán pulled a wrinkled pink shirt over his head, his gaze caught the faces of Gabriela and Josefina staring back at him from the shrine. He walked over to the dresser and picked up the statue of la Virgen de la Caridad.

"Please. Please. Just get her here. Just make this end." He set down the statue, put two fingers to his lips, and pressed them against the photo of Gabriela. "I know you can do this, Gabi. I'll see you soon."

★

Mona Passage

Pat's alarm went off. Groaning, he pulled back the rack curtain and silenced it. It took him a moment to realize where he was, as he'd only been asleep for three hours. He swung his feet onto the carpeted deck and stumbled into the shower. The sea state had picked up, and he had to use one hand to steady himself. It wasn't until the hot water sprayed onto his face and sore shoulders that the night before replayed itself in his mind.

Chief Landis was right. Somehow, someway, Pat would have to answer for what he had done.

The midmorning messdeck was empty, so at least Pat could enjoy a banana and a cup of bitter coffee in peace. When he finished, he took a deep breath and climbed the ladder to the bridge.

Other than abruptly ending their debate about Cam Newton and Drew Brees, the watch team didn't acknowledge Pat's presence. Instead, the conning officer and quartermaster began cleaning the windows, and the engineer disappeared to do a round in the engine room.

Refusing to give his shipmates the satisfaction of icing him off the bridge, Pat sat down at the gun console and stared out at the fat cumulus clouds hanging just above the horizon. Out of the corner of his eye, he noticed the conning officer put away his Windex and pick up the sound-powered telephone. Pat couldn't hear the hushed words.

A moment later, the captain appeared at the top of the ladder and motioned for Pat to join him outside.

"What happened last night?" asked the captain, closing the pilothouse door behind him. He had circles under his eyes, and his face looked more concerned than angry. "People are saying things."

Pat held the captain's gaze. He thought he would be more nervous than he was. Maybe he was just too exhausted. "I didn't feel comfortable with disabling fire," he finally lied.

"Yeah? But why?" asked the captain, his brow furrowed. "You guys were only doing fifteen knots. It was flat. That was nothing new to you or Chief or Martínez." He began to take a sip of his coffee but decided against it. "From what Chief says, you weren't yourself."

Pat could tell by the way the captain shifted his gaze that Chief Landis had probably said something slightly more colorful. He could only imagine what, though. Pat turned his head and watched the *Strickland*'s wake shoot off toward the horizon. He didn't know what to say.

"Was it because of the machete?" asked the captain. "That's what Chief thought."

Pat kept his eyes on the foaming wake. The blood had meant nothing to him, not after seeing Galán's sister. There had only been so much his mind could process.

But now Pat realized that the machete was a gift.

"Yeah, that didn't help, sir." Pat looked down at his scuffed boots. He tried to sound affected without overdoing it. "Things just seemed to be going sideways. I don't know. I just had a bad feeling about those shots." He looked up at the captain's patient face before returning his eyes to the deck. "But who knows? Maybe I was wrong."

Pat could feel the captain studying him. He expected his superior to call bullshit at any moment. Pat almost wanted him to so that they could put an end to the charade. Instead, the captain nodded.

"Fair enough, XO." The captain grabbed the aluminum door handle. "Get some rest. I can cover your watch."

"Thanks, sir."

Pat waited for the door to close behind the captain before walking over to the rail. He knew the watch standers were eyeing him from inside the pilothouse, so he did his best to maintain a thousand-yard stare.

Just sell it, he told himself, and thank your lucky stars for that machete. That's all you have to do. Time will take care of the rest.

34

Mona Island, Puerto Rico

The sleek orange helicopter descended from the intermittent clouds, hesitating above the dirt before landing hard. The door slid open, and a man jumped out wearing what Gabriela thought looked like an astronaut's helmet. The park ranger who had found the migrants roasting under the afternoon sun handed the astronaut a packet of papers, which the latter signed and returned. The park ranger waved over the first group of migrants.

Gabriela was less than thrilled to run underneath the helicopter's spinning rotors, but there was no other way off the island. Maybe, finally, Galán would be there on the other side.

"Careful with your head," yelled the astronaut in Spanish over the roar of the engine, as he helped Gabriela aboard.

She found a seat on the deck of the cabin next to the woman whose husband had been slashed. None of the migrants spoke. Gabriela felt a jerk, and suddenly they were airborne. She could've fallen asleep were it not for the view out of the open door, which, although stunningly beautiful, reminded her that she was no longer tethered to earth.

Just when Gabriela thought they couldn't climb any higher, the pilot pushed the cyclic away from his body, and the aircraft accelerated forward. Gabriela's lower back pressed against the fire extinguisher mounted behind her as the eastern cliffs of Mona disappeared. Suddenly, there was nothing below but the turquoise waters of the Caribbean, waters that seemed a lot less scary than they had the night before.

Five minutes later, land reappeared. The helicopter sped above a coherent grid of neighborhood streets, neatly maintained homes, and even a few backyard swimming pools. Gabriela had only ever seen those on television. These must be very rich people, she thought. Was Galán that rich? She hoped not, because she didn't know how to be a rich person.

The helicopter descended, and the roofs below became distressingly close. Just as Gabriela braced for impact, the neighborhood ended and a tarmac began. The helicopter touched down with a thud, sending a wave of pain up Gabriela's *yola*-battered spine. The astronaut helped her and the others onto the tarmac and directed them toward a group of stern-faced men with short haircuts and sunglasses.

This new group of men hustled Gabriela and the others to a nondescript concrete building as the helicopter roared into the sky and disappeared. Gabriela followed the group into an overly air-conditioned waiting room.

"Wait here," said the youngest, most muscular man. He had a strange Spanish accent.

Gabriela sat, cradling her arms to her body to keep warm. Every few minutes a different migrant was summoned to talk to one of the stern men. She tried to overhear the conversations, but she quickly fell asleep.

A nudge woke her up.

"Betances, right?" asked the woman whose husband had been cut. "Your turn."

Gabriela approached a mustachioed man in bifocals seated behind a desk. Keeping his eyes fixed on the large computer before him, he motioned for her to sit. After several moments of typing, he began to sift through a pile of paper while sipping from a Styrofoam cup of coffee. The cup was larger than what they drank in Cuba.

He finally looked up. "Your nationality?"

"Cuban," said Gabriela, barely above a whisper.

He tapped away at the keyboard. "Do you have your identification?"

Gabriela produced her blue passport with the gold República de Cuba crest. The man studied it, looked at her once, and clattered some more information into the computer.

"Do you have family here?"

"Here?" asked Gabriela.

"Yes, here."

Gabriela stared at him.

"Puerto Rico," he said. "Do you have family in Puerto Rico?"

Puerto Rico. Hearing the words made it finally seem real. This wasn't the Mona Island version of Puerto Rico where only birds and lizards lived. This was the Puerto Rico where Galán lived, the Puerto Rico where she was going to live. Gabriela's face tingled, and she blinked away tears.

"Anybody?" the man asked again, before taking another sip of coffee.

"Yes," she stammered. "My brother. My brother, Galán. Galán Betances."

She pulled a plastic baggie from her filthy sock and extracted a folded scrap of paper. Yunel had written down Galán's phone numbers the morning he dropped her off at the airport. Fingers trembling, Gabriela handed the scrap to the man.

The man studied the paper and picked up the phone.

☆

San Juan, Puerto Rico

The phone rang at la Fonda del Ciego. Sefora gave a construction worker his change before answering it. "Somebody for you," she said to Galán, shrugging her shoulders.

Galán took the receiver. There had been numerous false alarms over the past week, but suddenly the prospect of bad news seemed worse than no news. Before saying anything, he sat down at an empty table, the spiral cord stretched taut.

"Yes?"

"Galán Betances?" It was a man's voice, a smoker's baritone.

"Speaking."

"This is Agent Delgado with Customs and Border Protection in Aguadilla. We have a woman here who says she's your sister."

Galán's lip began to tremble. He tried to hide his face, but two taxi drivers stared at him as they waited for their *mallorcas*.

"Is she okay?" Galán finally managed to ask.

"Yeah, she's fine," said Agent Delgado quickly. "But I need you to confirm that you are the brother of Gabriela Betances."

Galán wiped his eyes. He struggled to speak, like in his dream from the night before.

"Sir?"

"Yes!" said Galán, half shouting. The rest of the patrons stared. "Yes, I'm her brother. Where is she?"

"I told you. The CBP station in Aguadilla."

"I'm on my way," said Galán, standing. "I'm coming from San Juan. I'll be there in two hours."

"We'll be waiting."

"I swear to God, if anything happens to her . . ."

"As I said, we'll be waiting." There was a click.

Without a word, Galán hung up the phone and went through the front door. The bells jingled behind him, and the taxi drivers turned back to the sports page of *el Vocero*.

★

Mona Passage

There was a knock on Pat's stateroom door. He had just gotten out of the shower after an abbreviated workout and was putting on his boots.

"Come in."

Chief Landis stepped into the cramped space and closed the door without asking. He leaned against the aft bulkhead and folded his arms. His face was stone, and he and the shellback tattoo on his forearm stared at Pat. "We need to talk."

"All right," said Pat, trying to appear relaxed. "Let's talk."

"What the hell happened to you last night?"

Pat exhaled, glancing down at the maroon carpet before looking back up at Chief Landis. "It was that migrant that got sliced. It messed me all up."

"Don't bullshit me, sir."

"What do you mean 'bullshit' you?" Pat refused to break his gaze from Chief Landis's icy blue eyes. "Pulling that guy from the water? How close we were to Mona? All those migrants squeezed into that *yola*? I had a bad feeling about it."

"About what?" Chief Landis's nostrils flared with each breath.

"About disabling fire. About making a bad situation worse. And as the mission commander, my ass was on the line if we shot one of those migrants. Or even if shrapnel from the cowling nicked one." Pat's explanation was weak, but at least it was consistent with what he told the captain.

Chief Landis didn't say anything.

"Your career would have been on the line, too," continued Pat. "With your sixteen years as a coxswain, some lieutenant commander conducting a use of force investigation would expect you to know better."

Chief Landis shook his head and laughed. "You're going to have to do better than that."

"Better than that?" Pat narrowed his eyes.

"There was something else going on last night, and we both know it. You were acting strange before that old man got cut. Hell, you've been acting strange this whole patrol."

Pat tried not to swallow.

"I don't know what your deal is, sir. All I know is that you haven't been you. And as the command chief, it's my duty to make sure you don't do something stupid, something reckless, that hurts this crew."

"Look, Chief," said Pat, leaning back in his chair and folding his untattooed arms. "I appreciate the concern. But me not being me isn't any of your business, and I don't have to explain myself to anybody. To you, to the captain, to anybody. Because I didn't do anything wrong. I stand behind what I did last night. So unless you have something else to say, I think we're finished."

Chief Landis's mouth curled into a sneer, and he shook his head. He opened the door but stopped at the threshold. "I never took you for a liar, sir. I thought you were one of the good ones." He stepped out, slamming the door behind him.

Pat closed his eyes and tipped his head back.

I was one of the good ones, he thought. Or maybe I never was until last night.

35

Aguadilla, Puerto Rico

Gabriela woke up in the waiting room where the grumpy men with short haircuts and sunglasses worked. Feeling warm for the first time since Mona, she looked down and saw that somebody had draped an oversized CBP sweatshirt across her chest.

"There's somebody here to see you, Betances," said Agent Delgado, emerging from behind his desk. He looked just as annoyed as before. "Up, up."

Gabriela stood. She was lightheaded from anticipation and hunger, and she hardly noticed the soreness that radiated throughout her body. She followed Agent Delgado into a lobby containing two armed men and one of those machines that she had first seen at José Martí Airport. Another man was crouched over, lacing his shoes.

"What's the problem?" asked Agent Delgado. "That isn't him?"

The man finished tying his shoes and stood.

It was Galán.

It was really him.

Gabriela lunged forward and threw herself into her brother's arms, her pent-up fear and anxiety pouring out. She cried into Galán's chest. Teresa hadn't lied. Neither had Yunel.

"It's over," said Galán into her ear. "It's over. You're here. It's over."

★

North of Puerto Rico

The wrapper of the dry Macanudo was peeling off, but Pat smoked it anyway. The cigar's taste and smell calmed his nerves. Even with the *Strickland* running on only one engine for the short evening transit back to San Juan, the blue smoke quickly whipped into nothingness.

Pat took another puff and thought about the chase. The crew would get over his erratic behavior—hell, the married ones were already thinking about their honey-do lists, and the single ones were trying to decide at which bar to get drunk that first night home. And the captain, the only person whose opinion truly mattered, was too busy with his applications to law school.

Chief Landis, however, was a different story. Pat hoped that the old adage that time heals all would prove true, but he wasn't confident. But even still, what could Chief Landis say that Pat couldn't refute? It would be he said, he said. Plus, Chief Landis didn't know anything about Galán or Gabriela, or the scrap of paper with the patrol dates.

And what about the rest of the Coast Guard? Pat knew that the failed pursuit would be mentioned at the next day's briefing at headquarters in DC. Some lieutenant would pull up a slide and tell the flag officers that a dozen Cuban nationals landed on Mona after an ineffective pursuit by the *Strickland*, and that the case had been transferred to Customs and Border Protection. The admirals would nod and sip their coffee, and the lieutenant would move on to the next slide about a drug interdiction in the eastern Pacific or a change to the pay and personnel manual.

But what happened off the coast of Mona mattered, and Pat smiled as he imagined Galán and Gabriela's reunion. Soon enough, Pat himself would be back on the terrace with them, his Puerto Rico family. He didn't know what he would say, if anything, to Galán about what happened out there in the shadow of that uninhabited piece of America. Probably better to just keep your mouth shut, he thought.

Just as Pat began to feel like himself, he remembered yet again that some human smuggler had made a lot of money off of his information and actions. Somewhere in the concrete labyrinth of metropolitan San Juan, a criminal was celebrating, a criminal who couldn't have cared less who lived or died on that *yola*. Pat tried to ward off the unsettling thought by taking another puff from the Macanudo.

Whatever, he thought, exhaling the smoke. What's done is done.

☆

Aguadilla, Puerto Rico

The sun had set by the time Galán and Gabriela stepped through the glass doors of the CBP station and into the nearly empty parking lot. As Galán turned the borrowed Corolla onto Route 110, he felt like he had just robbed a bank. Galán was afraid that Agent Delgado would have a change of heart, that any minute there would be flashing lights in the rearview mirror. With each passing kilometer, though, he allowed himself to relax just a little bit more.

As they merged onto Highway 2, Galán thought about asking Gabriela about her trip. They hadn't had a moment's privacy in Aguadilla, and he wanted to make sure that she had been okay, that nothing unspeakable had happened at the hands of Adonis's henchmen or the fellow migrants. But maybe he should just give her some time, especially since much of his curiosity stemmed from a guilty conscience.

Never again, he thought, before saying a prayer of thanks to la Virgen de la Caridad.

With the radio off, the only sound was Gabriela's snoring. Even the jarring capitalism of Puerto Rico, which screamed for their attention at every intersection, couldn't keep her awake. Businesses like Encanto Title Loans, with its green *coquí*, and Burger King, *la Casa del Whopper*, fought each other into a continuous neon stalemate.

At a red light in Hatillo, Galán pinched his forearm just to make sure that he wouldn't wake up with the cat, and not his sister, by his side. A prick of blood rose from his arm, and Gabi was still there.

By the time they reached Manatí, Galán was struggling to keep his eyes open. He took the exit for the outlet malls and pulled into a McDonalds. He killed the engine and nudged Gabriela awake. She jumped, her mind perhaps still somewhere in the Mona Passage. When she recognized her brother, though, she smiled.

Gabriela's first meal in the United States would be a Big Mac with fries and a Sprite. Galán wanted to make a joke about how cliché it was, but he knew she wouldn't get it. They stepped into the bright restaurant that smelled of grease, and Galán found a booth as far as possible from a group of teenagers huddled around a smartphone watching a *reggaetón* music video. The kids stared at Gabriela, who looked like a child in the oversized sweatshirt. They could probably smell her, too.

Galán went to the counter to order, his eyes darting back to Gabriela every few seconds. She had come too far for him to lose her now. Once the chunky server filled the brown tray with sandwiches, fries, and drinks, Galán brought the bounty over to his sister.

Gabriela devoured her value meal in minutes.

"When was the last time you ate?" asked Galán in amazement.

Gabriela thought for a moment. "I don't know. I was more thirsty than anything, but that big man with the mustache gave me some crackers."

Galán nodded. He had an idea and smiled. It was probably a bad idea, he thought, but who cared? There had been more than enough bad ideas recently. "I'll be right back."

"Okay," said Gabriela, "but please don't go far."

"Don't worry. I won't."

When Galán returned to the table with an ice cream sundae, Gabriela looked up at him, her eyes wide.

"Who's that for?"

"For you." Galán smiled.

"Are you sure?" She looked concerned. "It's too big for one person."

Galán produced an extra spoon. "Then we'll share it."

Just then, the door opened and a young man entered with a familiar scar running from his nose to his lip. He walked past the counter and headed directly to Galán and Gabriela. Just as the man reached their table, Galán recognized him as one of the bartenders from Bar Punta Cana.

"*Provecho*," said the man to Gabriela, smiling.

Gabriela looked down at her lap.

The man turned to Galán, still smiling. "That looks like a delicious treat."

"Did you pay full price for it?"

Galán nodded slowly. His mouth was too dry to speak.

"That's good," said the man. "You should always pay full price. Otherwise, the manager could come out here and demand you give the treat back. And that would be a shame."

Galán swallowed.

The man's smile disappeared. "You have a month."

Galán nodded.

The man grabbed a fistful of french fries and departed.

"Who was that man?" asked Gabriela. "I didn't like him. He seemed like a bad man."

"It's okay," said Galán, breathing shallowly. "Just an acquaintance. I don't like him, either."

Gabriela waited.

"Don't worry about him, Gabi." Galán forced a smile. "Just enjoy your ice cream."

"Okay." Gabriela spooned some of the whipped cream and chocolate sauce to her mouth. She smiled. "Wow. That is good."

Galán smiled again, naturally this time, and relaxed his vice grip on the plastic bench. One month. Nothing to worry about now.

Now, all he had to do was share a dessert with his sister. Now, his only task was to enjoy this moment.

They were together. Like they were always supposed to be.

Part Four

36

Santurce, Puerto Rico

Goddamned Adonis, thought the young *machetero*, as he hit the blunt in the Mitsubishi's backseat. He hated Adonis, and he was tired of taking his orders. He could deal with the crossings—they were simple—but he was sick of having to handle the old man's "business disputes."

The *machetero* had vowed to find another line of work the moment he walked out of the Customs and Border Protection station in Aguadilla several weeks prior. His luck was bound to run out soon. Not only did the Coast Guard inexplicably break off its pursuit of his *yola* just yards from Mona, but CBP fell for his Cuban refugee story. How he wasn't behind bars or at least on a Dominican navy ship headed back to Santo Domingo, he would never know.

But before the *machetero* could disappear into San Juan or maybe even move north to Lawrence, he had to take care of Don Gerónimo. This other old Dominican had become something of a competitor to Adonis, and competition wasn't good for profits.

The Arcángel song on 94.7 FM ended, and the young *machetero* took the commercial break as his cue. He patted the Glock in his waistband and nodded through the rearview mirror at the fat driver in the Miami Marlins jersey.

The driver barely looked up from his phone's Instagram feed.

The *machetero* stepped out into the heat and crossed the street. Cars cruised by in both directions, but rush-hour gridlock had thankfully come and gone—traffic and getaways didn't mix.

Moving slowly, the *machetero* checked for passersby before ducking into an alley behind Barbershop los Primos. The rear door was unlocked, as he was told it would be. He was ashamed that his heart was beating a little fast. He had killed before, but in a reactive way. This premeditated business bothered him.

He wiped his fingers on his tight, bleached jeans and checked the pistol one more time. He pulled the slide back slightly to reveal the brass of the chambered round and disengaged the safety. He took a deep breath and pushed in the door to the dark storeroom, careful not to knock over any brooms or cardboard boxes full of combs, picks, and gels.

Standing in the closet, the young man could hear the bachata and smell the Barbicide that emanated from beneath the opposite door. The song reminded him of his first girlfriend. Aventura was her favorite group, so much so that he had been jealous of Romeo Santos.

Forget her. Just commit.

He looked down at the pistol's glowing sights and took one more breath. He pushed open the door, and stepped into the bright space lined with barber's chairs and a wooden bench.

Neither the two barbers nor the handful of customers noticed the *machetero*'s arrival.

"Don Gerónimo," said the *machetero*, raising the Glock.

An older man with a prodigious belly turned, shaving cream around his temples. He didn't react, but his skinny barber yelped and dropped the straight razor.

The *machetero* squeezed the trigger twice in quick succession, just like he'd been taught in the narrow streets of San Cristóbal. The bullets exploded through Don Gerónimo's skull and lodged in the barber's narrow trunk. What remained of Don Gerónimo's head slumped forward, and the barber collapsed onto the tile floor.

The *machetero* turned and retraced his steps out of the barbershop. He was moving through the dark closet when he felt an inevitable bullet rip into his shoulder. A moment later, he heard the gunshot. He kept moving.

But the Mitsubishi wasn't in the alley.

Thinking that Adonis's boy had somehow forgotten the plan, the *machetero* sprinted to where he had been dropped off. His shoulder felt like it had been torn from his body, and he was amazed that his arm was still attached.

There was no Mitsubishi there either.

Fuck, he thought, looking up and down the street, his good hand both holding the pistol and supporting his shredded arm.

Pedestrians screamed and scrambled for cover.

The *machetero* tossed the Glock down a storm drain and took off running, a thin trail of blood marking his path. When he reached the end of the block, he looked over his good shoulder to check for Don Gerónimo's crew. Just as he saw them emerge onto the street, a bumper struck him in the side of his knee, knocking him down.

It was a white, blue, and yellow Policía Estatal squad car.

"Freeze!" yelled the stocky officer, throwing the door open and drawing his weapon.

The *machetero* peeled himself off the hot asphalt and continued running. Once again, he felt the bullet before he heard it. This time it was the back of his leg. He slid face-first onto the pavement.

He tried to crawl forward, but the pain was overpowering.

Motherfucking Adonis.

☆

San Juan, Puerto Rico

Pat stepped through the front door of la Fonda del Ciego, the bell jingling behind him. He smiled and waved to Gabriela, who was standing on a stepladder removing Christmas decorations. She smiled at him shyly before turning back to the red-and-white stockings and miniature wise men.

"The usual?" asked Sefora, not bothering to bring Pat a menu.

"Yes, please," said Pat, sitting at his favorite table—the one in the corner beneath the blown up panorama of Ciego de Ávila. He had been coming to the diner more often in recent weeks since Galán could only pay back Pat's $1,000 loan with free meals. Pat felt bad about it, but Galán had insisted.

As Pat waited, he fingered the lone silver bar on his ball cap. In just a few months, he would be promoted to full lieutenant. Maybe Galán could come down to the Coast Guard base to swap the shoulder boards at the promotion ceremony. Galán would get a kick out of that, Pat thought, smiling.

But just then something on the WAPA newscast caught Pat's eye. The president was speaking.

Galán emerged from his office and picked up two *cafecitos* from the counter. He sat down in the chair across from Pat.

"You seeing this?" asked Pat, pouring a packet of sugar into the coffee. His eyes were fixed on the television.

"No," said Galán, shifting in his chair to get a better look. "What is it? It's been a busy morning. Good for business, especially since we'll be closed during the San Sebastián parties."

The English captions announced that President Obama's final act in office would be the repeal of the "Wet Foot, Dry Foot" policy. Moving forward, Cubans would be dealt with the same as other migrants—no special treatment upon arrival, just life in the shadows of society.

Galán looked at Pat, his mouth open, and then turned back to the screen.

A reporter interviewed a group of *balseros* who had arrived in the Florida Keys just hours before the change went into effect. One of the rafters, his hair wild from the journey, talked excitedly before bursting into tears. He and his seven dehydrated friends would be the last ones put on the fast track to citizenship.

"I told you this was coming," said Pat softly, not taking his eyes off the television.

Galán didn't say anything.

The reporting shifted to the southwest border in Nuevo Laredo, Mexico. A different reporter interviewed a group of Cubans who had crossed the Yucatán Channel by boat before traversing Mexico on the tops of trains. They had been queued up on the Mexican side of the border, waiting to present themselves to US immigration officials, when the change happened. The migrant being interviewed also wept.

He was too late.

The newscast switched to a baseball montage promoting the upcoming Caribbean Series, featuring Puerto Rico's Criollos de Caguas.

Galán turned back to Pat, mouth still open.

"I told you," said Pat, sipping his coffee.

Galán pulled a rag out of the bottom pocket of his guayabera and wiped his brow. He mumbled something under his breath and turned toward Gabriela, who was wrapping the Christmas ornaments in old newspaper.

Pat put his hand on Galán's shoulder and left it there.

37

Carolina, Puerto Rico

The *machetero*, pretending to be asleep in his hospital bed, watched the portly detective out of the corner of his almost closed eye. The large man in the gray suit had appeared sometime after the arrival of the morning banana and orange juice. The detective had only gotten up once, and that was to refill his Styrofoam coffee cup. Otherwise he remained engrossed in a folded *el Nuevo Día*.

The hell with it, thought the *machetero*, shifting his legs under the dingy sheets. The chain on the shackle connecting his left ankle to the bed rail clinked. Blinking several times, he feigned waking up.

The detective smiled and set the newspaper on his lap. He handed the cup of orange juice to the boy. The *machetero* took it in his good hand and sipped. He didn't make eye contact.

"I just want to know why," said the detective, loosening his maroon tie and unbuttoning his collar. "I just want to know why some kid like you takes that old man down in broad daylight. While he's getting his whiskers trimmed. I just want to know why."

The boy had known a lot of Puerto Ricans through his line of work, but for some reason he found this guy's accent particularly annoying. The condescension in the detective's eyes and his well-manicured fingernails were equally off-putting. The *machetero* looked up at the curtain that hung between his bed and his neighbor's and thought about what to say.

"Look," said the detective. "It's okay to talk to me. You have nothing to lose. Your shoulder is splattered all over that barbershop.

There's a trail of blood from there to where Officer Ordóñez got you. We found the pistol in the sewer. And you forgot to pull that stocking from your pocket and put it over your head." He shook his head, smiling. "But I still don't understand why."

The *machetero* didn't say anything. If the detective wanted to tell the story himself, so be it.

"Do you know who that man was?"

Still nothing.

"Osvaldo Marín de la Vega," said the detective, answering his own question. "But he went by Gerónimo."

The ceiling fan spun slowly, its blades covered in dust.

"If you're waiting for a lawyer, suit yourself. But right now this is between me and you. Think of this off-the-record conversation as a golden opportunity."

The *machetero* didn't know any lawyers.

"Anyway, you don't strike me as the kind of man who would be enemies with Gerónimo," said the detective, sipping his coffee. "But enemies he had, enemies he had indeed." He picked up the newspaper and fanned himself. "Maybe somebody asked you to do it? Maybe as a favor?"

The *machetero* only listened.

"You know," said the detective, leaning forward in a conspiratorial manner, "you seem like a good kid. You don't seem evil. And I would know. I deal with a lot of evil." He picked up his coffee cup, looked into it, and put it back down. "I think you were just doing somebody a favor."

The *machetero* exhaled slowly but didn't say anything. He watched the fan spin.

"Do you know what Gerónimo does for money?" asked the detective, unfastening his belt to allow his prodigious stomach some more room to maneuver.

"No," lied the boy. He hadn't heard his own voice since the barbershop.

"Well, I'll tell you then," said the detective, seemingly emboldened. "He's a people smuggler. He runs boats from the Dominican

Republic to here. Brings over Dominicans, Cubans, Haitians. Whoever. It doesn't matter, as long as they pay." He sat back and regarded the boy as if they were meeting for the first time. "Anyway, I don't think I'm telling you anything you don't know. I heard about how you and a bunch of other Cubans arrived at Mona Island a few weeks ago."

The *machetero* glanced at the detective before looking back at the fan. He regretted it immediately.

"But what strikes me as funny," continued the detective, a grin spreading, "is that you're the most Dominican-looking Cuban I've ever seen."

The *machetero* swallowed. Where was this clown going with all this? He decided to hear him out before saying something stupid.

"So the way I see it," said the detective as he turned to watch a nurse in tight pants walk past the room, "is that somebody had a problem with Gerónimo, and that same somebody told you to take care of it."

The young man licked his lips, eyes fixed on the fan.

"And to me," said the detective, finally turning back from the open door, "to me, it's sad that a young man like yourself, with all his life ahead of him, needs to get burned for something he didn't even want any part of."

The fat detective was good, thought the *machetero*, closing his eyes. He tried to think of what to say, but instead he saw the blood explode from Don Gerónimo's head.

And then he saw Adonis.

The *machetero* and Adonis first met two years earlier at the beach in Camuy, Puerto Rico. The boy had just delivered a mixed load of Dominicans and Haitians, and he and his partner were preparing to return to the Dominican Republic when Adonis emerged from the predawn brush. The boy wanted to get going because the sun was about to rise, but Adonis assured him that there was no rush, that the Puerto Rican Policía Estatal "had other engagements." Adonis then selected a teenage Dominican girl from amongst the huddled migrants, took her into the palms, and raped her. It wasn't until he emerged, zipping up his jeans, that he finally gave the boy and his partner their money. The boy could still remember how the girl cried from the shadows of the trees.

"It's just sad," said the detective, opening the newspaper again. "But don't worry about what I think. There is more than enough blood being shed in my country for me to be able to pay the bills." He crossed his ankles. "I'm just saying all this as an unbiased observer. As an anthropologist." He turned the page.

"They call him Adonis," said the boy, still looking at the fan. A feeling of weightlessness came over him, and he thought he could float up and touch the whirring blades. "You can find him at Bar Punta Cana."

✭

San Juan, Puerto Rico

Pat was walking along la Calle Norzagaray when his phone rang. He pulled it out of his arm band. UNAVAILABLE. Normally he wouldn't answer, but he had just finished a jog and had nothing else to do other than a cool-down walk to el Morro.

"Hello?" Pat's gaze bounced across the rooftops of la Perla to the blue Atlantic.

Silence.

"Hello?" he said again.

"Pat," said a familiar voice. "Pat, it's me."

"Danny?" Pat tried to shield the phone from the ocean breeze.

"Yeah, it's me, Danny."

"Where are you?" It was a dumb question, but the words came from habit.

"You know where I am," said Danny, laughing. "Same place I was last time I tried to call you. This shitty little jail outside Manch-Vegas. Trust me, I'd like to be somewhere else, but they have these guys here called 'corrections officers.'"

"Last time you called me? When was that?"

"A few weeks ago. You must have been out on the ocean or something. Anyway, I only have a few minutes."

"Okay, yeah, no problem," said Pat. "So what's up? How are you?" He turned off Norzagaray and onto the immense lawn that led up to el Morro.

There was a pause, but Pat waited.

"I just don't know how to say it," said Danny finally, his voice becoming serious.

"Say what?"

Danny sighed. "I'm sorry. I'm just calling to say I'm sorry."

Families picnicked on the hill below. Children chased their kites, laughing and squealing.

"You have nothing to apologize for," said Pat finally. "You went through too much. More than a person ever should. It's okay."

"No," Danny choked. "It's not okay. Other guys went through the same shit over there, or worse, and they didn't fall apart like a baby."

"Don't say that. That's not what happened."

"It is," said Danny, regaining his composure. "It is. But what matters is that I promise you I'm going to change."

"Okay." Pat's own eyes would have been watering were it not for the wind.

"I'm going to change, and I'm going to be like you."

"Like me?"

"Because I'm proud of you, Pat." Danny cleared his throat. "I'm proud to be your brother."

Pat swallowed. "Thank you," he finally said softly. "You know I'm proud to be your brother, too."

"I know. I've always known."

Pat didn't know what to say, so he waited.

Danny coughed. "Anyway, I think I have to go. I wasted the first three minutes of my allowance dialing the wrong number. Some Puerto Rican dude kept getting angrier and angrier every time he answered."

Pat laughed and wiped his eyes. He turned left off the pathway and walked across the grass toward the fortress walls. He used to come here with Michaela and look at the bay, the Bacardi distillery, and the distant mountains.

"But just remember what I said, okay?" said Danny. "I'm going to get out of here in a few months, and I'm going to turn this shit around."

"I'll remember," said Pat. "Don't worry."

"Good." Danny paused for a moment. "I love you."

"I love you, too."

Sitting on the top of the fortress wall and watching a pilot boat trail a crisp wake, Pat realized how good it felt to say those three words. The sweat had dried from his skin, but his cheeks were still wet.

38

Santurce, Puerto Rico

Two weeks after the *machetero* spoke Adonis's name from the Carolina hospital bed, a black armored truck rumbled down the streets of el Barrio Obrero. A woman pushing an elderly Chihuahua down the street in a baby carriage stopped and stared. Two young boys walking home from school sprinted down the opposite sidewalk in an effort to keep up with the ominous vehicle, their Spiderman and Nemo backpacks swinging wildly. The wiser residents sought refuge.

A black helicopter circled overhead with a silver stripe and the letters FURA emblazoned across the cabin. The aircrew from this tactical wing of the Puerto Rican Police hadn't been told who the target was. Too many similar operations had failed in the past thanks to leaks from within commonwealth law enforcement—the officers' paychecks were too small and the payoffs from criminal networks too big. The pilot, careful not to linger right on top of Bar Punta Cana, ensured that all means of egress were blocked by white and blue Suburbans from Homeland Security Investigations.

With all units in place, the operation's leader spoke into his encrypted radio from the passenger seat of the black armored truck.

"All units go."

His commonwealth and federal partners, clad in black bulletproof vests and balaclavas, spilled out of their vehicles and burst through the nightclub's front doors.

"Freeze!" yelled the point man into the darkness of Bar Punta Cana. "Don't move! Show me your hands!"

The bartender with the butterfly tattoo screamed, and the operators threw her to the ground. She twisted her head and spat at the closest agent who pushed her face into the concrete floor. She chipped a tooth and drops of blood fell from her lip.

The rest of the agents searched the main dance hall, while a four-man team stacked at the door to the narrow internal hallway. Ignoring the sign that read AREA RESTRINGIDA, the leader made a chopping motion with his hand. The point man pushed through the plastic curtain, and the team advanced down the dark corridor. The red dots from their M4 rifle sights danced off of cardboard boxes of Medalla and Presidente.

They stacked up on both sides of the office door and caught their breaths. The leader formed a hook with his pointer and middle fingers, and the rest of the team nodded.

The point man kicked open the door and the team burst into Adonis's office.

"Freeze! Homeland Security!"

There was no response but the sound of an afternoon radio talk show and the scent of Chinese food.

"What the fuck?" said the leader, lowering his rifle barrel and engaging the safety. He pulled the balaclava from his sweaty head and keyed his radio. "Negative results in the office."

"Roger."

The team waited in silence for their fellow agents to complete the sweep of the rest of the nightclub. A blond, tattooed HSI agent put a pinch of Grizzly into his lower lip. His eyes lingered on the pinup model hanging from the wall.

"What was that?" asked the point man, straightening up from where he was leaning against the desk.

"What was what?" asked the leader.

"Listen."

Sure enough, above the din of the dance hall being tossed, there was a faint rattle coming from somewhere in the office.

The point man smiled.

"This is Bravo Seven," said the leader calmly into his radio. "All units stand by. We may have something here in the office after all." He pulled the ski mask back over his face.

The noise sounded like a metallic shaking.

Bravo Seven raised his rifle and clicked the selector from SAFE to SEMI, aiming at a coffin-like storage container.

The point man stepped forward, his body turned away from where the cabinet would open. Bravo Seven nodded, and the point man flipped open the container's lid.

"Freeze!" shouted Bravo Seven, his finger on the trigger.

Curled up in the fetal position, his hands covering his face, was Adonis Guzmán.

The agents ripped him out of his aluminum womb and threw him face-first onto the concrete floor. Blood streamed out of Adonis's nose, mixing with years of splattered takeout grease.

"Adonis Guzmán," said Bravo Seven, as one of his lieutenants applied the handcuffs. "You are being placed under arrest by US Homeland Security Investigations. You have the right to remain silent . . ."

As Bravo Seven recited the Miranda warning, Adonis licked the blood from his top lip and considered his options.

There was always a next move.

☆

San Juan, Puerto Rico

Pat waited for Chief Landis to finish spreading mustard onto his turkey sandwich with the plastic packet. As the in-port officer of the day, Chief Landis had his duty radio sitting next to him at the mess-deck table like a little companion.

"What are you still doing here, sir?" asked Chief Landis, finally looking up.

"I'm married to this cutter," said Pat, patting the bulkhead. "You know that."

"Tell me about it," said Chief Landis. He laid some potato chips on top of the mustard and squeezed the two pieces of bread together with a crunch. Chief Landis's wife and three children hadn't bothered following him from Duluth to Puerto Rico.

Pat and his former sea daddy had developed a working truce ever since their disagreements in the Mona Passage. But a truce was no way to lead a ship.

"Look," said Pat, his eyes focused on the salt shaker that sat between him and Chief Landis, "I've been meaning to say this for a while now. I was wrong. I was wrong, and I'm sorry."

"What are you talking about, sir?"

"The way I was during that Mona patrol. Being a jackass to you and everybody else."

Chief Landis took a bite of his sandwich and looked at Pat.

Pat waited for him to finish chewing.

"I wasn't upset," said Chief Landis, his face conveying no emotion. "I've been in this business long enough to not take shit personally. I was disappointed more than anything."

Pat nodded. Through the porthole, one of their sister ships rocked against the neighboring pier. Several nonrates balanced on a paint float and scrubbed green marine growth off the white hull. "It's no excuse," said Pat, "but I had stuff going on back home. I let it get to me."

"Is it all good now?"

"I guess," said Pat, looking back at Chief Landis. "You remember my girlfriend? Well, she's long gone. I messed that one up good."

Chief Landis either grunted or chuckled. "There's worse places to be single."

"I guess," said Pat. "And my brother, he's been going through some stuff."

"The one from the army?"

"Yeah. He's had it kind of rough since he got out. One thing led to another, and now he's doing a little bit of time."

"The boys in green get rode hard and put away wet," said Chief Landis. "My nephew went through the same shit. It's messed up how they do their own like that."

Pat nodded. "Anyway, I just wanted to say I'm sorry. And I want to say thanks for looking out for me."

Chief Landis nodded.

Pat thought about saying something else but didn't.

"All I'll say, sir," said Chief Landis, cracking open a can of Diet Coke, "is that this is a small service. Your reputation precedes you."

Pat nodded.

"If you shit away your integrity, the word gets out. From the captain down to the fireman cleaning the bilge, people will know."

Pat swallowed.

"So I'm not going to ask any more questions about what went on during the last patrol, and it sounds like you have your reasons for not being you, but just don't let it happen again."

Pat nodded. "It won't."

"Good." Chief Landis sipped his soda, and the corners of his mouth ticked up in a subdued smile. "Because I still think you're one of the good ones."

Pat smiled and got up from the booth. He was still smiling as he walked through the athwartships passageway and out into the steamy San Juan afternoon. The restlessness in his gut subsided for the first time since he had written down those patrol dates for Galán.

☆

Hato Rey, Puerto Rico

Inside an interview room at the US Attorney's Office on the twelfth floor of la Torre Chardón, Adonis fingered the baggy sleeve of his orange jumpsuit and listened to his lawyer argue with the prosecutor. Adonis hated himself for having been pulled from the filing cabinet like a rodent from a trap—he was supposed to be a street soldier. But then again, he was alive. And as long as he was alive, he could make moves.

Adonis's attorney leaned back from the table and folded his hands behind his head. "I'll just get right to the point," he said.

"Mr. Guzmán possesses information that the government may find useful."

This overpriced schoolboy better be right about this strategy if he wants to earn another pair of those Ferragamos, thought Adonis, noticing the cordovan loafers with the gold clasp. Adonis was still confused as to how he was here in chains, like a dog, despite his faithful tithing to government officials on both sides of the Mona Passage.

"And what is that information?" asked the prosecutor. She was also young, barely over thirty, and wore a tight navy-blue skirt and white blouse. Adonis undressed her with his eyes, but she seemed unfazed. He liked that.

"Mr. Guzmán has friends," said the defense counsel. "Friends all over this island, all over the Caribbean, really. We can name names."

Adonis never saw himself as a snitch, but the only other option was to rot in federal prison. To hell with that, he thought. The orphan from Jimaní had made it through life alone. If that pissed off his associates and gave them an appetite for vengeance, so be it. He could defend himself.

"Your client has friends," said the sexy prosecutor, scrolling through her phone. "Great. Then start naming them. I have an appearance in courtroom six in twenty minutes."

"We can start naming names when you offer us some terms. But there's more than a handful with Puerto Rico PD. A few with FURA as well."

"I'm floored," she said. "Come on. We both know how many of them are on the take. You're going to have to do better than that."

"You want federal?" asked the defense attorney. "Well, we have those little science nerds, those park rangers, on Mona."

"I'm serious," said the prosecutor, shaking her head. "I have work to do."

"We have CBP."

"CBP?" She looked up at the defense lawyer. "That's a start. We might be able to work with that."

The lawyer smiled, his arms folded across his pressed pink shirt. "We even have Coast Guard."

"Coast Guard?" Her eyebrows raised. "If you're talking about one of those Puerto Rican kids who's been in for a year, you're going to have to do better."

The defense attorney laughed. "No, I'm not talking about that. I'm talking about an officer. A white boy."

"Really?" The prosecutor smiled. "You know this guy? You can identify him?"

"I know a Cuban," said Adonis before his lawyer could stop him. "You follow the Cuban, you'll find the white boy."

"Who is this Cuban?" asked the prosecutor. "Is he also in your line of work?"

Adonis opened his mouth but his lawyer gave him a look.

"You give us something to work with," said the lawyer, "and we'll produce. Mr. Guzmán is nothing if not reliable."

"I'll see what I can do." The prosecutor uncrossed her legs and stood up. She looked down at Adonis. "I'm glad you see the value of cooperation."

Adonis gave her a leering smile and stared at her tight backside as she walked out the door.

Yes, the orphan from Jimaní always had another move.

39

San Juan, Puerto Rico

Galán poured water onto the wood chips and covered the smoker. He learned how to barbecue back in Key West, and the smell of the pork shoulder and apple juice reminded him of Esperanza and the brief life they had shared. Maybe he would go to California just to say hello. She probably had a man and some kids by now, but that would be all right.

"I think we're looking pretty good," he said through the open window to Gabriela. She was mopping the floor, and the orange cat, lanky in his adolescence, scampered from chair to dresser to table, watching her every move. The mop had been asking for it for some time.

"You know," said Galán, "you don't need to do that. Just come out and relax. You're already working hard enough as it is at la Fonda."

"But I want our house to look good for Patricio," she said through the window.

"Trust me," said Galán, smiling. "He doesn't care. Anyway, it's going to be a nice sunset, and I don't want you to miss it."

"Okay, okay. I'm almost done."

Galán took a swig of his Medalla. Several weeks had passed since his sister's journey, and he could still remember the anxiety, the stress, the guilt. He opened the grill and examined the pork. They'd been lucky. All three of them.

So, so lucky.

Gabriela came out onto the terrace, the cat trailing behind her. She sat down with a cup of orange juice and handed Galán another beer. The cat jumped into her lap, and the three of them looked out toward the harbor, waiting for the sky to turn orange.

"We should've been doing this years ago," said Galán.

"Doing what?" she asked, turning toward him.

"Nothing. Just being together." He wanted a cigarette, but he tried not to smoke around her.

"Oh."

"I wish Mami were here, though. She would've liked this. Us being together."

Gabriela smiled and stroked the cat's chin. "She is here. You said so yourself. You don't remember?"

"Yeah, I remember," said Galán, smiling. "You're right. She is here."

He was still smiling when he checked his watch. The pork would be ready by the time Pat arrived. Galán hoped the meat would taste as good as it looked. His brother had earned each and every one of these meals.

★

Pat was changing out of his uniform for Galán's barbecue when there was a knock. He pulled a Boston Celtics T-shirt over his head and opened his stateroom door.

A short, muscular man in a Hawaiian shirt stood at the threshold. Behind him loitered a uniformed petty officer in a gun belt and bulletproof vest.

"Something I can help you with?" asked Pat, making room.

He'd seen the muscular guy at the base gym before, but he didn't know who he was. He thought for a minute as the two visitors positioned themselves with their backs to the ersatz wood bulkhead. That's right, Pat remembered, the muscle-bound guy was with Coast Guard Investigative Service. One of the *Strickland* crewmembers must have gotten a DUI or mouthed off to a police officer over at la Placita.

"Lieutenant McAllister," said the squat man, presenting a gold badge and identification card, "I'm Special Agent Machado from CGIS. You have a minute?"

"Sure." Pat pulled his military ID from the slot on his computer keyboard and put it in his wallet. "I was just getting ready to head out, but I got time."

"Look, LT," said Special Agent Machado, eyes darting around the small stateroom, "I don't get any pleasure in this, but it's my job and my duty."

"Yeah, no problem. You got to do what you got to do. These young guys are always getting into shit. So what's up?"

There was a moment of silence before Special Agent Machado looked Pat in the eye. "It's not about your crew. It's about you."

Pat flushed. The petty officer stared at his boots. Special Agent Machado grimaced.

"It's about me?" Pat was taking shallow breaths and felt like he couldn't get enough air.

Special Agent Machado pulled a piece of paper from his pocket and showed it to Pat. "You recognize this?" It was a photocopy of the scrap that Pat had given Galán.

Pat swallowed. He could hear himself breathing.

"We recovered the original from a human smuggler, and we have reason to suspect it came from you. We also have reason to suspect that you provided $1,000 to your Cuban neighbor, knowing that it was destined for that same human smuggler." He shook his head. "Combine all of that with your erratic behavior on that failed pursuit near Mona . . . ? Let's just say it's a problem."

Pat didn't say anything.

"I've been with CGIS for eighteen years, and I've never heard of anything like this from an officer. Young guys from the islands who are strapped for cash and have family ties? Yeah, maybe. But an officer?" Special Agent Machado licked his lips. "I just hope there's something we're missing."

Pat felt like he was in some sort of bizarre dream, watching it all unfold from the upper rack next to him.

"So here's the deal," continued Special Agent Machado. "You're going to have to come with us so we can all get to the bottom of this. If we have to, we can put you in cuffs, but I'd rather not. I think it would be better for your crew that we don't. You good with that?"

Pat kept waiting to wake up from the dream.

"I'm asking you a question, sir," said Special Agent Machado. "Can you promise me we won't have any problems?"

Pat made a barely perceptible nod.

"If I were you," said Special Agent Machado, "I'd pack up anything of value. You don't know when you'll be coming back here."

Pat nodded again and slowly filled his backpack. The last item he grabbed was the picture of Michaela hanging next to his rack that he should have removed months ago. He looked at her smile and loving eyes one more time before dropping the photo in the trash. He shouldered his backpack and nodded to Special Agent Machado.

The threesome walked through the galley and out onto the weather deck. Pat moved slowly and tried to capture the feeling of his ship beneath his sneakers, but within seconds he was crossing the brow and stepping onto the concrete pier. They stepped over shore ties and puddles and approached the smoke pit where Chief Landis was lighting a cigarette.

Pat didn't make eye contact, but he could feel Chief Landis staring at him quizzically.

The armed petty officer opened the back door of an unmarked government sedan and motioned for Pat to get in. They drove through the base's front gate and up the broken pavement of la Puntilla. Stray cats darted under cars and into doorways, their all-knowing eyes watching Pat through the tinted glass.

As they approached the traffic circle by the old courthouse, Pat thought about who he would call first and when that opportunity might be. The thought of it made him cringe. His family was crushed by Danny, but they understood why he was behind bars. They visited Danny every week, and upon his upcoming release, Danny would be checking into one of the finest rehabilitation centers in New England thanks to their mom going back to work.

But this? How would they understand this?

The blue sedan turned onto cobblestoned la Calle Tanca, and Pat tried to clear his mind. He would have plenty of time to think, but right now he just wanted to see his city. It seemed like he had memories on every corner.

When they passed Mamajuana's on the left, Pat could faintly hear the bachata flowing out of the open doors. He thought about the first time he went there, the afternoon that Galán danced with Yadira. It felt like a lot more than a year and a half had passed.

Pat was about to turn away when he saw his landlord, Edwin. The old man was pushing a cart loaded with tamarinds, mangoes, and plantains up the narrow sidewalk. His paltry gray ponytail bounced on the collar of his black T-shirt, and the calf muscles of his thin legs strained with each step. What would Edwin tell the next tenant? That the last guy who lived there had broken his lease after being hauled away in handcuffs? Or would Edwin point with his long forefinger over the terrace wall at Gabriela feeding the kitten and say that if it weren't for the last tenant, she wouldn't be there?

Looking out the opposite window to the right, Pat saw el Flamenco. Pat had eaten brunch there with Michaela one Sunday before she left for the airport. He was so anxious that she not miss her flight that they left before she could finish her slice of *tres leches* cake—her favorite dessert. That was the last time he saw her.

The sedan lurched forward again, and they were at the base of la Plaza de la Barandilla. Pat craned his neck to take one more look, even though he knew he would just be tormenting himself. Sure enough, smoke drifted into the darkening sky from Galán's terrace. The famous pork shoulder was probably almost ready. He pictured Galán and Gabriela sitting side by side, waiting. He wondered how long they would wait before eating without him.

Pat leaned his head back against the cloth headrest. He took a deep breath and closed his eyes. Maybe the Coast Guard would send him to jail, maybe they wouldn't. The idea of being behind bars was too much for Pat to fathom. What he did understand, though, was that his future would be wrecked the moment he received his dishonorable discharge. With that perfunctory summation of the four years he'd invested into serving his country, a country he loved, Pat would be joining a fraternity of rapists, pedophiles, and thieves.

But like Danny, Pat had his reasons. They were sitting up there on that terrace. Together. The way a family should. The Coast Guard wouldn't get it. His family might not, either. But in Pat's heart, he knew.

He would always know.

Acknowledgments

Determining who to thank by name on these pages was not easy, as there are so many people in my life who deserve recognition. After reflecting on the journey that led to *Mona Passage*, however, I decided to focus on those people who introduced me to Latin America, those who played an influential role during my Coast Guard service, and those who have contributed to my writing. To everyone else who has shaped, taught, and supported me, thank you.

The path that would eventually take me to Puerto Rico began in a Spanish classroom at Saint Albans School in Washington, DC. Sherry Rusher and Gilda Carbonaro not only introduced me to the Spanish language and to Latin America but also treated me like a son. I can't repay them for their inspiration and kindness.

While Sherry and Gilda provided the kindling for my interest in Latin America, Jack and Tari Watson provided the spark. They allowed a sixteen-year-old they barely knew to accompany them on one of their many trips from Florida to Cuba, introducing me to their church family in Havana, Matanzas, Ciego de Ávila, and Santiago de Cuba. I treasure those experiences and those friendships (Pepe, Jairo, Luis, Lili, Leandro, Noel . . .) to this day.

As my interest in Latin America matured, another took root. My older brother Will joined the army in the wake of 9/11, and his example affected me greatly. My parents—reluctant to have another son go to war—encouraged me to look into the Coast Guard, a branch that would allow me to serve my country and return to Latin America. Indeed, my two years living in Puerto Rico and patrolling the Caribbean were two of the best years of my life. So thank you,

Will, for your selfless example, and thank you, Mom and Pop, for the nudge toward the sea.

Boarding scallopers in the Gulf of Maine, pursuing go-fasts off of Puerto Rico, and rappelling from helicopters into the Bay of Cartagena made for great stories, but it was executing these missions alongside my Coast Guard shipmates that made them special. In particular, I want to thank Charlie Totten and Tommy Carman for their love and loyalty.

In 2017 I was diagnosed with type 1 diabetes, and my days in the Coast Guard became suddenly numbered. Stationed in Puerto Rico but no longer allowed to go to sea with my cutter, I leaned heavily on Galen Gass and Charles Watkins for much-needed friendship and support. These two men will always be my brothers, and I dream of getting the band back together once more.

It was during my transition from the Coast Guard that I began to write *Mona Passage*. Initially, I harbored no illusions about publication. However, this changed once I began working with author Janet Benton, a born teacher. With her editorial guidance, *Mona Passage* became presentable. I'm so fortunate that our paths crossed, and I can only hope that *Mona Passage* is half as moving as *Lilli de Jong*.

Another author who went out of his way for me was fellow Coast Guard veteran Jim Howe. Despite having a day job, a large family, and his own writing career, Jim read my manuscript not once but twice. For readers particularly interested in the Coast Guard aspect of *Mona Passage*, I suggest you check out Jim's book *Red Crew*.

I would like to thank Ana Méndez-Villamil, a classmate at Harvard Law School, for reading *Mona Passage*, correcting my Spanish errors, and verifying that my depiction of her home island rang true. She did all of this while briefing cases and studying for exams. I look forward to when we meet again in San Juan!

My heartfelt thanks to Syracuse University Press for hosting the Veterans Writing Award and to Tobias Wolff for volunteering his time to review the manuscripts of the next generation of veterans-turned-writers. Thank you, Deborah Manion, for shepherding *Mona Passage* through the publication process and for being my advocate.

This novel made it across the finish line because you believed in it. Thank you, Lisa Renee Kuerbis, Mona Hamlin, and Gretchen Crary (February Media), for the tremendous marketing support and for cheerfully answering my many questions and accommodating my many suggestions. Thank you, Alesandra Temerte, for the awesome book trailer! And finally, thank you, Lynn Wilcox, for designing such an incredible book cover. An author could not ask for a better team.

As the youngest of five siblings, I still look up to and learn from my brothers and sisters. Thank you, Annie, for reading and rereading *Mona Passage*, especially when the story was in its embryonic stage. Your feedback kept the narrative from getting lost in Coast Guard weeds! Thank you, Tad, for reading *Mona Passage* during your commute. You have been an incredible role model as I follow you into fatherhood. And thank you, Nelly, for believing in the idea of *Mona Passage*, and hopefully you will actually find time to read it now that all of the kiddos are about out of diapers!

My brother Will deserves special recognition. As a veteran-turned-writer himself, he not only edited early drafts of *Mona Passage* but also educated me on how the publishing industry works. He has been one of my greatest allies throughout this process, and I would be fortunate if this story is even half as well received as *The Prisoner in His Palace*.

Thank you to my parents, Walter and Patricia. They have consistently put their children and grandchildren first, rarely having strung together more than a few days off since 1976. We joke that my mom went through K–12 six times—once as a child, and once with each of us. Little did my parents know when they were helping me with grade-school essays that they would still be helping me with writing two decades later. Of far greater import, however, has been their unwavering support and devotion. Mom and Pop, please know that none of us take either of you for granted!

Most importantly, thank you to my wife, Alie. She has read every iteration of every chapter, giving tough feedback where appropriate and encouragement when needed. Despite *Mona Passage* sucking up what little free time I had outside of work or school, Alie never gave me a hard time. She knew how much the story meant to me. Her understanding was particularly impressive once our daughter, Leni, was born, and my writing put the burdens of parenting disproportionately on her shoulders. Alie, I will always be indebted to you for your unwavering support, and I love you.

And speaking of Leni, I hope you enjoy this book one day when you're a young woman. I also hope that the story of Pat, Galán, and Gabriela gives you a taste of what your dad was up to in those years preceding your arrival, as well as an appreciation for what really matters in life. I love you.

Thomas "Buddy" Bardenwerper served five years in the US Coast Guard aboard cutters homeported in Maine and Puerto Rico. He participated in humanitarian and law enforcement missions from the Gulf of Maine to the Caribbean Basin. After being medically retired for type 1 diabetes in 2018, Bardenwerper began a joint degree program at Harvard Law School and the Harvard Kennedy School of Government. Upon graduation in 2022, Bardenwerper will be moving to Miami with his wife and daughter.